PRAISE FOR *THE FROZEN WOMAN* AND JON MICHELET

'The best Norwegian crime novel this autumn by far'
– ***Dagbladet***

'Jon Michelet hits back with interest… yes, this is Jon Michelet in sparkling linguistic and compositional form'
– ***Aftenposten***

'This is a story that left me feeling breathless, Michelet is a master'
– ***Netgalley***

'*The Frozen Woman* kept me awake all night… a Nordic crime masterpiece'
– ***The Daily Walk***

'*The Frozen Woman* has all the sophistication of a veteran writer at the top of his game'
– ***Nudge***

'Lavish and thrilling… Michelet writes with dramatic momentum, leaving the reader at the edge of the chair, ready to run for safety'
– ***Varden***

Also available in English translation

Orion's Belt
Under the Blood Tree

The Frozen Woman

JON MICHELET

TRANSLATION BY DON BARTLETT

NO EXIT PRESS

This edition published in 2017 by No Exit Press,
an imprint of Oldcastle Books Ltd,
PO Box 394, Harpenden,
Herts, AL5 1XJ, UK
noexit.co.uk
@noexitpress

This translation has been published with the financial support
of NORLA

ISBN
978-1-84344-292-9 (hardcover)
978-1-84344-774-0 (paperback)
978-1-84344-775-7 (epub)
978-1-84344-776-4 (kindle)
978-1-84344-777-1 (pdf)

Typeset in 12.75pt Garamond MT
by Avocet Typeset, Somerton, Somerset, TA11 6RT
Printed and bound by TJ International, Padstow, Cornwall

For more information about Crime Fiction go to @CrimeTimeUK

The Frozen Woman

I

'WHAT WAS YOUR FIRST reaction when you found her, Thygesen?' Stribolt asks.

Vilhelm Thygesen doesn't answer. He has his eyes fixed on a point behind Stribolt, who observes the distracted look on Thygesen's face and repeats the question in a sharper tone: 'How did you react when you found the frozen body of the dead woman?'

'There's a woman trying to get in,' Thygesen says, pointing with the stem of his pipe to the point he has been staring at. Stribolt wriggles on the leather sofa and catches sight of Vaage. She is standing on the glass veranda and fumbling with the handle of the door to Thygesen's living room cum office. The low sun in the middle of the day, which is the second in February, a Friday, causes the frost patterns on the veranda window to glitter. Through the windows of the large log-house in Bestum the light angles in, giving the burlap wallpaper a warm glow, and is reflected by the golden letters on the spine of *Norway's Laws* and other books on the shelves, causing the wisps of pipe smoke to become visible.

'It's not locked, but it's awkward,' Thygesen says, getting up and walking to the door.

Stribolt struggles to deal with the unreality of the situation. He is sitting here on official business in the home of a man whose sun he had thought had long since set. A murky legend who, it transpires, is a living legend.

Thygesen has a slight limp. His ponytail, which makes him look like an old hippie, swings back and forth. It doesn't go with the Italian-tailored charcoal suit which Thygesen is wearing and definitely not the white shirt and grey-striped silk tie which matches the man's hair almost too perfectly.

To Stribolt it is unimaginable that Thygesen should comb his mane into a ponytail and wear a fashionable suit on a daily basis. He had expected a scruffier turnout. Leaving to meet Thygesen, he had assumed he would be confronted by a wreck, a shipwrecked mariner washed ashore on the sea of life.

Stribolt makes a note on his pad lying on the coffee table: *T has tarted himself up for us.*

Thygesen kicks the door as he twists the handle.

A cold blast of air enters from the veranda. It is freezer temperature outside: minus 18 degrees. Ruddy-faced Vaage has frost on her dark fringe. She looks even more apple-cheeked and attractive than usual, Stribolt muses. Every time he works with Vaage he thinks he will have to have his hair cut as short as hers, take up squash again and get himself into shape. When he was last out on the town a slip of a girl told him he looked like a Buddha with a Beatles wig sliding off the back of his head. Not hard to say something like that when you are in the Buddha Bar, but he took it to heart and the sight of the clientele made him bristle with anger, all those tossers on financial steroids. Now it annoys him that Vaage is wearing an almost identical shiny blue pilot's jacket to his. They aren't in uniform. Although they look as if they are, just not a police uniform.

'More like taxi drivers,' Stribolt mumbles.

Vaage removes her gloves, shakes Thygesen's hand and introduces herself.

'I'm also a Kripos detective,' she says. 'A chief inspector like my colleague Stribolt here.'

'Coffee?' Thygesen asks. 'I've put a pot on.'

'No, thanks,' Vaage says.

Stribolt accepts.

While Thygesen goes out, Vaage examines the room, clearly with some disapproval. Perhaps she thinks it is repugnant that a couple of logs are crackling away on the fire while a very cold woman is lying under a tarpaulin in a corner of Thygesen's large, overgrown garden.

'I thought this bugger Thygesen didn't have two øre to rub together,' Vaage says under her breath. 'He'd gone to the dogs. Done for murder in the seventies, petty fraud in the nineties. Alkie and all-round dick. And then here he is, poncing around in this million-dollar pad in the West End of Oslo.'

'It's just a rambling old house,' Stribolt says.

'Imagine what he can *get* for this place, the plot alone. Why's he trying to trick old dears out of the odd krone when he has all this?'

'It's dangerous to give credence to rumours,' Stribolt answers, turning down the volume of the stereo, which is playing a jazz CD, possibly Miles Davis. 'Our friends at Grønland Police HQ are not always well informed. The two fraud charges against Thygesen were dropped for lack of evidence.'

'What we have in the garden is murder,' Vaage says. '*Premeditated* murder, I would think. The poor girl has been hacked about in every conceivable way.'

Vaage roams around restlessly and scrutinises a new, green transparent iMac on a computer desk, a thick book beside it, next to a south-facing window overlooking the garden.

'Is Thygesen a member of some morose sect?' she asks, lifting up the book.

Lichtturm is written on the cover in big letters.

'I think it's a stamp catalogue,' Stribolt says, trying not to let his voice sound too cutting. He has never got used to the sudden changes in Vaage's temperament and deals with her forthrightness badly every time. She can be as capricious as the weather on his childhood coast.

'Right, I thought it might be one of those sect books,' Vaage says. 'Lighthouse or whatever it's called. You've heard about *Watchtower*, haven't you, Smartie Pants?'

Stribolt has no time to respond. Thygesen makes his entry carrying a jug of espresso coffee and three small, brushed-steel cups on a tray.

'We want permission to carry out a detailed inspection of the site,' Vaage says.

'Aren't you doing that already?' Thygesen answers, nodding towards the windows. Stribolt looks in the same direction. Down in the south-east corner of the snow-covered garden, where the bushes and scrub appear like frost-ridden trolls, the SOC team, wearing white overalls over thermal suits, are inspecting the area around the spruce tree where the woman was found. Three Kripos officers are busy in Skogveien. They are crouched down by the wire fence that borders Thygesen's property from the road. Presumably they are looking for tyre marks in the snow. Two police cars are parked further up the road behind a cordon. One of them has a rotating blue light. Behind it there is a red Saab which Stribolt thinks he recognises – a press car from Akersgata, the Norwegian Fleet Street. A little crowd of curious onlookers has gathered by the cars, mostly schoolchildren by the look of it.

'I'm referring to an inspection of the *house*,' Vaage says.

Thygesen places the tray on the coffee table. He fills all three cups and sits down in the Stressless, which clearly belongs to the man of the house, rests his right foot on a stool and lifts his cup.

Stribolt notices Thygesen's hands trembling. He has small hands, surprisingly brown for the middle of the winter, with a number of conspicuous liver spots.

'The house,' Thygesen repeats. 'Is that really necessary?'

'The officers in charge of this investigation have stated

we *definitely* have to search your house,' Vaage answers.

'I see. I have a couple of legal objections. But I don't want to be difficult. Odd that you're both Nordlanders, by the way,' Thygesen says. He lights his pipe with a match. Picks an imaginary crumb from his beard, which is the same colour as the espresso cups and as well brushed.

Stribolt and Vaage exchange glances. Stribolt's Finnmark dialect has faded so much, in his own opinion, that you would have to be a Linguistics Professor to hear that he is from Hammerfest. Even a professor would be deceived by his Oslo-acquired 'a' endings. It is easier for a layman to hear that Vaage is from Helgeland, the most southerly district of northern Norway.

'You take the room at the end,' Stribolt says to Vaage. 'I'd like to finish this interview without any interruptions.'

'Cool worktop,' Vaage says, running her hand along the polished surface, which is made of a large piece of shiny black marble, three fingers thick. 'Must have cost a *fortune*?'

'It's home-made,' Thygesen answers. 'I used to work with stone once upon a time.'

Vaage must have forgotten she didn't want any coffee. She takes a cup, drains it in two or three quick sips, goes out on to the veranda and starts talking on her phone.

'Where were we?' Stribolt asks.

'You were asking me what my reaction was when I found her.'

'Let me rewind a bit. I need more accurate personal details.'

Stribolt checks his notes.

'It's correct that you're 63 and on disability benefit, is it?'

'Soon 64, and I prefer to call it a disability *pension*,' Thygesen says. He pulls a face which Stribolt finds hard to interpret: is he offended or is he acting offended?

'You have standards which do not seem to correspond to the image I have of people living on disability benefit.'

Thygesen leans forward, knocks the ash out of his pipe and splays his palms.

‘The house and furniture are inherited. I have no debts. I have some rental income and I earn a fair bit buying and selling stamps over the internet.’

‘Like those on the screen?’ Stribolt asks, pointing to the iMac.

‘Yes, they’re African stamps from colonial times. Rhodesia, Nyasaland and Tanganyika.’

Thygesen reaches over a stamp album and opens it at a page marked with a silk ribbon in Norwegian colours.

‘This is the closest I came to a Royal Norwegian Order of St. Olav,’ Thygesen says, holding out the ribbon. ‘This is the same page you saw on the screen. I photograph album pages with a digital camera and put them on the net. If I can sell this collection I’ll earn 200 dollars.’

Stribolt peers at the stamps, which have either the British Queen or an elephant as the motif. Kilimanjaro takes centre stage on one stamp.

‘Let’s drop the philately,’ he says. ‘Do you deal in badges and coins as well?’

‘On the odd occasion.’

‘I have a vague idea you run an unlicensed legal business.’

‘Your sources are not mistaken,’ Thygesen says. ‘Why wouldn’t I offer assistance to widows and the fatherless if they ask nicely? Society at large had no further use of me and dropped me like a dead fish. But in the micro-society around me there are deserving poor who may even need such a decrepit pedant as yours truly.’

‘Do you take a fee off them?’

Thygesen shrugs.

‘And declare your earnings to the tax authorities?’ Stribolt enquires.

‘I thought you were Kripos, not the Fraud Squad.’

Stribolt notices that Vaage's irritation with Thygesen has rubbed off on him. It is a risk working as a pair, with one officer acting as the aggressive partner and the other playing the more laidback, reserved part. If the play-acting fails it is easy to slip into the other's role. At the back of his head Stribolt hears the voices of the veterans there are left at Kripos when reports of the dead woman in Thygesen's garden came in: Off you go. Catch the bastard now, once and for all. He was one of us in a way. He was a cop in his day, then he became a murderer.

Now he is king of all he surveys here, Thygesen of all people, in a palace in the West End behaving like a mafioso. Teasing us with his under-the-table cash.

'So it's black money,' Stribolt states.

'Blacker than the night,' Thygesen says, bursting into laughter. He has brown stains on his teeth. 'But how I make a living should hardly concern a murder investigation. At least not as long as I have the status of a witness and not a suspect. I was skint for many years, scraping the bottom because of the demon drink. Then I managed to pick myself up by my bootstraps from the hell. Do you and your colleagues imagine I have lapsed into crime?'

Stribolt grips the marble worktop. He would have loved to deflate Thygesen. Stick a sharp point in his skinny carcass – much thinner than on the photos in Kripos's files – as he sits there shaking with extremely inappropriate laughter. Who gave Thygesen the idea that he was only a witness? He could become a suspect in a flash.

'You said you went down the garden to cut off spruce twigs,' Stribolt says. 'So you had a knife on you?'

'Indeed,' Thygesen says. His laughter had subsided. His eyes had narrowed. 'For Christ's sake, you don't think I stabbed her, whoever she is, do you? That I killed the little lady and left her under a tree in my own garden? Surely you can't have *such* a fatuous working hypothesis.'

'We're keeping all avenues open,' Stribolt says, annoyed that he lets such a cliché pass his lips. 'What about the twigs?'

'I've already told you.'

'Try again.'

Thygesen pours himself another cup of coffee and produces a little silver box from his jacket pocket. It contains snus, in pouch-form, to be placed under the top lip.

Thygesen repeats that he realised no birds had been in the two corn sheaves he hung from the veranda posts for Christmas, despite how cold the weather had been.

'Then it struck me I'd forgotten to add spruce twigs to the sheaves. As a landing place for tits. I went down to lop some twigs off the spruces. When I pushed apart the lower branches I saw a body lying there.'

Stribolt takes notes.

'*That* is extremely suspicious,' Thygesen says. 'A man tending his Christmas corn sheaf in February.'

'Spare me the sarcasm,' Stribolt says.

'Apologies. Do you think I'm made of iron or what? All this has been very upsetting.'

'You went out at a quarter past six. That's early, isn't it?'

'I usually get up early. I'd slept badly.'

'Any special reason?'

'It's got nothing to do with the case. I may come back to it. Someone close to me is in trouble. Maybe because of uranium. It's a long story.'

Stribolt sips at the espresso. It tastes of mafia, ergo Italian, ergo absolutely excellent. He asks whether Thygesen minds if he lights a cigarette, and is told, as he had expected from a smoker, that of course it is fine. He can feel the pressure, which always builds during an interview, lightening.

'We have a time gap here,' Stribolt says. 'You found her

at around six. But you didn't alert the police until six forty-two.'

'I needed time to think straight. Get over the shock. I knew I would come under suspicion, because of my criminal record.'

'You said just now that suspecting you was a fatuous working hypothesis.'

'OK. Forget it. I thought time wasn't important. After all, she must have been there a good while. She was like deep-frozen. And then there were the tracks… they slightly unsettled me.'

'What tracks?' Stribolt asks, even though he knows the tracks he means: the tiny animals' tracks around the body, which made him stop and swallow several times before he could continue examining the body.

'You saw them yourself when you were down there doing a recce. Mouse tracks, I would say, in the thin layer of snow beneath the tree. Unless they were from a wild mink. I'm glad she was lying on her stomach. When I plucked up the courage to turn her over I was expecting the animals not only to have attacked her fingers but her face as well. And eyes. Thank God, though, everything was intact. I could see the blood on the light-coloured blouse was her own. I saw the rips in her clothing. After I'd seen enough I had to take a trip to the bathroom, if you know what I mean.'

Stribolt can understand the shock and the nausea. Even for a man like Thygesen, who has been around, it must have been distressful to find a dead woman in his garden. If he had found her, that is, if everything he is saying now is not a carefully prepared pose.

'Your first reaction before you touched the body?' Stribolt persists.

Thygesen takes out a snus pouch, which always reminds Stribolt of a used miniature tea bag, and puts it on the lid of the box. Stribolt crushes the ultra-light Marlboro in the ashtray.

'I thought she was a druggie who'd fallen over the fence,' Thygesen says tentatively. 'And was sleeping off a high. She was wearing a down jacket after all. I thought she was sheltered by the spruce. It didn't occur to me how bloody cold it was.'

Stribolt scribbles away on his pad.

'And then?' he asks.

'I'm sure you know from your own experience that your brain whirs for a few seconds before you realise you're standing in front of a corpse. My next thought was that she'd come a long way. She was… what do bloody politicians call them?… culturally diverse.'

'What made you think that?'

'I had a déjà vu experience. There used to be a reception centre for asylum-seekers down the road here. Very unpopular with the posh neighbours. One evening I found a man bleeding in my garden. He wasn't lying on the ground but on a garden bench. A Kurd. From Iraq, as far as I remember. He'd been in a fight at the centre and had been stabbed in the neck with a screwdriver. He didn't want to report the incident and didn't want to see a doctor. It cost me half a bottle of whiskey to thaw him out and put on a bandage. There was something about the dead woman that reminded me of him. The raven-black hair, the very pronounced eyebrows.'

Stribolt lights another cigarette and allows a silence to develop.

'There's something else you'd like to tell me about your reflections by the body, isn't there?' he says.

'A total absurdity,' Thygesen answers. 'It occurred to me that an estate agent might have dumped her there.'

'An estate agent?'

They are interrupted by the ring of Stribolt's mobile

phone, the ridiculous march jingle he hasn't been able to re-programme, and he unhooks the machine from his belt, presses the answer key and listens.

'This is private,' he says to Thygesen.

'Shall I go away?'

'No, I can go into the hall.'

In the hall it is as untidy, down-at-heel and cold as Stribolt had expected Vilhelm Thygesen's home to be. He trips on a threadbare rag rug, kicks over a bamboo ski stick that should have been in a museum – and sits down on the lowest step of the stairs leading to the first floor. A Kripos SOC officer in polyethylene coveralls, with blue gloves on his hands, steals past.

Stribolt has received a call from Akersgata. It is a female reporter, whom he knows, has occasionally advised and even taken for a drink to Tostrupkjeller bar.

'It is correct that we're performing a crime-scene investigation at the house of ex-solicitor Vilhelm Thygesen in connection with a suspected murder,' Stribolt says. 'It is correct that we've found a dead body in the garden. You must have seen that from your press car. But it is not correct that Thygesen is a suspect. We're interviewing him as a witness.'

Stribolt discovers that he is holding a cigarette butt that is still glowing. He stubs it out in a metal bowl with remains of what might have been cat food. Does Thygesen, the devil incarnate, keep cats?

'What do you mean by once a murderer always a murderer?' Stribolt says. 'Please spare me such nonsense. If I may offer you some advice, play this case down and do not splash Thygesen over the whole of the front page. You might have a vague memory of the wonderful Norwegian press's code of ethics poster? Stick to it. If Thygesen really turns out to be the murderer I'll serve you his head on a silver platter.'

Stribolt notices a movement against his trouser leg and feels the hairs on his neck standing up. It is a cat. A little tiger, as lean as her owner, though not quite so grey-haired. Stribolt has always thought he should be allergic to cats. Even though he isn't, he still reacts mentally. It is his firm conviction that all kinds of cats, whether big lions or tiny kitties, should be kept in a zoo. He kicks the mog away. Had anyone seen him he would have maintained that it wasn't a kick but a tap, no more violent than the kick-off at the start of a football match.

'How did you know the deceased was a woman?' he asks the reporter. 'All right, let's say it's a woman then.'

The mog is eating the cigarette end now. That should give it diarrhoea.

'No, we haven't identified her. She doesn't match anyone on our missing-persons list. But we did have a quick look at the list before we set off for the crime scene. You'll have to ask Vaage about an ID. Hello, are you there? There's a bad connection. I'm busy interviewing. Yes, I heard you say you don't get on so well with Vaage. But none of us in Kripos is in this business to be loved by our venerable journalists.'

The inquisitive puss doesn't eat the cigarette end after all. It is a smart cat.

'Hello, yes. No, we don't know who she is,' Stribolt says, pressing the 'off' button. He sighs with relief as he attempts to forget that he said x and thought y to fob off the journalist. And forces himself to return to deadly, literally deadly, serious matters.

The dead woman hadn't had her throat cut. On her neck he had observed only a few scratches. It was her breasts and her stomach that had taken the brunt of the attack. By some lunatic. So many cuts.

The SOC officer, Larsson, to be precise, comes down from the first floor.

'Do you know if Thygesen has a tenant?' Larsson asks.

'There seems to be a separate flat up here. The door's locked.'

'Ask Thygesen for a key. He mentioned something about rental income. He's probably got a tenant living there.'

When they arrived, Stribolt noticed there were two bells by the front door. He goes outside and the cold hits him in the face. Under one bell, an old-fashioned bronze affair, there is a brass plate saying *Fam Thygesen*.

Not much left of the family, Stribolt muses. Behind the façade Thygesen has erected it isn't hard to see a lonely soul. He lives alone, as the majority of city inhabitants do. If there are no ghosts haunting the loft of the hundred-year-old house, there are certainly countless demons haunting the owner's brain.

Beneath a modern, white bell there is a strip of Dymo tape with *VC Alam* written on it. So, judging by the name, the tenant is an immigrant. A Pakistani?

On the drive leading to the front door is one of the police's civilian vehicles, which most officers regard as an old banger, but Stribolt loves driving it. Alongside, by a garage overgrown with moss, built with logs like the house, stands a rust-riddled, snow-covered Fiesta, with no registration plates. It is dwarfed by Kripos's old 4WD Nissan with all their vital equipment on the flat bed.

The garage has a lean-to shed on the side, presumably for wood. Many cords of birch are piled up neatly along the wall. There is a chopping block with an axe sunk in it. Newly cloven logs lie scattered around. Beside the garage is a brand-new, illuminated greenhouse. Through the misted-up glass Stribolt can make out plants that are redolent of marijuana. They are most probably tomatoes.

A gust of wind causes the snow on the tall pine trees to fall by the wrought-iron gate facing Skogveien. Stribolt shivers and makes his way back indoors. In the corners of the hall piles of work and outdoor clothes hang from hooks. On a stool there is a chainsaw, which is dripping oil into a little pool on the floor. He concludes that Thygesen spends a lot of time working in the garden and cutting wood when he is not bodging legal jobs or trying his hand as an internet pedlar.

Or committing acts so unpleasant that not even a seasoned murder investigator likes to contemplate them.

From the belt of wadmal overalls hangs a knife in a leather sheath with silver ornamentation.

The shaft of the knife appears to be made of reindeer horn. There are some reddish-brown stains on the handle.

Larsson comes in and shows him a key.

'Thygesen said the tenant was a woman,' Larsson says. 'Apparently she's working abroad.'

'Check out the knife with the reindeer horn handle,' Stribolt says. 'Are they blood stains?'

'Looks like dried blood, yes. But I think the handle's made of ivory.'

'Coming from Finnmark, I know perfectly well what reindeer horn looks like. Besides, trade in ivory is forbidden.'

'Not antique ivory,' Larsson says, carefully slipping the sheath off the belt and putting the knife into a plastic bag.

'See if you can find a picture of the tenant upstairs. A passport photo. Anything.'

'You think it's *her*? You think he murdered his own tenant?'

'I don't think anything.'

In the living room Thygesen is bent over the soapstone stove, warming his hands. Stribolt coughs. Thygesen straightens up.

'Let's sit back down, shall we,' Stribolt says. 'Tell me about your tenant.'

Thygesen takes a seat and stares vacantly into the room, where the light has begun to fade.

'Why?' he says. 'Vera's been in the Balkans since just after Christmas. She knows even less about what has happened than I do.'

'Vera Alam?' Stribolt asks, and makes a note.

'Vera Christophersen Alam. Norwegian mother. Father was from Bangladesh. She's a kind of stepdaughter to me,' Thygesen says, and falls silent.

'Oh, yes?'

Thygesen rummages through his jacket pockets. Finds the pipe he put down on the marble table top, but doesn't fill it, just sits polishing the bowl with his fingertips.

'As you get older you have so many stories to tell,' Thygesen says at length. 'I'll give you the edited highlights. Vera's mother and I were a couple. She was murdered. Little Vera went out into the world. Started working for idealistic organisations. More coffee?'

Without waiting for an answer, Thygesen fetches a copper kettle he has put on the stove.

He was suspected at that time in the eighties as well, Stribolt reflects. For the murder of a female journalist. Was that murder ever cleared up satisfactorily? The alleged murderer shot himself by the River Lysaker.

'It's old-style coffee,' Thygesen says. 'I realised you liked espresso, but I haven't any more Lavazza.'

He has brought out bigger cups and a little jug of milk.

Stribolt reflects that it will take more than coffee with milk to sidetrack him.

'Vera came home five or six years ago,' Thygesen says. 'She was going to study at Blindern University. Serbo-Croat. She wanted to rent a room here. I liked the idea of that and I have more than enough space. She's been at home very little of the time, but has kept the two rooms as a fixed point in her life. We've agreed a price that is way below the market rate.'

'Where is she now?'

'In Bosnia, working for Norwegian People's Aid. She was home for a while at Christmas and went back on the 27th. She had a partner here, but now there is nothing that binds her to Norway, and an old fogey like me can't hold her.'

'How old is Vera Alam?' Stribolt asks.

'A bit younger than you. Thirty-three.'

Thygesen has started fiddling with the snus box. Stribolt tries the coffee, which tastes like coffee did in his youth in Prærien, the northernmost town in the world.

'You didn't have a relationship beyond the rental contract?'

Thygesen gives a crooked grin.

'I'm starting to be too tired for that kind of thing. And if I'd tried I wouldn't have had a chance.'

'Why not?'

'Quite simply because she's a modern girl and her partners are other women.'

They both give a start at the wail of a police siren. The sound dies away as quickly as it began. Stribolt has taken up a position so that he has a view of the glass veranda. He can confirm that now there are birds in Thygesen's sheaves, even though there were no spruce twigs in them.

Vaage and Larsson enter. Larsson has something hidden behind his back and Stribolt guesses it is the knife.

Vaage, who is either unusually fierce or pretending to be, lays a colour photo on the table.

'Is this your tenant?' she asks.

'Bloody hell, not much sacrosanct to you, eh,' Thygesen sighs. 'Is it absolutely necessary to rifle through *her* things?'

Stribolt looks at the picture. It shows a dark-haired woman leaning against a jeep and squinting into the bright sun, with her sunglasses perched on top of her head.

He and Vaage exchange glances. She pinches her mouth. They are both thinking the same: there is a striking similarity between Vera Alam and the murdered woman.

Thygesen, almost as a reflex action, takes a cigarette from Stribolt's packet and lights it with hands that are trembling a lot now.

Confess, Stribolt thinks. Confess this very minute. We have the body, we have the knife, we have the motive: jealousy.

'I can read your thoughts,' Thygesen says, his lips quivering. 'If you can call them *thoughts* or anything so exalted. Shit for brains! I know Kripos has the highest clear-up rate for murder in the world. What clever cops you are, eh! But if you really think I killed Vera you're the two least talented detectives ever to have worn shoes. Sherlock Holmes will be turning in his grave.'

'Relax,' Vaage says.

'Relax?' hisses Thygesen. His lean face is as red as the embers in the stove. 'I've never had any children. The girl I've regarded as my daughter isn't lying under a spruce tree in Norway. Vera's lying in hospital in Sarajevo. And if anyone has snuffed her out it isn't Mr Thygesen but fucking NATO.'

'*NATO?* How come?' Stribolt asks.

'She's had a tumour lasered off her oesophagus. She emailed to tell me the lump was benign. Her colleagues have phoned to say they're not so sure. They reckon she might have been poisoned by depleted uranium. During the mine-clearance programme she went to every bombed village in Bosnia. She drank water and ate vegetables there. Since then she's worked in Kosovo and recently in Serbian districts of Sarajevo where people think they've been poisoned on a regular basis.'

'We don't need a party-political broadcast,' Vaage says grumpily. 'How can we get confirmation that Alam is in Sarajevo?'

'Easy as wink,' Thygesen answers. 'Ring Norwegian People's Aid.'

Vaage fans her face.

'I'm going crazy with all the smoke in here,' she says, walking towards the veranda door; she gives it a hefty kick, frightens away the sparrows and tits, stands outside and barks down her phone.

'We'd better get Vera Alam checked out,' Stribolt says. 'You mentioned something about estate agents, Thygesen?'

'Yes, just blather. It struck me as a remote possibility that an estate agent might have put a body in my garden. They've been hovering over me like vultures, these agents, to get me to sell so that they can build terraced houses on this site and shovel in the millions. The perverse idiots might even succeed if they can get me locked up for another murder.'

Stribolt had to stifle a smile.

'You haven't got any better theories that might be able to help us Kripos cripples?'

'One,' Thygesen says. 'Her ending up in my garden is completely random. I think she was killed somewhere else, transported to a quiet part of town and thrown over the fence where the spruces would hide her. The person or persons who did it needed time to make their getaway. But they weren't frightened the body could lead the police back to them when she was found.'

Stribolt writes this down. He notices he has lost some of his steam.

Not so with Vaage, who reluctantly has to confirm that Norwegian People's Aid's information tallies with what Thygesen has said. She hasn't closed the veranda door after her when she came in; she is a fresh-air fiend. She beckons to Larsson, who slips in from the wings and places the knife on the table.

Thygesen doesn't react noticeably at the sight of the knife.

'Here we have a blood-stained knife,' Vaage proclaims.

'Beef,' Thygesen says. 'I was sent a load of beef by a

friend, Bernhard Levin, former solicitor colleague. Now seized by an insane fear of mad cow disease. I cut up the meat with a hunting knife, which is the sharpest I have, and put it in the freezer.'

'And the other knives?' Vaage asks.

'They're around. You'll find them,' Thygesen says, looking at his watch, an Omega with a manual wind facility. 'If you would excuse me… I have to go to a funeral. I suppose you must have guessed from my attire. A mourning suit doesn't gather moths when you get to my age. The show gets under way at half past three. In the awful Ullern church at the top of the hill. One of my best friends from school. We bought a car together to celebrate the end of our schooldays, a Packard. It would be best if you posted someone in the house until I'm back, so we don't have to bother with keys.'

Stribolt accompanies Thygesen out. From behind all the work clothes in the hall Thygesen hauls out a beige camel-hair coat, which is one of the most elegant Stribolt has ever seen.

'Who owns the little Ford with no plates?' Stribolt asks.

'It's Vera's wreck. I haven't had a driving licence for many years.'

'I'll stay here until you get back, and then we can continue the interview.'

'Fair enough,' Thygesen answers, heading for the gate. He has forgotten to change into outdoor shoes.

He'll freeze his toes off, Stribolt thinks.

'I've put a tail on Thygesen,' Vaage states.

Stribolt doesn't reply. He suspects now that winter and spring could pass before they find a solution – or they are facing the unsolvable. He doesn't tell Vaage though. She won't want to hear that.

2

VAAGE BURSTS INTO STRIBOLT'S office unannounced. He has been daydreaming that he is Michael Douglas and hurriedly clicks on to his screensaver, which is showing Catherine Zeta-Jones in a becoming evening gown.

But he is too slow, as usual, and Vaage shouts 'Dirty old bugger!' – as usual – they have their little rituals. Another screensaver automatically appears, of another actor, Stribolt's fellow Hammerfestian Bjørn Sundquist, in the role of Hamlet, with the skull held out at arm's length.

It is Monday 12 February. More than a week has passed since they found the body of the frozen woman. And the bitter reality is that they have less than nothing to go on. The only thing *he* has, as the interviewer, is that he trapped Vilhelm Thygesen in a bare-faced lie. Thygesen told him in the interview that on 27 January he had dinner with Bernhard Levin and his partner at Restaurant Arcimboldo. It was physically impossible and Thygesen is trying to cover up something by lying about this restaurant visit. But is what he wants to hide such a sophisticated murder that there isn't a single clue? Or is it some minor sleaze?

Thygesen didn't lie about where his tenant, Vera Alam, is. Norwegian People's Aid has confirmed that she works for the organisation in Sarajevo and she is living there for the moment.

'I suggest we have another bash at it,' Vaage says. She is wearing her office outfit: college sweater and wide-fitting training pants. It is the same Yankee get-up she wears when she pumps iron. She has lifted tons in the last week, bitterly frustrated that she, as leader of the forensic section, has nothing substantial to go on. Not the tiniest drop of relevant blood or anything else that contains DNA, no decent tyre tracks, no footprints. Worst of all, no identification of the deceased. The only clue she has is what she in an initial burst of enthusiasm called 'plaster stripes', which were the remains of glue on the dead body. These stripes show that the woman wore plasters over something she wanted to hide and they suggest drugs. But all Vaage has to show for her efforts is a couple of desiccated lumps of hash, which are of as much use as last year's snow, and four morphine ampules from the Second World War.

Oslo's telltales have no tales to tell. The general public is unusually quiet. Even the usual crop of mad tip-offs is thin.

The newspapers are showing a surprising reserve and have lost interest in the whole affair.

'Anything new on your front?' Stribolt asks. He has left foreign leads to Vaage.

'The Swedish guy from Västerås who claims that his Assyrian – or was it asylum Syrian? – girlfriend has gone missing in Norway is coming over tomorrow to have a look at Picea.'

They have given the unidentified woman the name Picea after the Latin word for spruce. It had been Stribolt's spur-of-the-moment suggestion, and he regrets it because its Norwegian pronunciation rhymes with Ikea, and in Ikea he suffers from claustrophobia and an acute refusal to buy.

The man from Västerås has been convicted of rape and charged with molesting under-age girls. Picea wasn't sexually abused. They know that with as much certainty as they can know that sort of thing, based on the pathologist's examination of the body. They are spared the repulsion of having to hunt a sex murderer; however, a motive which often leads to an arrest is lacking in this case.

'Anything from Interpol?' Stribolt asks.

'Nothing of any use, but wickedness on a grand scale as far as women are concerned. I'm a bit shocked at how many non-European women have been reported missing in Europe. And perhaps even more amazed by how many dark-haired girls and women are found murdered in our part of the world every year, and the percentage of those who are never identified. They have lists kilometres long in the Lyons archives. Three to four hundred women from countries outside the Schengen Area are killed every year in Europe. Interpol never finds out who many of them are and hardly anyone is ever caught for these crimes.'

Vaage has spoken for an unusually long time and with a melancholic tone to her voice. Her expression wasn't the usual dogged grimace. A shadow of sadness flitted across her face. For a short while she stepped out of the role she normally plays. They both play roles to keep their routine encounters with death at bay, to keep emergency psychiatrists at a distance.

Stribolt, who, after working with Vanja Vaage for many years, knows her better than her own father does, waits for her to revert to her role and become the tough female cop she is reputed to be. Vaage, with her arms stiffly down by her sides, sways. She will never be a reed in the wind though; she is too robust for that. But she has shown a certain vulnerability which she knows is in her, even if it is rarely seen.

'Take a seat, Vanja,' Stribolt says, and clears his throat loudly.

He has tried to follow Thygesen's example by slipping a snus pouch inside his lip. Without success. He might just as well have inserted powdered cat shit.

In front of him on the table is a close-up of Picea's face. It is there to remind him how depressing the material they are sifting through is. Picea's ear is deformed as a result of an injury and ought to be able to help them towards identifying her. The pathologist believes it may have been caused by a bite, a dog bite maybe, most probably when she was small. The odontology expert considers the fillings she has – very few of them, bearing in mind her age, thirty to thirty-five – to be typical of the Middle East. There is a fresh tear in the undamaged ear. The perpetrator, or perpetrators, might have torn off an earring.

'Her coat is a cheap brand,' Vaage says, starting up the laptop she has placed on her knees. 'The label is Portofino. Produced in Slovenia. Sold all over the EU and in Greenland. Maybe Picea was an Eskimo?'

'They're called Inuits nowadays,' Stribolt points out.

'Sorry, poor joke,' Vaage says. 'Picea's boots were so worn down we can't find a trademark on the soles. The rest of what she wore was clean, unsexy ladies clothing.'

'And Thygesen's blood-stained knives?'

'Grouse, trout. The man knows something about nutrition anyway. Full freezer. Enough redcurrants to feed a battalion.'

'He makes wine with the berries. Fortified wine, not half bad either. The knife with the so-called ivory handle?'

'Beef, as he said. No question. And the tyre marks which I hoped would reveal something turn out to be no bloody good.'

She places the photos of the tyre mould on Stribolt's desk. He moves away a pile of books; on top are two volumes by Frans G Bengtsson about King Charles XII of Sweden.

'It was pure ice at the side of the road,' Vaage says. 'We have a bit of a tyre print in the snow close by the fence. The lab folk think it's a standard Continental. The most common in Norway. Could have been on a little van. The mould doesn't give us any special features to go on.'

'No other footprints in the garden apart from Thygesen's?' Stribolt asks.

'Nothing. Nothing in the lower levels of the snow either.'

'I'm going to break Norwegian law and light up.'

'Then I'll scream for the Head of Health & Safety,' Vaage says sweetly, gets up, opens the window and stands next to it. 'Tell me what you reckon now, equipped as you are with mental radar that can occasionally scan beyond the visible horizon. I don't want any trifling details or abject facts. Give me a typically full Stribolt panorama.'

Stribolt puts away his packet of cigarettes and takes out his crystal ball, which has been hidden under loose papers, shakes it, lets the snow flutter down over the Eiffel Tower; it is a present from his mother after a pensioners' outing to France, and he chants: 'The Arctic Wizard sees what is hidden to the eyes of the common man and...'

'Get on with it,' Vaage says.

'Right, I see a young girl running on the outskirts of a dusty village by the upper reaches of the Euphrates. She's playing with a dog. It bites her. Fortunately for her the dog doesn't have rabies. She gets over the ignominy of her deformed ear. But there's something about her – she doesn't get married and wear a shawl like the others. Is it a taste for adventure perhaps? A desire to break out of the tedium, poverty? She goes to the city. Beirut, Istanbul, Samarkand. She gets into bad company. They promise her riches if she does just one gig. They stick heroin bags to her skin. Perhaps she's in a situation where she has nothing to lose. She travels north. In Norway, or Sweden for that matter – she can be transported long after she's dead – something goes wrong when she is met. Something triggers the drugs gang's suspicions or fears. Picea may have been noticed by someone who shouldn't have seen her. The gang isn't the most professional in the world. If they were, they would have liquidated her with a small-calibre pistol and dropped her in a fjord or a lake. The gang kills her with whatever comes to hand, the customary knife. But the person, or persons, who did it haven't got the gumption to check that she can't be traced, at least not easily, and so Picea is dumped in a peaceful district of town one quiet night.'

'Nice scenario,' Vaage opines. 'But you've forgotten one thing: Thygesen's role in this mess.'

'I'll leave that to the satanic Thinker from Træna for further deep analysis.'

'And up yours!'

Stribolt offers her a Ricola lemon mint sugar-free herb drop. Vaage accepts hesitantly, crunches the sweet in record time and announces: 'I also have a partiality for the drugs hypothesis. I include Thygesen, and possibly Vera Alam. She operates in the Balkans. She may have a connection with the Kosovo-Albanian mafia. We know she smokes hash.'

'Hang on a minute,' Stribolt says. 'The grams we found in her wreck of a car were prehistoric. *Green* Lebanese, not red. Green with mould.'

'Don't interrupt me. Thygesen's at the receiver end. He's a weak point. West End wuss, on his way out of drugs and into stamp paradise. The gang needs him anyway. No reason to give the elbow to Schloss Thygesen. What he wants is a warning. The hoodlum boys think: let's kill a mule we don't have any use for. We'll dump her at Thygesen's. The message is: next time you try to flap your dishevelled wings, Grey Eagle, the same will happen to you. They assume he'll find her and bury her in his compost bin. They never imagined that *we* would find Picea.'

'B+ for the theory,' Stribolt says. 'You would've got an A if you'd remembered it was Thygesen who gave us the tip-off and we have sweet FA tying him to drugs or any form of organised crime.'

'Tell me what Thygesen said about his fraud cases then,' Vaage says.

Stribolt clicks on to his interview report, neatly entered into the forms on the police intranet. What he lacks in organisation on his desk he makes up for on the computer screen.

'One man's fraud is another man's… both cases appear to me to be neighbourhood squabbles.'

'Squabbles?'

'Comedies played out in the finer part of town. The first report came from a neighbour who claimed that Thygesen had cheated him over some birch logs. This neighbour had given Thygesen permission to cut down some trees on his property. In the report he asserted it had never been agreed that Thygesen would get the logs free.'

'The cheapskate,' Vaage says.

'That's what Thygesen said, and he added – I'm quoting from my notes: "Kyrre Svendsby, my neighbour, is so pathologically mean that he probably used the wood-shavings I left to wipe his arse. I imagine Svendsby reported me because he became envious when he looked over the fence and saw all the wonderful wood that came from the birch."'

'Next episode in the West End soap opera.'

'This time we're dealing with a *frøken*, a breed that will soon be extinct. Frøken Meidell from Sollerud. A rich old dear of the kind we used to call a skinflint. Thygesen had to help her go through her share portfolio and set up a will.'

'And he sold her shares for less than face value and named himself as the main beneficiary?'

'No, he bought two sets of enamel Olympic pins – lapel badges really – off Frøken Meidell. Thygesen says of the transaction: "These were pins made on the occasion of the 1952 Oslo Winter Olympics. All the schoolchildren in town were given a couple of sets which they had to sell. The money was meant for a charitable purpose.

This Meidell crone refused to let her nephew sell them for charity. She considered it to be beneath the family's dignity and confiscated the sets. I found them in her piles of documents. She asked if I wanted them. I thought she would recuperate them by reducing my fee, so I offered to buy the sets for a hundred kroner each. I admit this was a symbolic sum and I knew this was a coup. But business is business, and the old trout agreed. It was only when, sadly, she found out how much they were worth that she reported me."'

'What did *he* get for them?' Vaage demands.

'They're supposed to be the only two completely intact sets in the world. Thygesen said he got ten thousand for the set of silver enamel badges and eight thousand for the bronze ones. I can understand you won't be charmed by his wheeling and dealing, but I hardly think this is a matter for the Fraud Squad.'

'If he's so good at stitching up everyone he deals with, perhaps he doesn't *need* to push dope.'

'We've got the morphine anyway,' Stribolt says consolingly.

'Shit morphine!'

Vaage has nothing further to add about the morphine the Kripos SOC officers found in a discarded medicine cabinet in Thygesen's cellar, except that Thygesen's explanation seems likely. He claimed they were ampoules he found in a lifeboat once when he did a stint at sea in his youth, on board a tanker. He was supposed to tidy up the equipment in the lifeboat and throw away any provisions or medicines that were past their sell-by date. The morphine he kept as a souvenir when he signed off was soon forgotten.

'And that's probably how it is with *this* case,' Vaage says.

Stribolt's office phone rings. Central switchboard says they have received a call from someone who sounds plausible, but wishes to remain anonymous.

Stribolt introduces himself. He busily takes notes while Vaage sits in silence.

'I've got a real pompous prick on the line,' Stribolt says, covering the receiver with his hand.

'Give him a mouthful,' Vaage says.

Stribolt asks: 'Where was it she came from, this missing house-help of yours? Some island in the Caribbean is not very useful. We have to know which island, sir. You took her over from a business connection in London and *assume* she's Jamaican? But you must have seen her passport when you organised her work permit, didn't you? No work permit, I see. Saying there's no visa requirement for Jamaicans in Norway until the Schengen Agreement comes into effect is of no interest. What I need to know most of all is what colour her skin is. No, no, I'm not going to scream racism at you if you say she's black. Darker than Merlene Ottey? Noted. You think I could have been less rude. Fine. If you're going to help us, sir, we have to know who you are.'

The bellowing at the other end is so loud that Vaage leans forward to listen.

'You prefer not to?' Stribolt says and can feel his head getting warm. '*No name, no shame*, you say. The discreet charm of the upper classes, eh?'

Stribolt slams down the phone, but carries on talking: 'I have to tell you, sir, that you're worse than the most contemptible poacher. I hope you get caught in your own trap, you *profiteering bastard*.'

'Rare for you to say "sir" to anyone,' Vaage says.

'You can stop your whinnying. This was a troll from the very top of Holmenkollen Ridge.'

'Is that a *name* you scribbled down while you were ranting and raving?'

'A name?' Stribolt murmurs absent-mindedly,

examining the yellow Post-it. 'It says ØJ Bones. That can't be right, can it?'

'No, sounds a bit funny,' Vaage says.

'Probably one of my stupid anagrams.'

Stribolt leans back in his chair, puts his hands behind his head, stares at the ceiling and says to himself: 'If I may say so, our poor Picea is definitely not black.'

'Are you going to do a bit of TM?' Vaage asks. 'Or shall we go through the results of the door-to-door search again?'

'NTR.'

'Which means?'

'Sort of acronym. Nothing to report. All we've got is the two witness statements saying they heard voices, the bang of a car door and the revving of an engine near where the body was found at around four on the morning of 29 January. One witness is Thygesen's neighbour, Svendsby, who was woken up by the racket. The other's from two boys who were kissing at the crossroads between Skogveien and Bestumveien. One says he saw a light-coloured van. The other was absolutely certain it was a yellow taxi. I put the squeeze on the latter and he admitted he'd been on ecstasy and was wearing dark glasses, even though it was the middle of the night.'

'What does Thygesen say?'

'He claims he didn't hear anything. He was sleeping like a log after returning from the restaurant in a taxi. The receipt shows he came home at half past two.'

'You think he was bluffing about where he was though? Why?'

'I don't know why he was bluffing. What I do know is that he can't possibly have been at Arcimboldo because the restaurant's in Kunstnernes Hus in Wergelandsveien and that particular building has been closed all winter for renovation.'

'Not somewhere I frequent,' Vaage says. 'But I've read in the paper that the art gallery was closed. What are we waiting for? Why aren't we already heading Thygesen's way to grill him? I'll join you as far as Bestum if you don't mind.'

3

'WE'RE A BIT UNSURE about your movements, Thygesen,' Stribolt says. 'So we'd like to have another conversation.'

'Is this a formal interview?' Thygesen asks, planting his elbows on the kitchen table and leaning forward.

His eyes are bloodshot, as though he hasn't slept for several days. Or as though he has been crying, it strikes Stribolt. The drained facial expression is reinforced by his apparel, not the suit, as during the previous Kripos visit, but scruffy working clothes. Thygesen is wearing a Nordic sweater with holes in the sleeves, heavy-duty trousers for use when handling a chainsaw and coarse woollen socks inside his clogs. His hair is hanging down loose, no hippie pigtail, under a cap that looks as if it was knitted during the Inca period in the Andes. When they first arrived they found Thygesen in the woodshed where he was yanking at a chainsaw pull cord and cursing that the machine wouldn't start.

'Yes,' Vaage says.

Snowflakes drift across the high kitchen window. On the floor by the zinc basin unit, which has to be as old as the house, there is a paraffin burner on a low flame. Thygesen has offered them a coffee. Stribolt thinks it tastes as if it has been made with the dregs left over from a day or two ago.

'Am I going to be photographed, and is there going to be another house search?' Thygesen asks.

Vaage has a Kripos camera hanging around her neck and a headlight around her forehead. They argued about this in the car coming over; Vaage insisted police equipment increased their authority and put the interviewee at a disadvantage. In which case, Stribolt retorted, the simplest thing to do would be to brandish a pistol.

Vaage doesn't answer Thygesen's question.

Stribolt puts his notepad on the wax cloth with the Delft-blue windmills. He tries to catch Thygesen's eye, but his eyes are evasive.

'You said you've been to the centre of Oslo twice since the New Year,' Stribolt states. 'The last time was the first of February, in other words, the day before you found Picea dead in your garden.'

'Picea?'

'Our nickname for the deceased.'

'So you haven't identified her. You don't have a clue who she is,' Thygesen says.

'We have a number of leads,' Vaage answers, 'and are confident we'll have a clear ID as we speak.'

Thygesen gets up demonstratively, takes the coffee pot and empties the dregs into the sink. With his back to us, he says: 'You can't kid me. I'm afflicted by a terrible far-sightedness at the moment.'

He fills the pot with water and puts it on a hotplate on the stove, the only item in the kitchen which isn't old-fashioned. He continues to talk to the police with his back to them: 'I can see from here to Sarajevo. I apologise for not showing more interest in your business, but I've received bad news from down there. The worst possible, apart from news of a death.'

Thygesen says he has received a message about the tumour that Vera Alam had surgically removed.

'We're sorry to hear that, of course,' Stribolt says. 'But we have a job to do. So you went to the demonstration?'

'Yes, I did,' Thygesen says, sitting down on the creaky wooden chair. 'I went to the torchlight procession to pay my respects to the boy who'd been murdered by neo-Nazis.'

'What motivated you to do that?' Vaage asks.

'I don't think I have to justify my actions,' Thygesen says. 'Let's say I delved into my inner self, down to a kind of old political bedrock hidden under several layers of sediment. Vera called from Sarajevo to tell me she would've gone to the procession to commemorate Benjamin Hermansen if she'd been at home. So I went for her as well.'

'Alone?' Stribolt asks.

Thygesen nods.

'Did you meet anyone who can testify to your presence?'

'Did someone recognise me, do you mean?'

'Yes,' Stribolt answers.

'Fortunately hardly anyone recognises me in the street any longer. The thirty to forty thousand people in the procession were probably busy keeping an eye out for the Crown Prince and his squeeze.'

'Squeeze. Really!' Vaage bursts out.

'Fiancée then,' Thygesen responds, in a mock-submissive voice, with a sudden glint in his eye. 'Let me add that I also carried a torch because it's my twenty-five-year celebration this year. It's twenty-five years now since I was convicted for the wilful murder of an old Nazi with an Iron Cross. The fight against Nazism cost me a few years of my life, maybe half of it. Without a tear of bitterness I think I can say that I'd never have been charged today – it was the hysterical climate of the seventies that sent me to Ullersmo Prison. If you've considered the irony of me returning from the procession to commemorate the murder of a young man with an African father to find a young woman, from distant parts, in my garden, who had also been stabbed, in the midst of this Norwegian idyll, I can tell you it wasn't lost on me either. It may sound like black magic, but I don't believe in voodoo.'

Thygesen pours coarsely ground coffee into the pot. He tells them he has something to do while the coffee is brewing.

Stribolt doodles a magnificent fish on his pad. Vaage shines her headlight on a corner cabinet that serves as a store for coffee and shelving for cookery books. She pulls out one and shows it to Stribolt. It is Slettan and Øie's *Crime and Punishment – Criminal Law Manual.*

'Wonder why he's got a matchstick on page 445, about petty theft,' Vaage says.

Stribolt has no answer, nor any questions. He stares out of the window. The snow is getting thicker now.

'If it isn't drugs, it's sex,' Vaage carries on. 'Thygesen sells stamps over the internet. So he might also be looking for women. Poverty-stricken girls. He lures Picea. She isn't having any of it. Men's impotence can be a cause for murder. In blind frustration he kills her. He's more bloodthirsty than we thought. Imagine him using his knife on her in the woodshed. There won't be any trace of blood in all the oil, wood-shavings and general gunge covering the ground. And he leaves her there until she is frozen through. Then, after days – or weeks! – he carries Picea down the garden, hides her under the spruce and pretends he found her there. He threw the murder weapon into Bestum Bay ages ago. The other knives he holds on to are just a blind.'

'One snag with your hypothesis is that the bay has been frozen over since before Christmas,' Stribolt says.

'So there's a frost-free marina, an open… what the hell was that?'

The sound of an engine exploding into life is what shocks them into silence. They see Thygesen coming out of the woodshed with the chainsaw on full blast and a grin on his chops. He revs the saw.

Before Stribolt has a chance to be truly shocked Thygesen presses the stop button. The roar dies like the death rattle of a beheaded dinosaur.

Vaage marches out. Stribolt stares through the kitchen window. She gives him a good tongue-lashing. In his defence all he has to say is that he went to the outside toilet and as he passed through the woodshed he was tempted to try the Jonsered, which often roars into life when it has cooled down after a few failed pulls.

Thygesen tries to put on the charm and says that one of the few pleasures he has in life is getting the saw to start.

'Pathetic,' Vaage snaps.

In her harpy moods she wouldn't be charmed if the Angel Gabriel himself came down from the sky, Stribolt thinks, and doodles an angel.

A barely chastened Thygesen washes his hands with Sunlight under the kitchen tap. The smell of the soap reminds Stribolt of the washroom in the Findus factory where his mother and several aunts earned their crust, and where he had his first kiss, with a fish-gutter from Kuusamo.

Coffee and a cigarette will help him out of the mental vacuum. You are allowed to smoke in Thygesen's kitchen. It is a liberal house. On the face of it. Stribolt can't bring himself to think that it is the house of a murderer.

'Thygesen, you stated that you went to a restaurant with your friend Levin and his partner on Saturday 27 January,' Stribolt says in as forceful a tone as he can muster and notices a little uncertainty on Thygesen's face.

'That's right,' Thygesen answers.

'Was there any special reason for choosing this restaurant?' Stribolt asks.

'None except that Bernie wanted to show that gentlemen prefer blondes or vice versa.'

'Which means?' Vaage grunts.

'He'd pulled a blonde bimbo in his old age and was childishly proud of it.'

Stribolt takes a computer printout from his bag on which he has circled Arcimboldo and Kunsternes Hus with a red pen. He puts it on the table so that Thygesen can see.

'You said the dinner was in a restaurant in Kunsternes Hus,' Stribolt says. 'Anything about that statement you'd like to change?'

'No,' Thygesen says, taking off his cap and wiping his forehead with his hand.

Vaage gets up, heads for the kitchen door, turns suddenly and asks: 'What if we tell you the restaurant's been closed since October for building work?'

'Then I'll say we had our cod dish served on a pile of planks.'

'This will be easier if you cut the crap,' Vaage says.

'Fair enough,' Thygesen says. 'From my point of view I'd say everything would be easier on both sides if you'd cut out the good cop, bad cop routine. If I said Arcimboldo, it was a slip of the tongue.'

Stribolt lets a silence develop and carefully counts the number of times the restaurant, named after an Italian artist, is mentioned in Thygesen's statement. Four, he concludes. He tells Thygesen, and adds: 'You don't seem like the sort of person who is prone to such lapses.'

'Oh, I am,' Thygesen answers, tight-faced. 'Can't a lot of what we've said over a lifetime be characterised as lapses? Chit-chat and rubbish.'

Now it is Stribolt's turn to get up and go for a walk, on the pretext of collecting his phone from the car. The snow falls on his head. Perhaps it will clear his brain so that he can find a crack in Thygesen's mask.

In all theatres of the world there is one mask on the wall smiling and one crying. The double mask is a valid symbol not only for comedy and tragedy on the stage but all of life's scenes, that has always been Stribolt's opinion. One moment his idol Sundquist is gaping at a skull; the next Sundquist is grasping a stupid banana and acting in a Beckett play.

Stribolt takes a visible position outside the kitchen

window and pretends to be talking on the phone.

Vaage sits inside and seems to be trying to stare Thygesen into the ground. It won't help. They have nothing on him. If the restaurant faux pas had really been fatal for Thygesen, he would have shown some sign of it, perhaps he would have cracked already.

Stribolt goes back in, brushes the snow off his clothes and pours himself more coffee. Silence has descended over the kitchen table with the windmill cloth. He breaks it with a question, not directed at Thygesen but Vaage: 'Perhaps we ought to consider a charge of giving false information? I've asked our lawyer for advice.'

'Now you're taking this business much too far,' Thygesen says.

He says he hadn't realised that the Kunsternes Hus, or Huset, as he calls it, has been closed all winter. It used to be one of his fixed watering holes when he liked to hang out with bohemians, but it is many years since he has been there.

'If Huset really was closed obviously I was wrong when I said we ate there. But if you think this little lie can clear up a murder investigation you're fooling yourselves. We were at Lorry pub, very close to Kunsternes Hus. If it's of any interest I'm sure I have hundreds of witnesses there. Bernie had a bit to drink and sang what he thought were Jewish songs from the Warsaw ghetto. I had a drop too much as well. Perhaps that explains why I made the little boo-boo I did, about where we were at closing time.'

Stribolt steals a glance at Vaage and guesses she is thinking the boo-boo Thygesen wants to talk about is taking home an exotic young stranger, and then everything went wrong, and so he killed her.

'You were on the pull?' Vaage asks.

'Not at all. Bernie's blonde's stupid behaviour had cured me of any desire I might have felt for a woman that night.

But I did do something that might be considered a crime.'

'Come on then,' Vaage says.

'I stole a coat,' Vilhelm Thygesen says.

'You stole a coat?'

'Yes, I stole a coat. Yes, that's how deep I sank.'

'A *coat*,' Vaage sighs.

'A camel-hair coat, designed by the great Armani. If you report me, I don't think it will qualify as petty theft. I'll say it was a mix-up. The coat was similar to mine, which I couldn't find in the hurry to leave. Under torture I'll probably confess petty theft, but will plead "extenuating circumstances", as in clause 391 of the Penal Code, for the mildest possible punishment. I can claim that it was easy to make a mistake with so many drunken, jostling people leaving at the same time and impossible in the scrum to find the coat's rightful owner.'

'Spare us the legal niceties,' Vaage says. 'Can you prove you stole this bloody coat?'

'Well, it's here. Hanging in the hall, and your colleague was slavering over it the last time you were here.'

'What are you laughing at, Arve?' Vaage hisses.

'I'm not laughing at all, I'm coughing. I think I'm getting a cold,' Stribolt answers. 'Could I ask you for another drop of coffee?'

Thygesen isn't gloating, Stribolt observes, as though he had outmanoeuvred us and pulled the wool over our eyes with his coat wheeze. He quickly reverts to grieving over the news from Sarajevo, which probably – the world basically tending to be more of a tragic than a comic place – is that Vera Alam's tumour turned out to be malignant.

'I have to sort out a loan so that I can fly to Belgrade,' Thygesen says. 'I have a meeting with Levin at his place in Bjørnsletta in three-quarters of an hour. So I'll have to be off very soon. And I have nothing more to say, except about police work, and this I really mean.'

'I suppose we've finished here,' Vaage says and gets up.

'No, we haven't,' Stribolt says.

Surprised by his brusqueness, Vaage slumps back on to her chair.

'I was a cop in the last century,' Thygesen says. 'To be frank, I wasn't much of one, and in that sense have nothing I can teach you. But I've been round the block. Many times. In the twenty-first century Kriminalpolitisentral you're probably all good boys and girls, well used to reform and restructuring and whatever the terms are in bureaucratic language today. Nevertheless, I think you're not aware of the new reality – such as the case you're trawling through now. You don't know the identity of the victim and my guess is you never will know. So you won't find the murderer either.'

'Don't get too cocky now, Thygesen,' Vaage says.

'It's got nothing to do with cockiness. This is about an objective analysis. I've been on the open Interpol website in Lyon. You'll be horrified by the statistics on unidentified women from the Third World who have been murdered here in Europe. You can search the statistics that are not open to us and you probably know much more than I do about this. Perhaps the case of... what do you call her?... Pinea?'

'Picea,' Stribolt says.

'... gives us a glimpse of the future, also for cops in Norway, in the part of Fortress Europe that we constitute, where the visa-less refugees from poverty in Faroffistan are slipping through the cracks in the wall. Most to find happiness in the form of work and money, some to meet unhappiness in the form of a sudden death. Among the sudden deaths there appear to be more and more women used and abused, by pimps and drug dealers, by shady employers and cruel husbands who buy themselves a wife and then jettison her down the rubbish chute after they've had their use of them. There'll be many of these victims in the future: rejected women, mutilated. Frozen – like the woman I found. And then there are all the children. They'll be gone, scattered like chaff before the wind, blown into ditches, swept into landfill dumps, brushed into the gutters of the Boulevarde de Stalingrad in Paris, disfigured in a backyard in Berlin, shot in a shed in Skopje.'

Thygesen gets up and opens the fridge door, locates a carafe and takes three port glasses from a cabinet.

'Let's swallow the bitter with the sweet,' he says. 'This is a vintage redcurrant wine from the red seventies when we had a dream – insanely foolish, eh? – about humans not being treated as commodities.'

'I'm driving,' Vaage says.

'We came in the old Nissan jalopy, so I'll be driving, Vanja,' Stribolt says. 'It's no secret that with snow under the wheels I drive best on a dram.'

They gently touch glasses and soon take their leave. Thygesen dons a parka that matches the work clothes he is wearing.

From the Nissan, Stribolt watches Thygesen walk towards Skogveien, bent forwards into the snow, the parka hood over his head. Soon he is out of sight.

Stribolt puts the 4x4 into gear.

'Well,' he says. 'At least we cleared up the unreported theft of a coat.'

4

IT IS FRIDAY 2 March. Exactly a month has passed since the frozen corpse of the murdered woman was found in Vilhelm Thygesen's garden.

Vanja Vaage and Arve Stribolt have sat down on a bench against the sunny wall on the roof terrace outside the canteen of the new Kripos building in Oslo East.

The low afternoon sun doesn't warm much, but they are sick of sitting indoors and Stribolt is dying for a cigarette.

They have spent a couple of hours summarising how much, or how little, progress they have made after a month's work on the investigation. As from 1 March Vaage has been taken off the Picea case. Stribolt is left to run it on his own.

Vaage says: 'The mathematical odds of a woman being found in the garden of a man convicted of murder who has not been murdered by said man are the same as me winning ten million kroner on the Lotto.'

'I don't believe that's a very accurate calculation, Vanja.'

'Watch it or I'll send you out to find the murderer's missing sock in the Orderud case,' Vaage answers. 'Or I'll make you question one of the *knit*-wits who keep ringing to tell us the sock was knitted from a Serbian pattern or a Kosovo-Albanian one.'

Vaage is now in a position from which she can torment her colleague with sock investigations or at least have calls referred to him from women she calls the '*knit*-wits'. She has been appointed Duty Officer on the Kripos desk. The desk is the nerve centre for the processing and dissemination of information received.

In front of them on the brown wooden table are the new business cards that Kripos staff have just been issued.

'Have we actually deserved these gaudy cards?' Vaage asks.

She lifts the cup of coffee she has placed on her card so that it doesn't blow away and reads the English text aloud: National Bureau of Crime Investigation (Kripos), Communications and Service Section, Desk. Vanja Vaage, Detective Chief Inspector, Duty Officer.

'Yeah, well,' says Stribolt, fiddling with his own card. 'Detective Chief Inspector sounds more impressive than *førstebetjent*.'

He is enormously irritated by the way his home province of Finnmark has been drawn inside the Kripos logo on the card.

The Kripos logo is also mounted on the brick wall of the towering new building in Brynsalleen and on a flag flying from the mast in the lawn outside, the way the Merkantildata company flag flies in front of the neighbouring edifice.

It, the Kripos logo, consists of a map of Norway, drawn in blue lines, with KRIPOS printed across central Trøndelag. Around the map there is a yellow circle, and around that a wreath of stylised yellow oak leaves. Against a background of two crossed poles with spiked heads.

Whenever he walks to work from the Metro to the new Kripos palace and the wind unfurls the flag Stribolt cannot avoid seeing Finnmark. Once, in the middle of February, he said the following to Forensics Officer Gunvald Larsson, whom he met emerging from the underground car park: 'Shit, Larsson, on the Kripos logo Finnmark looks like it's just come out of the washing machine. There's not a single fjord in the right place.'

Larsson, for his part, was more annoyed by a little granite fountain that had been erected outside the main entrance. At the top a narrow channel for water had been carved out. When the two of them walked past, the water had been turned off for winter.

'I don't know what the bloody point of it is,' Larsson said. 'Only the crows drink the water. And watching it trickle down the narrow channel, I fear for my prostate.'

'Perhaps the fountain is meant to illustrate how much of our activity runs away into the Great Void,' Stribolt said.

'We have the highest clear-up rate in the western world for murder,' Larsson said, no doubt to console a colleague whom he knew was getting nowhere in an investigation for which he bore total responsibility.

'For as long as it lasts. We score high in the clear-up statistics because we're still a small, remote and sparsely populated other-land where everyone knows everyone,' Stribolt replied. 'The Picea case will be an example for me of what happens when the foreign pressure on our borders increases. Then we're going to find ourselves powerless time after time because there are no friends or acquaintances to report to us.'

Picea is still – now March is upon us and there is a touch of spring in the air – an unidentified murder victim.

'Picture?' Stribolt asks, stubbing out the cigarette on the upside-down flower pot doubling as an ashtray on the roof terrace.

'Nothing,' Vaage replies. 'I cannot fathom why we were told not to publish a picture of Picea in the papers.'

'Snafu,' Stribolt says.

Vaage stares at him in puzzlement.

'American acronym from World War Two,' Stribolt explains. 'Situation normal, all fucked up.'

Vaage laughs a short, throaty laugh.

'You know my hypothesis for why it's fucked up, don't you?' she says.

Stribolt knows her hypothesis about administrative cock-ups, concedes she might be right and elaborates.

Norway has recently acquired another directorate: the Police Directorate. Such a senior organ has of necessity to busy itself with questions of principle to define the rules of the police's various activities. The question of whether to publish photos to identify victims in criminal cases is tricky for the Police Directorate. Here there are two conflicting considerations to bear in mind. One is clearing up the case through identification. The other is the general public.

The general public is often called 'the great detective'. But they are a collection of amateurs who don't have the training in the world of murder that the police have.

Stribolt imagines an executive officer, a calm legal bureaucrat who has a photo of Picea's face placed before him, with a request from Kripos for permission to publish immediately.

Picea was found in a frozen state and kept in a coldroom at the Institute of Pathology where the body was transported after the autopsy. So she wasn't swollen, as bodies are after drowning. And, having been found in Thygesen's garden, she was far from being so disfigured, like Ole Johan, the horse which was found 'far, far away in Håstein's garden' in Jakob Sande's naturalistic poem 'The Corpse'. Once Stribolt got into hot water for reading it aloud at a Kripos Christmas dinner, where mutton ribs were being served, and one of the more seemly lines described the fleshless skull.

The executive officer, however, perhaps thinks the public might take offence at seeing a photo of a dead Picea. He determines to examine earlier practice and concludes that, as regards the publication of photos of murder victims it is, so to speak, non-existent. A lack of precedence makes legal practitioners quake at the knees.

On top of which there is another consideration: privacy protection. Here any bureaucrat in any Norwegian administration risks having the ever-alert Georg Apenes from the Data Directorate down on them after the slightest misdemeanour.

This is a legal nut the executive officer has to crack. Is a person unknown to the Norwegian public entitled to protection of her identity? She is not only dead and thereby unable to attend to her interests personally but also unidentified so there is no one else who might be expected to represent her.

'We should hear the Police Directorate's decision today,' Vaage says and rings a number on her phone. 'I'll check to see if it's in.'

Stribolt gets up to stretch his stiff legs. From Ringveien, which goes behind the Kripos building, there is the regular drone of cars leaving Oslo. The weekend rush has started. He himself isn't going anywhere even though he could have used a break from the town and the office. He has decided to spend the weekend trying to make some headway in the Kurdish, Iranian and Iraqi areas of the capital, to see if anyone can identify Picea from the photo of her he carries in his wallet.

'Latest news,' Vaage says, putting her phone into her pocket and pulling an ironic grimace. 'The Police Directorate say they're considering giving us permission to publish an identikit sketch.'

'*Identikit?* When we have a perfectly good photo?'

'The boss says they'll complain again. So there'll be another angry exchange of notes between the desk and the Directorate.'

'In the worst-case scenario, a waste of ink. A clatter of sabres and the publication of a photo comes to naught.'

'If the Justice Department gets involved it'll be hawk on hawk,' Vaage says, flapping her arms. 'Ingelin Killengreen versus Hanne Harlem. Going at each other beak and claw in the upper stratosphere. Feathers flying. Time passing.'

'Shit,' Stribolt mutters. 'What a shit scenario.'

'I can hear Killengreen from here,' Vaage says. 'Do you Kripos folk really think we'd agree to have pictures of a body splattered across the newspapers?'

'Did our dear Police Commissioner say that?'

'I don't know. The point is that she *could've* said something like that. All the intrigue makes me so depressed that I think I'll take the weekend off.'

'Have a good weekend then,' Stribolt says.

'And you?'

'I'm going to sit down and go through my notes.'

'We've hit a wall in the Picea case,' Vaage says. 'You'll have to console yourself with the fact that almost all walls have cracks.'

'There wasn't one in the Geiranger case. We were banging our heads against solid concrete.'

'You have to see the Geiranger murder as the exception that proves the rule.'

Stribolt goes to his office. Clicks Zeta-Jones off the screen. Stares in a melancholy frame of mind from his window on the second floor down at a little spruce tree growing in the lawn between Kripos and Merkantildata. Some girls in the company are sitting at the tables by the main entrance smoking. One is wearing a coat like Picea's.

In Hoffsveien, where he lives, one rainy evening he met a woman he thought was Picea for a few giddy seconds. The woman was startled by the look he sent her, took refuge behind her umbrella and ran down the pavement of Smestaddammen.

Stribolt pulls out the top drawer of his desk. Under the glass plate he has, among other memorabilia, a photo of one of his police idols: Rolf Harry Jahrmann, the Head of the Murder Commission in his time, the predecessor of Kripos. Neatly folded under the glass is a newly written version of the letter in which Inspector Arve Stribolt resigns from Kripos.

He unfolds the letter and reads: 'I find it hard to work in an institution where the media are continually trying to set the agenda for what cases we take, and to some degree they succeed, the result of which is that our concentration fails us in cases where the media are less interested. The triple murders at Orderud Farm and the double murders in Baneheia are, by Norwegian standards, very big, important cases. However, I have been entrusted with the responsibility for a murder case which, although it hasn't captured the media's interest, is in principle at least as significant as those of Orderud and Baneheia. I think it is lamentable that so few resources are being invested in this case. One reason for my resignation is that my suggestion – to send a detective to Sarajevo to question Vilhelm Thygesen's tenant, Vera Alam – was turned down on 7 February 2001, with the justification that it was not financially viable.'

Thygesen went to Sarajevo. They were in telephone contact a couple of times while he was there visiting the cancer patient.

Stribolt brings up a Word document entitled 'Thygesen's Travels' on screen. From Sarajevo Thygesen went to Paris, in his words because he had a plane ticket via Paris and he wanted to do some business with stamps and coins in the French capital. He stayed there for ten days and claimed in a telephone conversation that he had made such good deals he reckoned he could pay back the loan he had received from his friend Levin for the journey down to visit Vera.

The customs officials who examined Thygesen's luggage at Gardemoen Airport found nothing out of the ordinary. They considered it perfectly normal to have one bottle of wine too many.

Thygesen is in no way eliminated from the Picea case. A shadow of suspicion will hang over him until a murderer is found who is not Thygesen. But it is a flickering shadow, in the process of dissolving.

In Stribolt's opinion, it was right not to focus the investigation on Thygesen and his circle, even though it is scandalous that someone wasn't sent to Sarajevo to interview Vera Alam. The phone interview with her was doomed to failure because she was so ill and could barely talk after her throat operation.

Stribolt clicks on his self-critical list of areas where he might have failed: 1. Too much focus on drugs? There are so many other reasons for having tape stuck to your body when arriving in Norway legally or illegally, such as travel documents (genuine/false), names of contacts, personal letters, personal photos, etc. 2. Did I accept far too quickly that Picea had just arrived in the country? Could have been here for a long time, held as a slave by some bastard or other? 3. Could we have been deluded into thinking Picea hadn't been sexually abused? The perp might have used a condom so as not to leave DNA. If she was a prostitute a client might have used a condom during the act and then run amok and drawn a knife. 4. Have I got too hung up on the idea of a Kurdish trail, like some latter-day Swedish Hans Holmér, in the intuitive belief that Picea could be a Kurdish refugee? Have I spent too much time questioning Kurds? All the interviews were negative. The Kurds have a solid network. If she really was Kurdish, someone would have known about her. But no Kurds recognise her or admit they do.

The list has a dozen more points, which he can't be bothered to go through for the nth time.

Stribolt holds his head in his hands, studies his reflection in the glass.

What was it Thygesen, clearly well-oiled, said to him on the phone from Paris?

'You know, Stribolt, when I picture your face I see you with a smile and you remind me of a dolphin.'

Right. Better than grinning like a shark.

Stribolt clicks on the computer's media player and chooses a CD on which Lotte Lenya sings songs by Kurt Weill with lyrics by Bertolt Brecht.

Und der Haifisch, der hat Zähne
Und die trägt er im Gesicht
Und Macheath, der hat ein Messer
Doch das Messer sieht man nicht

Oh, the shark, babe, has such teeth, dear
And it shows them pearly white
Just a jack-knife has old Macheath, babe
And he keeps it, ah, out of sight.

Winters have gone, he thinks, and perhaps springs will go too. But my Mack the Knife is somewhere, and the wall will crack and I will see him.

5

'BANZAI, SAMURAI, BANZAI!' SCREAMS the young man sitting on the pillion of the motorbike. The rider turns the bike into a clearing by the road through Våler Forest where there was once a gravel pit. He comes to a halt in front of a damaged building with rusty reinforced steel protruding from the concrete. The man, twenty years old, slides off the seat, raises his arms in the air and does a jig on the gravel.

'Tell me, Kykke, that it's not shit cool to be out again,' the young man says, pinching himself on the upper arms. He removes his helmet and reveals a head of hair that is dyed bright yellow, combed and gelled into tufts.

'You look like something the cat brought in, Beach Boy,' says the man called Kykke.

'My sis said the same at the funeral, and if my mother'd been able to say anything she would've probably had a go at me as well. But no one bothered to ask me whose hair was like this. I modelled myself on the drummer in Marilyn Manson to celebrate my freedom,' Beach Boy says and switches on the Walkman attached to his belt.

It isn't a Manson song that reaches his ears via the earplugs. It is a song by a singer called Laurie Anderson, whom he had never heard of before he was given the CD by his sister after the funeral.

He spins the helmet round on the index finger of his right hand and is all smiles and summer happiness. Then he listens to what the American lady sings and he repeats the verse with his face creased in grief: *When my father died we put him in the ground, when my father died it was like a whole library had burned down.*

Beach Boy switches off the music and takes out the earplugs.

'I'll tell you one thing, Kykke,' he says. 'If my father really had been a library it would've been one crammed with instructions on how to assemble nuclear rockets.'

Kykke isn't listening. He is lost in his own thoughts and polishing the speedometer on his bike with a cloth.

'You certainly came out with the summer, Beach Boy,' Kykke says at length, dismounting with an effort because he is so big; he flicks the heavy bike on to the stand, takes off his helmet and places it on the seat. 'Brontes' is written on the petrol tank in ornate golden letters, and underneath, in smaller letters, 'Son of Uranus and Gaia'. The bike is a standard black Kawasaki, the largest model, KZ 1100, which is so old that, as Kykke often says, 'if Brontes had been a trotting horse it would've been taken behind the stable and shot'.

Kykke leans against the bike and stretches his legs. Massages his elbows and knees.

'Think I'm starting to get rheumatism in my joints,' Kykke says. 'I s'pose that's the sort of shite you have to expect when you've been sitting on a four-stroke pot-boiler since you were fourteen.'

'You've been riding a bike for half an eternity then,' Beach Boy says with reverence.

'It's thirty-five years since I burned rubber through the school playground in fuckin' Arnes on my first Kawasaki Samurai,' Kykke says, looking at his watch, which is a Rolex Oyster. The superb timepiece doesn't match the style of the man, who looks like a labourer, someone who has done heavy manual work. 'It's only ten. It's going to be boiling hot today. You still like being called Beach Boy, boy?'

'Beach Boy, Banzai Boy or Nike Boy. The name I use

depends on my mood. The psychologist at Trøgstad said I've got a split personality, but my personality as a whole is a fountain of talent. Does it matter if the water in it isn't as pure and clear as in the psalm at the funeral?' Beach Boy says, not caring that Kykke isn't listening with even half an ear.

'Am I in a good mood now or what?' the boy shouts, dancing a jig and causing the dust to lift in a cloud towards the concrete wall. 'God, how I've yearned to be back here at the clubhouse. You picking me up and bringing me here to The Middle of Nowhere is almost too good to be true.'

He catches sight of a tiny figure drawn in a black felt pen on the wall. The childish line-drawing represents a stick man hanging from the gallows. Underneath there is a name in weather-beaten letters, and that name is Vilhelm Thygesen.

'That's the devil I painted on the wall,' Beach Boy mumbles to himself. 'A little snot-nosed kid painted a big sack of shit.'

He pokes at the concrete. A flake peels off and the stick man has one leg less.

'Serves you right, Thygesen,' Beach Boy whispers. 'You should have been knee-capped because you screwed up everything for the Seven Samurai.'

He dances back to the big Kawasaki.

'Thanks for picking me up, Kykke. You came bloody early this morning. Before the sparrows had farted and Mum had her slippers on. Thank you, thank you, thank you. Banzai!'

'That's enough now,' Kykke says. 'If you saw the sexy beast waiting for you inside the bunker, you'd pass out, my lad.'

Kykke pulls down the zip on his leather suit, takes out a handkerchief and wipes the sweat from his thinly haired scalp and from his throat, which is covered with a carrot-coloured, grey-stippled beard, and straightens the string that keeps the black suede patch in place over his right eye.

'You sexy thing, you sexy thing!' Beach Boy sings, sitting on an imaginary motorbike and going vroom-vroom. He stops suddenly and asks worriedly: 'You did remember to bring the key, didn't you, Kykke?'

He points to a solid padlock on one of the tarred doors.

Kykke rattles the bunch of keys attached to his belt.

'How drunk are you actually?' he asks.

'I'm as sober as Mette-Marit after her engagement to the Crown Prince,' Beach Boy answers and laughs so much he splutters. 'I might've OD'd on anabolic steroids in the slammer. It's just rubbish, though, that they do your nut in.'

'They don't seem to have done much for your body either,' Kykke says. 'You're just as skinny as you always were.'

'If you lift wood all day at the saw mill in the perishing cold, you don't feel any need to pump iron in the Trøgstad fitness studio in the evening. You're too knackered to do any proper bodybuilding,' Beach Boy says apologetically. 'Shall we go in then?'

'Hang about,' Kykke says, holding the boy's shoulder. 'We just have to have a serious chat first. And I have to wipe off the sweat.'

Beach Boy asks if they still have running water or if the bastards on the local council have turned it off for winter. Kykke replies that the water has been cut off for the winter, but he has rigged up a cistern under the gutters.

'Happy times are here again,' Beach Boy says, taking a mouthful of Coke he has conjured up from the folds of his baggy army trousers. '11 May. A week to go to Independence Day and it's full summer.'

'It came in one day.'

'Kind of instant summer.'

'Well put. I've always had you down as a clever lad, you

know,' Kykke says. He produces a packet of Marlboro from the breast pocket of his leathers.

'Fag?'

'Prefer roll-ups,' Beach Boy says. 'In pallet-nailing hell you're soon hooked on Rød Mix. That's the only tobacco they have in the kiosk. It's real shit tobacco, but after smoking it for a couple of months filter cigarettes taste of diddly squat.'

'I don't smoke manufactured cigarettes either,' Kykke says. 'I just bought a packet in your honour. I've always thought of you as a smart lad and don't you listen to all the mud-slinging.'

'I appreciate that,' Beach Boy says with a smile, revealing a row of teeth so perfect they could have been in a chewing-gum advert, and dances a few steps. His basketball shoes kick up dust. His trousers sag fashionably. He picks up an empty Castrol container, sees a stick and starts drumming while Kykke regards him in the way a patient dog watches a frisky pup. Beach Boy takes off his reefer jacket and hangs it over the handlebars of the Kawasaki. There is a wad of newspapers sticking out of one pocket.

'Heard the latest about Jennifer?' he asks.

'Jennifer who?'

'Jennifer Lopez of course,' Beach Boy says, pointing to the motif on his T-shirt. 'Some crafty bugger managed to film her while she was shagging a guy.'

'I couldn't give a damn about Hollywood whoring,' Kykke says. 'I'm off for a piss.'

He lumbers by the concrete building which, according to what he has gleaned, was built as a garage by the Germans during the war, whatever Hitler's lot would want with that in the middle of a dense spruce forest. Younger locals, who don't have a clue, say the construction was erected as a NATO bunker, to protect the R120 road if the Russians advanced down it in their tanks heading for the Nike rockets in the Våler battery.

Kykke walks round to the lee side, kicks the Seven Samurai sign he threw there in the winter and studies the thermometer on the wall. It is mounted on an enamel plate with IG Farben on. The enamel hasn't cracked and the thermometer has never shown anything but what the weather forecast says. The screws holding the plate in place have crumbled to flakes of rust though. Obviously the Germans wouldn't use acid-proof screws to put up a simple measuring instrument on a remote wall somewhere in Norway.

He pees and confirms there is nothing wrong with his kidneys; his urine is the same colour as a pils, not a heavy lager. A layer of birch pollen floats on the surface of the water in the cisterns. He rinses his hands. Then tugs the German thermometer off the wall as a souvenir from The Middle of Nowhere.

'Twenty degrees,' he shouts to the lad. 'Reckon it'll be twenty-five before long.'

'Great, then I'll go to the sea in Fuglevik and get some sun on my body,' Beach Boy answers, beating his chest like Tarzan. He rolls a cigarette with fingers covered with splinters after the saw-mill shift in Trøgstad, lights up and coughs.

He studies the clubhouse. Above the brown doors, which tend to smell of tar when they get really hot, the name The Middle of Nowhere MC, motorcycle club, is still visible. It is painted in big, white letters with a silver shadow effect. The white has peeled off more than the silver. Someone has been busy with a spray can and there is graffiti on the concrete wall and the doors. Taggers, perhaps, or more likely school leavers. They usually come to this deserted place, pissed up, in their traditional red gear, park their traditionally red vehicles behind the building and do what Jennifer does. And there are splodges of red paint that look fresh. But the piglets and piglettes haven't reached The Middle of Nowhere yet. The name stands there as a souvenir of the times when the Easy-Rider Chopper freaks had their quarters here and Beach Boy was an ankle-biter.

In those days a plane mechanic by the name of Ottar Strand had a permanent job maintaining the rockets at the Nike battery. It lasted until 91, when the Nikes apparently reached their sell-by date. The Easy Riders packed up the year after and got an absolute palace in Spydeberg, thanks to the Socialist Party. Old Man Strand retrained. That was before the golden handshakes, before there were parachute payments, even if you weren't a parachutist, just a lousy major.

The Middle of Nowhere stood empty, and then, thank God, the Seven Samurai turned up and established themselves with the full MC Club turnout and secret initiation rituals for kids who hung around the clubhouse wide-eyed. Kykke began to build up a workshop which, in his words, would be the best Jap bike place in the whole of Østfold.

'You know how to do almost everything and better than anyone else,' Beach Boy says, straightening up. Hasn't he shown he can think positively and work creatively the way Ragnhild, his welfare officer in prison, tried to inculcate in him?

He is wondering what happened to the Seven Samurai sign. It couldn't have rotted or fallen down by itself. He'd had to help mount the teak sign and he remembers all too well how Kykke insisted they used proper, stainless steel bolts. If the sheriff and the council big shots have damaged the sign, then…

Beach Boy fiddles with his tufts of hair. However dead cool he thinks the Manson drummer's hairstyle is, it feels odd, as though it should be on some space creature that had just landed on Planet Earth.

'Fixing your new dreads?' Kykke says.

Beach Boy is startled and turns to the giant who has come up behind him. Kykke is not exactly every mother-in-law's dream, unless she wants her daughter to have a one-eyed troll. Imagine if Queen Sonja had taken the man from Moss into the palace.

'You could give anyone the heebie-jeebies,' Beach Boy says.

'Do those chimps from the Kamikaze gang still go out to the nick in Trøgstad and whack tennis balls full of speed over the fence?' Kykke asks.

'Not that often,' Beach Boy answers with a laugh. 'Could be more often if you ask me.'

'Bloody risky and a childish way to do business,' Kykke says grumpily. 'There's been a lot of fuss because they let you out way before time. Was it just because your father kicked the bucket?'

'Lots of people are released before time now. If you cop more than sixty days and your urine tests are negative, you only need to do two-thirds of the sentence. And then dad died, so I had social reasons as well.'

'But you know how Borken and Lips talk and call you Song Boy and Singing Bird,' Kykke says. 'Stupid people might be tempted to believe you'd brown-nosed or blabbed your way out of jail.'

'I know.'

'You'd sold your pals' arses to someone who doesn't deserve their own arse. But don't give it a thought, Beach Boy. You don't need to stand there staring at a hole in the ground like some schoolboy who's been caught beating the bishop in the changing room. Old Kykke doesn't believe everything he hears.'

Kykke covers his ears with both hands to illustrate his point.

'The sun's so hot your brain goes mushy,' he says.

'Get over it, as they say up in northern Norway. That's what I was told when I skidded big-time, crashed on to the pebbles on the beach in Lofoten and ended up with a face as flat as a flounder. Get over it, said the doctor at the hospital in Gravdal. That's what you have to think in critical situations. Fight the pain.'

He reaches over for the newspapers from the reefer pocket. Unfolds the *Verdens Gang* over the bike tank, leafs through and finds a drawing of a woman's face. The portrait of the dark-haired woman looks like an identikit picture of a suspected criminal. Kykke reads aloud the text under the picture while Beach Boy watches. His face exudes both pride and fear.

'This is the worst bit of mischief we've ever seen at the club,' Kykke says, planting his index finger on the drawing. 'That's why you and I need to have a little heart-to-heart, however bloody hot it is here and however sweaty I get listening to your schizophrenic chatter.'

He produces a bottle of Farris mineral water from the pannier on the bike and drinks half in one go, pours the rest on his handkerchief and knots it round his head.

'You should be glad Borken isn't here,' Kykke says. 'Borken's really pissed off. He told me to ask you some questions. First up, who's the woman?'

'No idea.'

'Second up, do you know who killed her?'

Beach Boy pokes the gravel with the stick. 'I thought it had to be someone from Kamikaze.'

'Why?'

'Because I found a ladies bag I imagined was hers in the house in Halden, the shack up in Aspedammen which Bård the Board had rented out to the Kamikaze lot.'

'How did you know it was hers?'

'Well, I mean…'

'Spit it out,' Kykke says.

'Did you say you had a Marlboro?'

'The packet's yours.'

Beach Boy lights a cigarette, unable to hide the fact that his hands are shaking.

'Well,' he says, 'there was so much damn blood on the kitchen floor and cupboard doors.'

'The Kamikaze could have killed a chicken,' Kykke says.

Beach Boy laughs and says he doubts anyone has seen a chicken left alive, except for the workers on chicken farms. He breaks the stick and tosses one part in an arc over the road. A couple of seconds later a red Transit van drives up from the north, more kids celebrating the end of school. The driver hoots his horn, staccato. Beach Boy gives him the finger.

'Let's sit down, shall we,' Kykke says. He walks around the concrete building and returns carrying a bench. He places it in front of one door.

Beach Boy tries to peep through the cracks in the woodwork.

'Is there really a cool bike in there?' he asks.

Kykke nods and sits down on the bench.

'Positive?'

'Jesus, you don't think I'd lie, do you?' Kykke says. 'You can trust me. Lips and I are the last friends you have in the Seven Samurai. Borken said I should wallop you over the skull with a spanner and bury you in the green hell.'

'Green hell?' Beach Boy echoes, staring at Kykke in fear, as though the man might produce a spanner from up his sleeve.

'The forest, Mongoloid Features,' Kykke says. 'Relax, lad. Do I look like I intend to smash your head down into your belly?'

'No,' Beach Boys answers, but steps back, kicks a small stone, and then another.

'Can you stand still or sit down on the bench,' Kykke says. 'All your kicking's making me nervous.'

'What about me? I'm getting a bit stressed with all your talk of killing me and burying me and all that.'

'You know what I mean by the green hell, do you?'

'The jungle in Vietnam.'

'Or the jungle in the Amazon. Surely you didn't think I'd transport you all the way to the banks of the Amazon to bury you in the mud there, did you?' Kykke laughs. His laughter sounds like the roar of a Kawasaki driven in an unusually low gear without a silencer.

'You were just kidding then?' Beach Boy says.

'Have I ever hit anyone?' Kykke asks.

'Not that I know of.'

'I'm a big guy, so I don't hit.'

Kykke points to the edge of a wood beyond the R120 where birch striplings, sallow and rowan trees display light green leaves against the background of dark spruces. A flowering wild cherry tree stands out amid all the light green.

'Think it's my style to bury a young lad in the forest, like a second Thomas Quick?'

'No, serial killing isn't really your style,' Beach Boy says, and sits down on the bench beside the man with the eyepatch and a dripping handkerchief on his head.

'If Borken had put a knife to my throat and ordered me to bury you, I would've refused,' Kykke says. 'Now you've heard what nasty thoughts chief Samurai Borken has about you. You can thank your Maker that I, as deputy, and Lips, as cashier, are of a different opinion.'

Kykke pulls off the top part of his leather suit and ties the sleeves around his waist. He is wearing a lumberjack shirt underneath, soaked in sweat. He removes the shirt and hangs it from a nail on the door. Walks around in a vest and gets himself a green can of beer from the left-hand pannier of the Kawasaki. It is a Carlsberg covered with beads of moisture. Beach Boy asks how he has kept the beer cold and is told he has icepacks inside a little cooler bag in the pannier. Beach Boy looks longingly at the beer can, but he is informed that as he is going to test-ride the bike he will have to stick to Coke.

It surprises Beach Boy that Kykke, who has been in the club for so long, has only one tattoo, at least only one that is visible on the winter-pale skin he reveals. It is a finely drawn affair on his upper left arm. Shaped like a diamond. Once, years ago, when he was a clingy, snot-nosed hanger-on, he asked Kykke what the tattoo was supposed to be. He was told gruffly that it was a souvenir of his days as a pirate, and he almost fell for it.

'We have to talk a bit more about what happened this winter,' Kykke says, wiping froth from his beard with the back of his hand. 'So you went to the house in Aspedammen? How did you get there?'

'In a car I nicked.'

'What kind of car?'

'Nothing special. A rusty old Opel Corsa.'

'What the hell did you do out there?'

'I wanted to see if there was any dope hidden in the house. It was a couple of days before I had to do bird in Trøgstad. I was crazy for something, anything. Bård had said he thought the Kamikazes used the shack as a depot for all sorts of goodies.'

'Did you go alone?' Kykke asks.

'Completely alone, late at night. It was dark and really cold. And spooky in that shit-heap of a house.'

'How did you get in?'

'Levered the rotting front door with a crowbar. And then I shone a torch round the haunted house and searched pretty systematically.'

'Find any dope?'

'Bit of powder in a kitchen cabinet. Tasted like amphetamine, but I wasn't sure. Could just as well have been rat poison and there wasn't enough for a decent dose. So I left it. Behind the kitchen door I found a ladies bag, and a bunch of crumpled plasters inside an envelope. And written on it was the name of that rich guy… the bag was empty. But it was a nice bag, crocodile skin.'

'And you took the bag with you?'

'I wanted to give it to a girl I was going out with, called Anita, as a goodbye present before I went to prison. So I went to the block of bedsits in Remmen where she lives. She's a student. Anita liked the bag a lot. But then another girl appeared. Her name was Dotti. When she saw the bag she said she'd seen it before. Actually it belonged to a foreign woman she'd been sitting next to on the Göteborg train. It was all very embarrassing for me, but I managed to blag my way out by saying I'd found it in a litter bin at the railway station.'

'In Halden?'

'In Halden, yes.'

'OK,' Kykke says. 'You find a ladies bag in an empty house and someone connects it with a woman she saw on a train. What makes you think the owner of the bag was murdered?'

'It was all the blood, as I said. And then there was the drunk who came as I was leaving.'

'A drunk came to the house?'

'Yes, as I was leaving there was a drunk standing in the doorway. I almost leapt out of my boots. The old man reeked of booze. Said he lived next door, asked me if I was a cop. "Are you the police, young man?" He said he'd rung the police some days before because he'd seen something very suspicious in Reidar's house. Reidar is Bård's uncle who couldn't care less about the shack in Aspedammen because it's falling to pieces and he lives in Lanzarote. The old man grumbled on about how the police never took him seriously when he saw mysterious goings-on and could prove the presence of drugs gangs and terrorists and so on. I told him I wasn't a cop but Reidar's nephew and it was my job to keep an eye on the house. Then I asked the old boy what suspicious things he'd seen.'

'The suspense is killing me,' Kykke says with a grin. But his expression is wary. The eye covered by the patch squints vigilantly into the sun.

'He said he'd seen a couple of guys forcing a gypsy woman – that's what he called her – out of a car and into the house. And then he heard screaming.'

'I see,' Kykke says. 'Did the old boy give any details of the two men and the car they came in?'

'No, and I didn't ask. I told him the men he'd seen were friends of mine I'd sent to show the gypsy woman around. She was looking for somewhere to live, but she thought the house was too isolated and the rent much too expensive. She went all surly, made a scene, screamed and took off.'

'And he bought that?'

'He was rat-arsed and drooling. Tried to bum money off me. I freaked, made for my car and roared off to the sound of tinkling ice. Afterwards, when I'd calmed down and heard about the woman on the train, I put two and two together and reckoned the Kamikaze gang had been settling a score with a drug mule in the house. One who'd perhaps cheated them and had to pay the bitter price.'

Kykke takes a sip from the beer can, a pinch of snus, spits majestically and praises Beach Boy for an excellent account. He asks why the lad thinks it was the Kamikaze renting the house and hears that it was Bård, Bård the Board, the skateboard freak, who had told him. Kykke says a lot of strange things go on in Aspedammen, as there is a motor circuit and everyone interested in cars knows the place, and it is close to Sweden. Pretty deserted. Great place for anyone who runs a little business over the border and needs somewhere to store goods.

'You haven't heard of or suspected anyone else who could be involved, apart from the Kamikaze?' Kykke asks.

'Nope,' Beach Boy answers.

'And the million-dollar question. Why did you think there was a connection between a woman killed in Aspedammen and the murder victim at Thygesen's place in Oslo?'

'When I went to Trøgstad there was a bit about the murdered woman in the papers and…'

'Hang on,' Kykke says. 'Was there anyone in the slammer who knew you had something to do with the Seven Samurai?'

'No, luckily, not at first,' Beach Boy says with a wide grin. 'I realised then how incredibly smart the rule of secret membership was. Because at Trøgstad there were two guys strutting about telling everyone they were Hells Angels and a third I was sure was a Kamikaze. There could have been all sorts of trouble if they'd known I was a Samurai. And then there were the poker-faced Albanians, who hate bikers, and the desert rats from Somalia, who don't like our kind either.'

'What did the other inmates make of you, lad?'

'I was who I said I was. A petty thief from Hobøl who lived with his mother in Tistedalen.'

'You said *at first*?'

'Gradually I began to feel more comfortable. The two Hells Angels left right after I arrived, and the guy I thought was a Kamikaze was transferred to a prison in Mysen because he stabbed a guy with a fork in the dining room. And then I got a cell-mate from Frederikstad, nothing suspect about him, in for fiddling the dole, who dreamed about riding a big bike. He was a Harley fan. I tried to redeem him, told him about Kawasakis and the Seven

Samurai, hinted that I knew a bit about the club.'

'Fine,' Kykke says. 'What I'm getting at is: did you say anything to the warders or welfare officers, that sort of person?'

'Not a peep. Are you out of your mind?'

Kykke slings his scarf, rolls a fag from Beach Boy's pouch, lights up, asks about Thygesen and blows out a cloud that hangs in the still air.

'One of the Hells Angels worked with me in the workshop where we reinforced the wooden crates,' Beach Boy says. 'He said the big guys in the Hells Angels had been to see Thygesen once to get advice about their magazine *Scanbike*. It was something to do with freedom of expression, and Thygesen was supposed to give legal support for a good fee. But it went pear-shaped and the Hells Angels were so angry they considered burning down his house. I wondered if the Kamikaze had used Thygesen as well and got so annoyed they dumped the dead woman in his garden, as an act of revenge, sort of.'

'You're a sharp thinker,' Kykke says. 'But is your memory as good? Can you remember me mentioning we'd also used some lawyer at The Middle of Nowhere?'

'No, first I've heard of it.'

'We, well, I, in my capacity as the mechanic in the Seven Samurai, hired a legal consultant at great expense to try to prevent the local council from expropriating the bunker and stopping us drinking and so on. All because of some damned environmental project the bloody Våler mayor wanted to push through. I lost because my legal bodger didn't see the time limit for an appeal and so I couldn't take out a civil action, and in the end I lost the chance to buy the farm and build a proper, authorised garage here. You didn't hear about this? You didn't tell anyone about it?'

'No,' Beach Boy says, staring at the ground.

'Look me in the eyes, boy.'

'I hadn't heard about it, and if I had, I wouldn't have told anyone, would I?'

'That sounds logical,' Kykke sighs. He gets up, walks over and points to the figure on the wall. 'D'you remember who daubed this? It was a kid we took care of when he pedalled past on his mountain bike, a real little racer from Ringvoll with an alcoholic dad and a Valium-addicted mum. Good at drawing. A little Edvard Munch. Perhaps you can remember the lad in that foggy brain of yours? And why on that autumn day in 1993 he stopped drawing atomic rockets and started drawing Thygesen on a gallows? Because little pitchers have long ears, and the kid had heard how mad we were with the bum lawyer from Oslo West.'

Beach Boy hides his face in his hands.

'There's no point lying through your teeth to me,' Kykke says, sitting down heavily with a creak of the bench. 'Was everything else you told me true or was that all lies too? Such as you being all alone in Aspedammen?'

'Bård the Board was with me. He kept watch in the car we'd stolen.'

'He never saw the blood or the bag?'

'No,' Beach Boy says, crossing his heart and drying his tears.

'That's the easy stuff over with,' Kykke says. 'Now we come to what really made Borken see red and Lips to look on the dark side. They almost went berserk when you called from the phone box in Trøgstad to say you were moving heaven and earth to get the photo of the murdered woman in the paper. They didn't think it was possible and, to be honest, neither did I. But today I told them you'd actually pulled it off, your pièce de résistance. Do you think Borken went berserk? Give me the CD player on your belt.'

Beach Boy unhitches the Walkman and passes it to Kykke. He takes out a little screwdriver from a side pocket in his leather trousers and unscrews the lid with quick, practised twists of his wrist. Removes the insides and examines them. Puts them back and replaces the lid.

'What was the point of that?' Beach Boy asks.

'Looking for a police bug,' Kykke answers calmly, and talks about the time he was part of a strike committee on a rig called the North Sea Star and the company bugged the cabins of the most militant gang leaders. That was when he had to learn how to look for hidden microphones.

'You don't bloody trust me at all, do you?' Beach Boy shouts. 'You have no reason to suspect that I'm a dirty, low-down spy.'

'Kiss my arse,' Kykke replies coldly.

'So tell me what the point of taking my CD player was.'

Beach Boy goes right up to Kykke and screams in his face, but Kykke stands with his hands in his pockets without responding.

'You just stand there, calm as a stone,' Beach Boy says.

'My calm is of the type the old Greeks called stoic. Stoic calm,' Kykke says. 'Now listen. Someone may have planted an especially adapted CD player, with a mike and recording equipment, perhaps even a transmitter. What I did, I did for the safety of the club and for yours too. The world out there is hard. The cops are trying to crush every biker club in the country and they have the very latest bugging equipment. What have we got? Year before last's old crap.'

Beach Boy has to concede this argument. He calms down and declares that if he were to spy for anyone it would have to be for the Russians. He could give them loads of information about the Nike battery in Våler.

From a little leather bag attached to the front of the Kawasaki petrol tank Kykke takes a shiny silver Dictaphone. They sit down and he places the mini-recorder on the bench between himself and Beach Boy.

'There's something that mystifies a simple soul like myself,' Kykke says wiping the sweat with a cloth he has taken from the bike. It is stained with motor oil. The stripes it leaves on his face are reminiscent of Indian war paint. 'If you wanted to put the squeeze on a rich bastard why did you contact the police?'

'I thought I'd kill two birds with one stone,' Beach Boy answers.

'How?'

'First, I wrote a letter to Ryland, Gerhard Ryland the admin director of that oil fund, and said I'd found his name and address in an envelope in the bag of the woman who'd been killed. I wrote that our silence had a price, and it was a million kroner.'

'What do you mean *our* silence? For Christ's sake, surely you didn't say anything about the Seven Samurai in the letter, did you?'

'Not at all,' Beach Boy answers quickly, running a hand through his yellow hair. 'No, I just wrote that I represented a gang.'

'Bloody hell, son,' Kykke groans. 'Now you're lying again. We can't have this. I'll have to turn this little mike off. Borken said he wanted a recording of the conversation if things went seriously wrong.'

'Don't give a shit,' Beach Boy says. 'There are no skeletons in my cupboard. But you can't expect me to remember everything perfectly. There are drugs that blow your mind if you mix them. Amphetamine plus four or five uppers, right?'

'Does that mean you're high now?'

'Bit of a hangover from last night, although my head's cleared after the Rohypnol. I didn't know you were coming to pick me up at my mum's this morning until you were at the door and frightened the living shit out of her.'

Kykke switches on the Dictaphone. The light is red; the tape is running.

And it runs for a good while.

In the end, Kykke gets up, switches off the machine and says he has to go and wash, and cool down in the stream. He crosses the tarmac road, which feels soft under his boots, plods through the birch scrub and mounds of wood anemones in full leaf – they remind him of snowdrifts bordering the Filefjell road in June – finds a hole in the streamlet, where some yellow flowers are pushing through; he would like to know their name, he will have to find out in his next life, then he can become a botanist if he isn't reincarnated as a bumble bee, that is. He takes off his eyepatch and sticks the whole of his head into the stream. The water is deliciously cool.

This is freedom. Finding a stream by a country lane and cooling down.

He waits for the surface of the water to become still. To reflect. He talks to his reflection: 'He wasn't a sight for the gods, except for Zeus, who set the Cyclops to work in Hephaistos's smithy where they forged hammers.'

Kykke breaks leafless twigs from a small tree which must have died in the summer drought. Places the twigs to form a lattice pattern over the hole. Sees his reflection again. This is how he will look behind prison bars.

'You're not a pleasant sight to behold from the normal view of beauty, but you'll be even more unlovely behind bars.'

A lack of beauty can be compensated for by cleverness.

'But your cleverness wasn't enough when you were going to create Hephaestus's smithy in The Middle of Nowhere. Cleverness will be dealt a fatal blow in a prison. What will be left of you is a big, heavy, hollow man slowly wasting away.'

Kykke dries himself with clumps of moss. Replaces the patch over his eye.

He conjures up the two Hells Angels leaders who in the spring of 2001 were both sentenced to sixteen years' imprisonment for smuggling 98.3 kilos of amphetamines.

Three to four carrier bags of speed. Sixteen years!

Sixteen tons. Sixteen ton-heavy years. The Belgian courier got fourteen. That is as long as it takes to become a teenager, and a teenager is almost an adult, a teenager has lived a little life.

The street value of one hundred kilos of amphetamines is more than half a billion kroner. Right, but if you buy shares worth half a billion in the Orkla Group, you are applauded at the shareholders' meeting and not one bugger asks you where you got it from, whether for example you sliced it off your grandmother's back in strips or laundered cocaine money or said you got the dough as a settlement for fish guts you sold to the Japs.

Even if a biker is innocent he risks being convicted for something, as an accessory. The authorities have made up their minds. Now people who started riding bikes because they loved the freedom of the road are hauled in to rot in clink until they reach pensionable age and are chucked out and can continue living like rotten apples in a basket, in a hospice.

'That won't happen,' Kykke mumbles, ploughing his way through the scrub forest like a bear, tearing up small trees by the roots, snapping them in half and throwing them into hell, if there is a hell for trees. 'You never know, you'll always walk alone, in the end.'

The sun stings his neck, unless it is the bumble bee he will become that has stung him.

'Hope that idiot of a boy has enough gumption to have cleared off.'

But Beach Boy's brain is on stand-by. He is sitting and smoking, cutting chunks off a piece of wood he has found, whittling away with his penknife.

'Why do you look so bloody angry, like a pitbull?' Beach Boy asks. 'You'll soon be frothing at the jaws.'

Kykke wipes his mouth.

'I thought I would get a bonus when I got out, I did,' Beach Boy says. 'The Hells Angels boast that they do. You said you had a sexy beast to show me? Were you teasing me or what?'

'I never tease. You'll see in two shakes. Do you know what Lips called you when he heard about all the commotion you've caused, about your great plan to make the club rich?'

'A genius?' Beach Boy answers.

'Lips said you were a loose cannon.'

'What does that mean?'

'Give it some thought and you'll work it out,' Kykke says, unclipping the bunch of keys from his belt. 'If you'd really managed to breach the ship below the waterline the cops would've surrounded your mother's house when you came home, and they'd have been swarming round here. I have to say no real harm has been done. I don't think Borken would agree with me, but I'm the one handling this. Borken isn't here.'

'Where is he?' Beach Boy asks, glancing towards the road where an articulated lorry is struggling up the gentle bend in the direction of Hobøl.

'Take it easy. Borken's at home on the farm arguing with his family about inheritance rights and his golf project. He won't turn up here to wring your neck.'

Kykke asks Beach Boy if he is willing to make a deal, to drop his plan. If he is capable of buttoning his lip and shutting his gob, of denying everything when asked.

'Christ, yes,' Beach Boy answers and kicks the pile of wood-shavings by his feet.

'Then let's draw a veil over the whole business, shall we? And you get a bonus from me, and Lips. It isn't one of the atomic rockets you always used to go on about, but it is almost,' Kykke says. 'Let's have a look at Lips's marvel.'

He finds the key that fits the padlock on the door, opens

it and pulls it to one side. Stale, oil-laden air hits them. The sunlight that tumbles in brings a gleam to the fire-engine red paint and nickel plate of a streamlined sports bike with a powerful exhaust pipe pointing upwards.

'Ninja,' Beach Boy whispers. 'Jesus Christ. It's a Ninja!'

'I hope you won't be disappointed to hear it's a ZX-11,' Kykke says.

'Disappointed? Like hell I am!' Beach Boy exclaims, goes over to the bike and strokes the side shield where it says 'Ninja' in letters that are almost as yellow as his hair, brushes some dust off the seat and grips the handlebars to get a feel. 'I didn't know Lips had bought himself such a beautiful hot rod.'

'You know what a cheapskate Lips is. He saved himself a stack of money by not buying the biggest race bike, the ZX-12,' Kykke says. 'But this one's not bad, is it?'

'Not half bad,' Beach Boy says. 'Sure I can borrow it?'

'You can have it for as long as Lips is in the States.'

'Great! This is the Samurai spirit, lending me a vehicle like this. Can we roll it outside?'

Before receiving an answer to his question Beach Boy starts trundling the bike on to the gravel. He straddles the machine. His face vies with the bodywork to beam brighter.

'Is Lips in the States?' he asks.

'His mother in Florida is ill,' Kykke replies.

'Does his mother live in Florida?'

'Don't keep asking questions and digging.'

'Sorry,' Beach Boy says and lets out an off-key whistle. 'Shit-hot machine. Could get a boner from less. How many cc is it? Nine hundred?'

'More than a thou. To be precise, one thousand and fifty-two. And it's got unbelievable thrust considering the cc. Lips says hi and he'll throttle you if you ride it like a maiden aunt.'

'Tell him that won't happen.'

The red van they had seen earlier passes by slowly, only one school leaver visible inside, and that is the driver. On the cab of the superannuated Transit the driver has put an orange roadwork sign, which says in black letters: Plantation Work In Progress.'

'Cool,' Beach Boy says.

The Transit disappears around the bend northwards.

'I don't like that red van,' Kykke says. 'Anyone would think they were spying on us.'

Beach Boy says it would be unusual for a cop to dress up in red as a nineteen-year-old school leaver, drive around in a red van, booze and make out with the girls. Kykke is forced to agree, but he tells the lad not to chat with the driver if he comes back and stops.

'You'll have to jump off now,' Kykke says. 'I'll go for a trial run and test the brakes. Think they're a bit tight.'

'Your helmet,' Beach Boy says, going over to Kykke's bike and fetching the helmet from the seat.

'Just going down to Joker's in Folkestad. Don't need it for such a short trip.'

'What about the police?'

'In their hammocks cooling down in this heat,' Kykke says, putting his leather top back on and wrapping a scarf round his neck.

'I fancy an ice lolly. Do you want one?'

'Please,' Beach Boy answers. 'Will you get me *Moss Avis* as well?'

'I reckon you've got more than enough newspapers,' Kykke says, pointing to the wad sticking up from his coat pocket and the *Verdens Gang* on the ground.

He starts the engine, revs up with a roar, lets the throttle go and does a speedway turn on the gravel, straightens and heads for the road on the rear wheel.

'Neat,' says Beach Boy.

He strolls into the concrete building. Switches on the light inside. Nothing happens. The tight-arse bosses at the council have probably cut the Seven Samurai off with another of their dirty tricks to get rid of the bikers in The Middle of Nowhere. His eyes slowly accustom themselves to the darkness.

The room seems empty compared to how it was when he was last here, in January. There is a boat on trestles, a plastic dinghy with a weak six-horsepower outboard motor at the rear. He hasn't seen that before. A lot of what he was used to seeing has gone: all the club's tools, the lathe, the drill stand. Kykke's blue toolbox is on the work bench. The camp bed where Kykke usually sleeps has been moved to the corner, with a sleeping bag on top.

Beach Boy opens the fridge beside the bed. It stinks of mould. He finds an unopened bottle of Farris. The lid is difficult to get off, but he manages and takes a drink.

With the curiosity of a thief he opens the big toolbox which Kykke brought back with him from the oil rig when the bastards on the North Sea Star gave him the boot.

If he has the Ninja all summer he will need to borrow some of Kykke's tools, and he has plenty of them. All of them top quality: Bahco. At the bottom of the box there is a big, military-green egg in a nest of oil-stained rags.

Beach Boy carefully lifts out the hand grenade and wipes an oil stain on his trousers.

'Cool,' he says, 'that Kykke's taking good care of the souvenir I gave him from Våler Forest.'

It is a Mills grenade which he found when he and Jens Petter broke into an overgrown bunker by Kasper's land one summer night eternities ago. They discovered that these small steel pineapples from the Second World War still had a bang in them when they tried a couple. They went off like bazooka shells and splinters whizzed through the scrub like a swarm of angry bees.

He hears Kykke turning into the drive, packs the hand grenade away and pats the cotton and rags round it. Wondering what Kykke actually wants with a live grenade in his toolbox. But, as he said before, it is a hard world out there.

'Crap shop,' Kykke says, sitting on the Ninja. 'They didn't have the new Manchester United lolly at Joker's. Can you nip down to the kiosk at the Skjellfoss crossroads and buy a couple?'

'Of course,' Beach Boy answers. 'But I'm a bit hard-up.'

'You'll get some start-up capital from the club, Beach Boy,' Kykke says, fishing out a note from his wallet. 'All I've got is a grumpy Sigrid Unset, but she'll do for a couple of lollies, a full tank and a bit more.'

He gives Beach Boy the silver-glinting five hundred-kroner note.

'I don't know what to say,' Beach Boy stammers.

'You don't have to say anything,' Kykke answers. 'Thought we should take care of you when you came out.'

He scratches his beard furiously and starts describing in great detail the big patches of snow on the slalom piste in Middagskollen and how this is a sign of the speed with which summer came.

'Right, I'm off,' Beach Boy says.

'I'll just adjust the brakes first,' Kykke says. 'They were even tighter than I thought.'

'It's very dark in the workshop.'

'Trust me. I can fix brakes blindfold. Even if I was blind in *both* eyes,' Kykke says, pointing to the eye covered by the black patch. 'You're probably wondering why the room looks so bare. We had to sell a number of items to pay the electricity bill and all the other council charges. As far as that goes, we could have used your million.'

He laughs and says the club will soon be back in operation. Beach Boy laughs too, but has to raise a finger to his eye and wipe something away.

'Don't be sad because of the council,' Kykke says.

'Everything's so bloody unfair. Why do we never get a real chance in life?'

'We will, we will.'

'There are just limits and restrictions everywhere.'

'Break them then,' Kykke says. 'Fuck them. You've been brainwashed by the prison welfare officer and have learned fine words, which actually only put a damper on your mood and sense of freedom.'

'I haven't been indoctrinated, if that's what you think,' Beach Boy replies. 'We had what are called constructive discussions.'

'Fair enough. That's what they pay the jug shrink to tell you. But when it comes to the crunch Zen has got more to it than all that psycho-babble people are so free with. With Zen and Greek mythology you can go from here to eternity, and a good bit further.'

'I'd like to learn more about them.'

'Here's Lesson Number 1,' Kykke says. 'Paradise is wherever you are now. The instant you flick your fingers or race along the road to Lofoten you're in the only place that can be called heaven.'

'It was Lofoten where you lost your eye, wasn't it?'

'No,' Kykke answers. 'It was on a trip to Czechoslovakia. We didn't know that Hells Angels ruled the roost in the country pub where we went. I had a smashed glass thrust into my face. That was a kind of eternity moment. You think you're gonna snuff it, it hurts like hell. But you get through it, into something new and better.'

'Jesus. Hells Angels,' Beach Boy says.

Kykke rolls the bike through the doorway and stands it against the work bench.

'You know I don't like having someone looking over my shoulder when I'm busy,' he says, and goes in search of a chilled Carlsberg in the cooler bag on Brontes. 'Sit in the sun and drink, but no more than half.'

Beach Boy listens to Kykke cursing and banging in the dark. He has enough flakes of tobacco in a little plastic pouch to roll himself a thin joint. He lights it and knocks back the beer in quick swigs.

A car coming from the south at great speed brakes and turns into the gravel drive, sending up clouds of dust. The car is a type Beach Boy has seen only in advertisements before: the latest Opel sports car, a shiny aluminium Speedster with the hood down in the sunny weather, two occupants – no room for any more – and German plates, easily recognisable by the four letters and EU logo. The woman in the passenger seat is wearing a scarf, as women do in convertibles. She opens her mouth and Norwegian, not German, comes out.

She asks for directions to Bærøe Farm.

Beach Boy says to drive north through the Våler bend, on to the straight and then take a right at the Skjellfoss crossroads. Then follow the signs on the gravel roads.

'But you can't drive right up to the farm,' he says. 'When you come to Lake Bærøe there's a sign that says "Trespassers Forbidden". They're pretty strict about that.'

'We've been invited to Bærøe,' the woman says in a saccharine tone.

'Can imagine,' Beach Boy says. 'Please pass on my regards to the farm-owner. He's the richest man in Østfold.'

The Speedster drives away. Beach Boy considers one finger is too little and gives them the full fist. He hides the empty beer can under the bench.

Kykke comes out, pushing the Ninja, with his toolbox on the seat. He straps the box to the back of Brontes.

He must have heard the car, must be able to see the beer can has gone and can perhaps smell the joint. But he says nothing.

Beach Boy says that now the rich are taking over the

best spots in the forests in Våler and Hobøl. The richest man in Østfold lives on Bærøe Farm. He's renovated the whole farm. All the yellow farmhouses have been painted and ditto the red barn.

Kykke answers, with weary intonation, that it is normal for rich people with yellow farmhouses and red barns to paint them, they can afford it.

'You don't understand what I mean,' Beach Boy says. 'I think there's something wrong with society when we get only shit from the council for wanting to spruce up The Middle of Nowhere while a rich man gets the go-ahead to take over a farm estate as easy as wink. Even if he can't comply with the requirement that he lives there and runs the farm and all that stuff. They're pampered while we're treated like pariahs, like beggars in India.'

Kykke polishes the tank until something invisible disappears.

'Now it's gleaming like the Emperor of Japan's jewels,' Kykke says. 'Fancy a ride?'

'Just guess, man.'

'Got instructions from Lips. You know how precise and finicky Lips is with everything and how hard he rides. He won't be very pleased if he returns from the States and finds his superbike knackered. Have you ridden anything other than motocross bikes?'

'Christ, yes,' Beach Boy replies with a laugh.

'Don't give me that. You're a motocross guy, we know that. When you came here and begged to become a member you were covered in mud. The biggest bike you've ridden is probably a Honda 350. The one that dickhead pal of yours, Jens Petter, had. And you rode it a bit last summer and autumn.'

'OK, you're right.'

'Remember this Ninja is three times more powerful than the old Honda crap, and a lot heavier. Before I entrust you with such a monster for the summer I want to see you ride it properly round bends. When you're back from the kiosk I'll stand here and watch you coming like a bullet out of the bend and leaning over at an appropriate angle. Not like in a road-racing comp, but at an acute angle.'

'I'll be coming like a bullet all right,' Beach Boy says.

'Oh dear,' Kykke answers, stroking his beard. 'Don't go all dreamy now. I can see you're going to get carried away. Listen to the following precautions from someone who has ridden from here to Mars, and the stretch from here to the moon was bends: when you accelerate out of here take it easy. The first bend comes on you faster than you think. Take your foot off the gas. Don't brake. Only boneheads brake into a bend. I never go into the Våler bend from the south at more than eighty. Lips thinks I'm a bloody wuss and I ride like an old codger. Lips takes it at a hundred. But I prefer to be safe and you should too. Especially when you've smoked a joint and drunk a beer. When you're in the first gentle bend and have started to lean over you can brake, but easy, easy, easy.'

'You should be a teacher,' Beach Boy says. 'Or perhaps, even better, a headmaster.'

'In my next life I'm planning to be a shrink.'

Beach Boy gets up on the Ninja. His smile has gone. He asks if the vehicle registration is all in order, and Kykke answers that they can check on his return.

'It's all yours, Beach Boy baby,' Kykke says and pats him on the back.

Beach Boy glances at the helmet on the seat of the Kawasaki.

'You didn't wear a helmet,' he says, 'on your little burn-up.'

'Right,' Kykke answers.

There is a silence. It is broken only by the chirp of

a blackbird in the trees across the road.

'Well?' Kykke says.

'Dunno. I've kind of lost a bit of my zing.'

Kykke brings his boots together and stands to attention.

'Will Private Viirilä explain to the colonel what he means by his anarchistic statement?' Kykke asks in a mock-fierce tone.

Beach Boy laughs and replies: 'Ha, ha, ha, ha... long live anarchy and blood-stained rags. May a storm arise and send socks skywards to dry on the polar star... heh heh heh.'

'Good, Private Viirilä! The next time they make a film of *The Unknown Soldier* you should apply for a job.'

'Does Colonel Karjula mean it is in order to make a better version than the one that became a cult hit in a certain Norwegian Bikers' Club?'

'Everything is possible, Viirilä. Fortune favours the brave. If Frederikstad-ers can become directors in Hollywood there's hope for other bold Østfold-ers. Here come the tanks by the way. The Russians are coming. Bloody Finnish sheep! Stay in your posts! Don't move. One step backwards and you will be shot!'

Beach Boy hangs over the handlebars, convulsed: 'Shit-hot, Colonel Karjula.'

'I believe you said something about a bowel movement?'

'Stop it before I piss my pants.'

'Did you allude to micturating in your trousers?'

'Stop it.'

'You are not in a position to give me orders, Private Viirilä. This is your Colonel speaking. You stop it! Where are you going?'

'To Lapland to fuck wolves,' Beach Boy gasps.

Kykke pauses for a dramatic effect, flings out his arms in resignation and shouts: 'Right, I see, pampered Finnish soldier. The wolves here in Våler Forest aren't good enough for you. You have to go all the way to Lapland to find a receptive vixen.'

Beach Boy laughs out loud. But his eyes are suddenly vacant.

'Not the forest, twat-face, the road,' he mutters to himself, and then louder, as if in supplication: 'Just do it!' He twists the throttle and sends gravel flying, roars on to the road, on to dry tarmac. Leaving a smell of burnt rubber. The wind catches his baggy trousers. He accelerates like a rocket, like a Nike off the launch pad. The engine whines like a tormented animal. Beach Boy must have been doing more than a hundred as he comes into the bend.

The roar falls silent somewhere, invisible to Kykke, in the gentle left bend. Again there is a silence. Kykke thought he heard the sound of metal on tarmac, of branches cracking.

He observes a tremor in his hands as he packs the boy's reefer jacket and the extra helmet and straps both on to the Kawasaki. The CD player and the Dictaphone he puts in the side pannier. He starts up and lets a post office van pass before turning on to the R120 northwards.

'Adios amigo,' he whispers. 'Adios The Middle of Nowhere.'

He snakes into the bend, glances to the right, stops, sees cracked branches glistening white like skeleton bones, and deep into the scrub a wheel spinning slowly, the spokes glittering. Even further in: a doll-like figure with spiky yellow hair on a blood-stained head. The body plastered to a tree. Arms and legs pointing in every conceivable and inconceivable direction.

Kykke, a lump in his throat, tells himself there is no point going to check. Carries on, taking it calmly. Meanders peacefully through the villages in Hobøl municipality.

At the Elvestad crossroads he sees a police car with a blue light coming from the Askim area and indicating to turn right on to the main road towards Våler and Moss. At the Shell station is the red Transit with the plantation sign.

Kykke swings right on to the E18. Goes through Elvestad, fucking Riverton in Beach Boy's translation. He always used to give Norwegian towns English names. A dump like Kroer became Pubs and Skotbu Shothouse.

He shifts up a gear. But adheres to the speed limit more or less. Daft to get stopped now.

The boy was out of his mind. May peace be with him.

In the middle of Fossum Bridge Kykke stops, loosens the bundle of clothes and drops the boy's reefer jacket over the railing. He watches it hit the springtide's brown waters of the Glomma.

'Vaya con dios.'

The water looks repugnant. Filthy.

He stops at the snack bar east of the bridge. Takes the phone from the tank bag and taps in Borken's number. Borken answers at once.

'Just to let you know the song bird has stopped twittering,' Kykke says. 'Crash-landed. Wings clipped.'

Borken says 'We're grateful for that' and switches off.

Kykke wanders behind the snack bar and throws up.

He buys a bottle of Farris to rinse his mouth. Goes into the toilet and washes the oil off his hands. Removes the patch from his right eye and massages his eyelid with a wet paper towel. He has to cover five hundred kilometres and will need both of them.

Once outside he stands squinting into the sharp sunlight for a while to get used to it.

He adjusts the bag straps. Mounts Brontes, pulls down his visor, swings on to the road to Sweden, to Stockholm. Borken will be waiting on the quay with the tickets for Tallinn. It is supposed to be a great town according to Lips, who has been motoring around the Baltic since the snows receded and bought a strip bar on behalf of the Seven Samurai management troika in the capital of Estonia.

But Kykke isn't sure he will ever go to Tallinn. Perhaps he will go to Lapland instead. Not to fuck wolves, but to go into hiding and dig for gold.

6

Ulrikke Enholm Johnsen is on her way along the R120 from Ringvoll to Moss Hospital in her own, personal, somewhat dented Citroën Xsara. She drives with the window rolled down. Her youngest is asleep in the child seat. In her imagination the young driver with the hennaed hair pretends her child is named after the car, Xanthippe Sara.

Fru Enholm, which she occasionally calls herself, is not in the best frame of mind. She has been ordered to do an extra shift at reception in Moss Hospital. On such a wonderful day, the first of the summer, she could have tried on her bikini and let the little one swim in their new inflatable pool instead of going to work.

She has a strong suspicion that some of her colleagues are not as allergic to pollen as they let on. Why, for example, do allergies have a greater impact in sunshine than rain?

This is what is on Enholm's mind as she scratches her newly pierced left ear, with a suitably punky, suitably discreet, stud – quite un-Christian, her partner said when she came home from the salon – as she passes the seventy-kilometre sign between Hobøl and Våler municipalities. She comes into the first bends in Våler and drives slowly to see the violets at the edge of the forest. This is a good place for violets. On the way home she can pick a bunch for her other half.

She sees something glinting in the scrub, possibly the spokes of a wheel. She sees cracked branches shining white, and she moves as far as she can on to the hard shoulder on the right. Activates the emergency lights. Checks her child hasn't woken up. No danger of that. Xanthippe sleeps like every parent's dream.

Enholm finds it strange there are no brake marks on the dry tarmac. Perhaps a mountain biker has skidded?

She crosses the road and sees several cracked branches. Stands on her tiptoes and sees a wheel which is too big for any normal bike. Someone has hurled themselves against a tree, thirty to forty metres off the road, in the middle of a spruce forest, as though he wanted to embrace the shaggy trunk.

Enholm swallows, and ploughs her way through the bushes and saplings, stumbles over fern roots and almost falls over the motorbike, which is red, like a toy. She pulls herself along by the branches as she covers the last metres to where the man, or the boy, because he is a boy, has smacked into the tree.

God almighty, there can hardly be a bone left intact, she cries, without any sense of a sound crossing her lips.

His head can't be whole either. There is a lot of blood on the outside, but his skin is as white as snow, as though all the blood has run out through the boy's nose and ears.

With a dry mouth, she gulps.

Come on now! You're not a surgeon, you're an office assistant. But you work at the hospital. And you've seen worse than this when the injured come in after head-on crashes on the E6. Take his pulse.

She touches his neck. The boy's head moves, as though perched loosely on his body, and she jumps back. Touches his neck again, even though it seems futile.

Zero pulse. Eyes stiff, pointing at eternity. Impossible to be deader than that. Considering what happened, the boy has been lucky and it was over within an instant.

He is wearing only a T-shirt. With some stupid film star on. No motorbike gear. And no helmet. Idiot. He could have saved himself the trouble with his yellow spiky hair.

What a wally. What a blinking wally.

But there is no helmet in the world that could have saved him.

She thinks she knows who the boy is. The strange hair confused her. Now she is sure. It has to be the Strand boy, son of Strand the flier, Strand the boozer.

Enholm leaps back through the scrub, to get away from the sudden death, to get to her phone. By the motorbike, which looks undamaged apart from the front headlamp, she smells the strong stench of petrol. Is she wearing any clothes that could produce static electricity and ignite the petrol vapours? No, she is wearing cotton trousers and a sweater and leather shoes. There is oil on her trousers, and blood, hers or the dead boy's.

She looks carefully before running across the road. It is precisely in situations like this you can lose concentration and do silly things, rush out into the road and get knocked down by someone speeding.

Her phone is where it should be, in the holder on the dashboard. Xanthippe is sleeping like a log.

Enholm taps in 113 for the ambulance service. Immediate response. She says she is reporting a fatal accident, a biker, just off the road, killed outright, very nasty accident. She is asked if she is sure it is fatal, she answers yes, she took his pulse and the result was negative. She adds she works at the hospital in Moss. Gives her name and location, the make of her car by the scene. On the first bend when you come into Våler from the north, in the trees, not so far from the turn-off for Kasper's land and a bit closer to the Bikers' Club…

'Something in English. On the tip of my tongue, something like Middle of Nowhere. Yes, I'll wait until you get here. No, I haven't rung the police. Will you do that? Best if I do it from the scene of the accident, OK.'

She rings 112 and has a woman on the line who calls herself the duty officer, probably it is the police station in Moss. The officer notes down the information Enholm tries to give as concisely as possible, asks her to wait and says an officer from Våler will be along soon.

She takes the warning triangle from the boot and walks a hundred paces along the road and sets it up. Walks stiffly back to the car, her heart hammering away and her pulse racing. Locates her partner's tobacco pouch in the glove compartment and rolls a cigar Fidel Castro would have envied her. Sniffs for petrol, can't smell any and lights up, drops hot ash on her light-coloured sweater and burns holes.

'Shit,' Ulrikke Enholm Johnsen thinks she has every reason to say, the whole situation taken into account, even though she represents the Christian Democrats on Hobøl council.

While she is calling the childminder to say she is going to be late a police car rolls up behind her. Out steps a constable in a short-sleeved, light blue shirt. His colleague remains in the car brandishing a pair of handcuffs.

'I thought you'd be coming from Våler,' Enholm says.

'We picked up a report of the accident on police radio,' the officer answers. 'We're on our way from Askim to a court session in Moss, with that dumb animal there.'

He points to an unfortunate on the back seat of the police car, who now has handcuffs clicked around his wrists.

The officer waves on a slow, inquisitive motorist.

'Was it you who phoned in?' he asks Enholm. She nods. He asks her to wait by her car, then makes his way through the undergrowth.

An unmarked police vehicle stops. Out steps a man in a uniform. He introduces himself as the Våler Police Chief, Harald Herføll. Before he makes a move towards the bushes, Enholm says: 'I know who the boy is. I can identify him.'

'Who is it?'

'Øystein Strand. Twenty odd. Actually from Ringvoll, but lives with his mother in Halden.'

Herføll says he knows of the boy. He thanks Enholm for her concise on-the-scene reporting.

'We modern women never stop surprising you chaps, do we, eh?' she answers, picking a handful of violets, and drives to Moss, where there is always a need for violets. This thought fills her with an insane joy, as if she has been drinking champagne.

Enholm knows the jollity will disappear, the way it always does, and she will have to live with the image of a dead boy embracing a spruce tree. She has never liked spruces much. If only it had been a pine, erect and magnificent, whose bark is illuminated by God's shafts of sunlight. Spruces always swallow all the light while pine reflects it and makes it even more golden, heavenly.

A red Transit stops at the accident spot, with a sign stolen from the Highways Authority mounted over the windscreen. The driver gawps as if he had paid to see a spectacle and is quickly waved on, after his breath has been smelt by police officer number two from Askim.

The ambulance arrives, all sirens blaring.

The rest should have been a simple matter of procedure for the police and paramedics who work with victims of biker accidents from the moment snow disappears to the moment it settles.

Had it not been for Herføll and his colleague from Askim finding there were several suspicious circumstances to this case. First of all, there is Øystein Strand riding such a powerful bike as a 1000cc Kawasaki Ninja without a helmet or leathers. Secondly, there were no brake marks. Thirdly, the bike must have been going at an incredible speed to have crashed through the undergrowth for such a distance. God knows it is speed that kills most motorbike riders, but what the Ninja must have been doing doesn't tally with even the most fanatical biker.

Herføll rings the duty officer in Moss and says he wants the crashed motorbike transported to the Moss Department of Transport branch, to undergo a thorough technical examination.

A thought, a wild idea, strikes him. The accident happened on the same day that the press printed an identikit picture of the woman who was murdered in Thygesen's garden in Oslo. The boy was in the Seven Samurai, as a kind of apprentice to the troll Terje Kykkelsrud. Thygesen, for a short period, was the legal adviser for the Samurai. Could there be a connection?

What that connection might be is extremely unclear to Herføll. But the wild idea won't let go of him.

The breakdown truck from Viking arrives. After dragging the bike out of the forest and lifting it up on to the truck Herføll asks the guy to have a quick look at the bike to see if there is anything unusual.

It takes a couple of minutes.

The Viking guy's response is clear: 'There are no damn brakes. Some bastard has tampered with them.'

On the way back to the office Herføll remembers Øystein Strand when he was first brought in as a fifteen-year-old under suspicion of having broken into the arms store by the Nike battery. Both he and his pal, Jens Petter Sundin, denied everything point-blank. Since no fingerprints were found at the site and none of the hand grenades that were stolen came to light the police initially had a poor case. It wasn't improved by the only witness withdrawing his statement. He, a mechanic friend of Øystein's father, said at first he had been out picking cowberries in the forest by Kasper's land and had seen and heard the boys setting off the grenades, but then he changed his mind and said he hadn't seen or heard anything.

Øystein had been a bright teenager, even though there was something shifty about him. He was full of wild stories and grandiose plans, and a bit of a blabbermouth. But when it came to the crunch, to the break-in, he was immovable and sat there with his turned-up nose stuck in the air.

Was it on the cards that Øystein Strand would end up on the wrong side of the law, regularly breaking into record and computer shops? Perhaps so. Nature and nurture. But the combination of nature and nurture had given him talents that, if realised, could have taken him anywhere, perhaps even to Mars, which was his ambition at that time. He wanted to be one of the first astronauts to land on the 'Red Planet'.

Instead he landed at a fearsome speed in the forest, covered in blood. It was enough to make you weep. Herføll doesn't weep. He has seen too many drunken killings and misery and drownings in Lake Vansjø for tears to flow because of a death. Nevertheless, when the young die in accidents something also dies in the adults who find them.

7

BACK IN HIS VÅLER office, Harald Herføll switches on the computer to write up a report about the fatal accident. He has phoned through the most important information of the case to Moss Police District and asked if there is any indication the Ninja could have been stolen. According to the way work is distributed in the district, the Våler station is responsible for further investigation, if necessary, with assistance from forensics officers in Moss or Kripos.

Herføll starts flicking through the documents he has on Øystein Strand. It is dismal reading for a law enforcer.

Trøgstad Prison was the boy's first taste of punishment. After two conditional sentences for petty larceny and car theft he received a stinging unconditional. Herføll rings Trøgstad and asks when Strand was released. Thursday 10 May is the response. To questions about his behaviour in prison, the answer is good, but his commitment to work was poor, otherwise he was co-operative and clean, according to his urine samples.

Herføll wonders if Strand had any enemies during his stretch. Not to the knowledge of the officer he talks to. Although inmates try to keep that sort of thing hidden, until eventually tempers fray and knives appear.

Strand enjoyed freedom for only a day before he careered off the road and collided with a tree. The poor fool. Fell straight into the trap.

On a hot rod. With tampered brakes?

Herføll notes on his pad: 'If the brakes on the Ninja

had been tampered with, causing Strand to ride to his death, we're talking premeditated murder.'

He receives a call from the Moss police to tell him that the plates on the Ninja were reported stolen from a bike parked by the council building in Ørje on the night of Friday 11 May. No Ninja bikes have been reported missing in the Moss Police District, but the officer says he will check all the other districts and with his Swedish colleagues.

Herføll notes: 'Plates stolen in Ørje. Bike stolen in Sweden? Must remember to ask the DoT people to examine the lock on the bike. If it has been forced professionally – hardly likely Strand stole the Ninja. Strand no good with locks and never steals vehicles alone.'

He leans back and looks up at Finken, who is smiling as he always does. Can that man never be serious? The picture of Finn Christian Jagge in the framed glass, taken on the victory rostrum after nicking the slalom gold from Alberto Tomba at the Albertville Olympic Games, is the only personal touch in the otherwise regulation sparse office. He has been teased a lot about the poster. Evil tongues claim he has hung up Finken because in 1993 a lady slightly the worse for wear after the Christmas dinner at Parketten in Moss told him he looked a bit like Jagge. Such tittle-tattle is water off a duck's back to Herføll. He knows Finken is hanging there because his slalom gold in the opinion of all true alpinists is among the great golds in the history of Norwegian winter sports. And Herføll is a fan. He doesn't often pray to the Lord. The times it has happened, with all due respect, it has been to remind the Lord that Østfold can't take any more mild winters if the extinction-threatened alpine sport in the county is not to be killed off for good. Last winter his prayer was heard and he had the pleasure of driving the snow-blower on Middagskollen and seeing the snow actually settle for one wonderful week after another.

Harald Herføll finds a Justice Department circular sent to police districts all over the country, in which they are requested to intensify their vigilance with regard to crime in biker circles. He calls the duty officer in Moss again. They agree that the best option for the Våler station is to contact Kripos directly.

It is rare for a provincial police officer to have anything to report that might capture the attention of Oslo. The fear of being treated unsympathetically and making a fool of himself weighs heavily on Herføll. He has to psych himself up before ringing Kripos.

Kripos mustn't get the feeling he has tied his colours to a particular hypothesis. In their eyes, there is nothing worse. If he is going to venture to suggest a possible connection with Thygesen he has to prepare what he is going to say and present it logically.

How did Thygesen come into the picture? How did he suddenly appear as a true *rara avis* in the council corridors of Våler? A lean man with grey hair tied in a ponytail, trembling hands and red eyes, but on the ball legally speaking.

When the Seven Samurai established themselves in the old garage from the war days the club reckoned on taking over the agreement the Chopper Freaks had had with Våler Council. Herføll had himself been involved with pushing through the agreement, as at that time he was on the building committee. Then the mayor, Wenche Rosefjorden, Conservatives, got it into her head that criminal bacteria accompanied biker circles and the bunker was a macho monument that should be razed to the ground. Rosefjorden couldn't say this aloud. Instead she decided the forest north of the R120 should be earmarked as a future conservation area. The mayor got the chief administrative officer on her side and later the executive committee and the local council's majority.

Of course there was uproar. The Samurai protested vehemently. They had a competent spokesperson in their leader, the businessman Borkenhagen, and they were able to wheel out the one-eyed Kykkelsrud. Despite his awful appearance Kykkelsrud had working-class charm and authenticity, which impressed the Labour Party and the Socialist Left. Behind the scenes slippery Lipinski was able to twist every communication, and very probably also forge documents.

However, what really created so much trouble for Rosefjorden that the events were commonly referred to as 'the fire in Rosefjorden's camp' was that she unwittingly stepped on the forest-owners' sensitive toes. Conservative mayors on forest councils who fall out with forest-owners have to expect to be thoroughly de-branched and de-barked.

Chainsaws met motorbikes in a strange alliance. In the midst of all this landed the highly dubious lawyer Vilhelm Thygesen from the capital to defend the Seven Samurai. His conduct of the case to ensure the bikers kept the clubhouse as their headquarters was in itself irreproachable. Thygesen's problem was alcohol. In his confusion he missed an appeal deadline for the court of enforcement. Rosefjorden and the chief administrative officer were on them like hawks and the battle to establish Kykkelsrud's authorised workshop was lost.

Shortly afterwards Kykkelsrud was found in a ditch near Lake Vansjø where he had been asleep with the heavy Kawasaki over him like a blanket. His blood test showed he was several times over the limit. Herføll interviewed the man when he awoke from his drunken stupor. His bitterness towards Thygesen was tangible. Jens Petter Sundin had arranged the club's contact with Thygesen, and Herføll said Kykkelsrud would crack every one of Sundin's fingers. Apparently a relative of Sundin's had once gone around with Thygesen.

Originally, the Seven Samurai must have noticed that Thygesen was willing to offer his legal services to bikers, whereas most lawyers wouldn't have touched them with a barge pole. When he helped the Hells Angels over the freedom of expression question there was quite a furore.

But Thygesen had to leave Våler with his ponytail between his legs, mission unaccomplished and negative PR in the local papers.

The forest-owners relaxed when the forests were downgraded to conservation areas in which the owners would still have full commercial use and rights. The fire in Rosefjorden's camp was extinguished.

Discussion at the provincial police station centred on whether the mayor's measures to fight possible crime in and around a biker's club would have the diametrically opposite effect to what she had intended. And on whether blocking the bikers' application to use and run the workshop would force the Samurai into more illicit activities. Would this stoke glowing embers?

Because chasing them out of The Middle of Nowhere was not so easy. They quite simply moved into the old German garage and attracted the young like flies. Kykkelsrud strengthened his links with the Social Democrats and the Socialists, talked the leader of the council's culture committee round and managed to market himself in idealistic circles as the most ardent patron of youth. Borkenhagen wrangled and wheedled himself deals with the local council and power plant to have water and electricity supplied. There were rumours that Lipinski had developed an amorous relationship with a forest-owner called Elisabeth Spetalen and thereby maintained relations between the bikers' club and one of the strong economic forces in the municipality.

Herføll writes: 'Could Strand have committed suicide? Had his stay in prison cracked him – did he leave the road deliberately? But why tamper with the brakes? So as not to give himself an opportunity to change his mind and brake at the last moment?'

From the bowels of the computer he elicits a list with the names and nicknames of the triumvirate in the Seven Samurai.

He pours himself a coffee from the flask. Clears his throat with a camphor drop and rings Kripos.

From the central switchboard he is put through to the duty officer. He gives a start when he hears the strident female voice and the name of Vaage. In police circles it is said of Vanja Vaage that she grew up in a sulphur mine on the Helgeland coast.

Vaage's reputation as remorselessly caustic is perhaps somewhat exaggerated?

Because she listens to what the officer from the outback has to say about the boy who crashes, the brakes and the bikers' club. Afterwards Herføll keeps Thygesen up his sleeve and allows Vaage to ask questions.

'Are the Seven Samurai in some way associated with the Hells Angels?' Vaage asks.

'More the opposite. They ride Japanese bikes, Kawasaki, and consider the Hells Angels their enemy.'

'Have the two clubs been at war?'

'No, but the club in our region has had a couple of clashes with a competing Østfold club called the Kamikaze.'

'Violent clashes?' Vaage asks.

'Once there was a fist fight outside By The Way, a pub off the E6 through Rygge. Recently the Kamikaze reported our Samurai for sabotaging their clubhouse in Kleberget, Moss. Apparently it was nonsense. School leavers had thrown a beer bottle full of petrol. A Molotov cocktail that never exploded.'

Vaage asks, with a certain levity of tone, if there was a bikers' club called Hara-kiri in Østfold. Herføll answers that most of the hara-kiri committed in his county occurred in cars on the E6 and E18.

'Are the Seven Samurai involved in much crime?' Vaage asks.

'Very little as far as we know,' Herføll replies, flicking through his papers. 'One member, Terje Kykkelsrud, has been convicted a couple of times for drink-driving, and once he got a conditional sentence for receiving stolen goods, selling on a stolen machine tool, a lathe I think it was. He was also accused of selling stolen motorcycle parts, but the charge was dropped through lack of evidence.'

'Just petty crime then?'

'We have suspicions of something bigger. We had an informant in the club, a young hanger-on, who reported that the Seven Samurai were planning to import drugs. Not heroin but amphetamines.'

'The informant wouldn't by any chance be the boy who killed himself?'

'No,' Herføll answers. 'But the two of them were childhood friends.'

'What's the name of the informant?'

'Jens Petter Sundin. Twenty-one. Lives in Kroer.'

'Kroer?'

'Yes, Kroer. Pubs in English.'

'Go on. What happened to the informant?'

'He was frozen out. The club leaders saw him as tainted. Which is also my opinion. He's unusually bad news.'

'Could it be that the club leaders saw Øystein Strand as a police informant?' Vaage asks.

'Possible,' Herføll answers. 'But there's nothing to support that view. We've had very little trouble from the Samurai since last winter and we have no one on the inside any more. Strand was generally seen as a blabbermouth, a fantasist and a schemer. Got excellent grades from

Kirkeparken, the upper secondary school in Moss. But loads of trouble at home.'

'The usual – dope, booze and violence?'

'No drugs, no violence. Booze and pills at his parents' house. We top the pill list in the county.'

'And I know why,' Vaage says. 'You've got no bloody mountains.'

'If the mountain won't come to Mohammed, Mohammed has to go to the mountains.'

'Meaning?'

'It's a proverb we have at our skiing club in winters when there's no snow. But Strand a copper's nark? I don't know. I simply can't imagine anyone in the club wanting to kill him. He was selflessly loyal to the Seven Samurai.'

'Who's at the head of the club?'

'I've mentioned Kykke.'

'Kykke?'

'Terje Kykkelsrud. He's known as Kykke. The name suits a guy who looks like a Cyclops from Greek mythology.'

Vaage says she had no idea ordinary Østfolders knew anything about Greek mythology.

Herføll continues his presentation undeterred.

'Kykkelsrud is the real motorbike fiend among the Samurai. Forty-nine years old. Divorced. No children. Officially lives in Krapfoss in Moss, but apparently he has a cabin in Finnskogen. He's more often there than at home. Mechanic by trade. Long time offshore, in the North Sea. He told me during an interview after a drink-driving offence that he was one of the first roughnecks on the oil rigs, but he was blacklisted after a strike and so came ashore to try and build up a fully authorised motorbike workshop. If anyone in the Seven Samurai had fiddled with the brakes of the bike Strand rode to his death, it would be tinkerman Kykkelsrud, I would imagine.'

Herføll hears Vaage tapping in the information on

the computer. He feels he has a listener.

'Noted,' Vaage says. 'Any more?'

'Kykkelsrud brought someone with him from the North Sea, called Lips. Richard Lipinski, originally a Polish American from Chicago, now a Norwegian national. He worked in catering on the rigs. Has two convictions, spent some time in a British prison for cheque fraud. In the days when cheques existed. Nothing illegal registered in Norway. Forty-seven years old. Lives in Skredderåsen, Kambo, Moss. Partner, two children. Acts as the club treasurer and has the reputation of being such a good bike rider he could have taken part in the world road-racing championship if he'd been younger.'

'The club has a leader, does it?'

'Yes, Borken. Leif André Borkenhagen. Thirty-eight years old. Single. Lives in Rakkestad where his family runs a farm. More of a car than a bike man, but rides a heavy Kawasaki like the others. No convictions, but he's disqualified from running a business after bankruptcy.'

'What kind?'

'Car body shop in Skiptvedt. Another company that imported paint. Video shop. Plus a great many more.'

'Any more names?'

'Not really. They were never seven Samurai, only a basic troika with young satellites floating round. The only one worth noting down is Sundin, whom I mentioned before. He was the one who provided the contact with Thygesen for the club,' Herføll says as casually as possible.

'Thygesen? Do you mean Vilhelm Thygesen?'

'Yes.'

'Oh, brother. Give me more.'

Herføll tells her about Thygesen's role as a legal adviser for a club in The Middle of Nowhere, somewhere in Våler. To his great satisfaction, it seems that the information has hit home. He can hear the keyboard in Oslo clattering away.

'I can't see a direct link,' Vaage says after Herføll has finished reporting back on Thygesen. 'Especially the role of the dead boy is unclear to me.'

'Something might have happened to Strand in prison,' Herføll says.

'Did you say prison? Trøgstad by any chance?'

'Well, I didn't say Trøgstad. But that was where Strand served his sentence until yesterday.'

'Yes!' Vaage exclaims. 'I think we've got something that is beginning to look like a case now. I'll have to check a number of recordings. It'd be good if you could be on hand so that we can reach you quickly, should we need to get back to you.'

8

'THE GREAT THING ABOUT you, Borken, is that you never trust anyone,' says Lipinski, taking a gulp of coffee. He grimaces to demonstrate the coffee is cold. He probably acquired the nickname Lips through his surname, not because his lips are particularly fleshy. The most pronounced feature of his face is his dark, bushy eyebrows which stand out even more now that he has shaved his head.

'I don't even trust myself,' Borkenhagen answers. 'Nothing is sure or reliable in our tiny human lives. Kykke's smart, but just as doomed to making fatal, childish mistakes.'

They are sitting in a room in the Sjöfartshotell on Katarinavägen in Stockholm. On the table is a gun, a Walther, type PP Super, along with its magazine. It is loaded with 9mm bullets of the kind known as 'Police'. On the table there are also more everyday items: a tray with a steel coffee flask and cups marked Scandic Hotels, a half-full ashtray, a six-pack of unopened Pripps Blå cans, three mobile phones and a couple of chargers. On the made double bed there is a map of Sweden spread out, the southern half. By the wall are two leather motorbike panniers with a helmet and gloves placed on top.

'In the worst-case scenario...,' Borkenhagen says. With his left hand he grips the ribbed metal of the pistol, raises the weapon, aims at the window where bright sunlight is falling between a gap in the curtains and pulls the trigger. The click of the hammer hitting the air in the empty chamber is surprisingly loud. He turns his upper body and arm and aims at a framed colour photograph on the wall. The subject is a passenger ship with a chimney on which there is a blue J inside a yellow star. He aims at the star and clicks the hammer again.

Borkenhagen puts the gun down on the arm of the chair he is sitting in.

He grabs a serviette from the coffee tray and wipes the oil off the pistol grip and dries his hands. They are small and brown, as though he has been in the south of Europe or a solarium. His face is not as tanned. There the brown is scattered between freckles, which redheads often tend to have. His wavy hair is short by his ears and neck and he has tried to flatten the hair on top by using gel. Unlike many redheads in the north he doesn't have blue eyes but brown. His glasses are tinted a soft brown, perhaps to match his eyes.

Both of the two men are lightly dressed because the summer heat has arrived in Stockholm too. Lipinski in a T-shirt and jeans; Borkenhagen in a light blue shirt and khaki Levi Dockers. Lipinski has a dragon tattoo curved round his left bicep. On his right he has the same tattoo as Kykkelsrud, an object that looks like a diamond, but which the Chinese tattooist in Aberdeen had designed especially for oil workers: a drill bit.

Borkenhagen has no visible tattoos. He adorns himself with gold chains round his neck and left hand, and he has a gleaming gold wrist watch round his right wrist.

'I can't work out how it can take our little friend so long to find a telephone box that hasn't been vandalised,' he says. 'Fuck Kykke for ringing from an unsafe mobile phone.'

Lipinski stifles a yawn, gets up and goes into the bathroom for water, comes back with a plastic glass. He sits down on the floor in a lotus position, blows bubbles in the water and studies them.

'We can take him out on board the ferry, get him loaded and give him a little nudge over the side,' he says.

'And then we come ashore in Tallinn, Lips. You and I minus the third name on the passenger list. On the car deck they find a large, antiquated Kawasaki by the name of Brontes. Who's going to ask any questions, eh?'

'We could get forged papers for Kykke. Bribe the customs officials in Tallinn. Everything's possible in Estonia with German dough.'

'Much too risky,' Borkenhagen says. 'And who's going to give the ugly bugger the nudge? We aren't built like him. If he's got rid of the grass, Strand, by putting him on a bike with no brakes, which is what we think, we'll have to use this.'

He pats the Walther.

'That's a bloody sight more decent than letting an old pal drown in the Baltic.'

'Poor bastard. He hates salt water,' Lipinski says. 'Well, that would be an unpleasant way to die. All the bubbles you release until you have no air left.'

He closes his eyes.

'How do you see your friend's face when he knows you're gonna shoot him?' Lipinski asks in a low, intoning voice.

'None of that psycho-babble, Lips.'

One of the phones rings. Borkenhagen grabs it. Lipinski is sitting with his eyes closed.

'Took your time, Bård,' Borkenhagen says. 'Where are you calling from? The kiosk in Sarpsborg. That's good.'

Borkenhagen listens carefully. Removes his glasses and massages the small, tense muscles in the corners of his eyes.

'Red van and red overalls? Right. Idiotic disguise if you ask me. But if it helped and no one saw you well enough to identify you, then maybe it was all right.'

He squeezes the phone between his shoulder and chin,

grabs one of the beer cans and opens it. Blows away the froth. Listens and rolls his eyes.

'Jesus,' he says. 'What a bloody fool!'

Lipinski opens his eyes. He too takes a can from the packet.

'Here's what you do, Bård,' Borkenhagen says. 'Get rid of the Transit. Hire or steal another car. Find a five-litre can of petrol. Go to Aspedammen and burn down your uncle's old shack. Do it at night and do it properly. Then you follow the plan. Take the ten thou, you know where it is, go to Ibiza and stay there for as long as you can. We'll send you more corn from Riga when we get set up there. Don't do any more of this school leaver bollocks. You did a good job, Bård. Have a nice trip.'

Borkenhagen presses *off*.

'Riga?' Lipinski says.

'He doesn't need to know precisely where we are. Fucking Kykke stole a Ninja, fixed the brakes and tricked Strand into ploughing through the forest and flying through the air like a rag doll. Five hundred metres from The Middle of Nowhere! That's so bloody stupid that even the muppets at the police station will know what's gone on. Bård the Board has done a great undercover job for us – in a clapped-out Transit – but what he had to say was really sad. Sad for Kykke. Kykke can take his bloody code of honour and stick it right up that big jacksie of his. Last winter he didn't even do one single decent run for us. And now this, sabotaging the brakes! The cops'll need about *this* long to get the picture, I reckon.'

He holds up the index finger and thumb of his left hand with the distance between them like the electrodes on a spark plug.

'We've got no choice, Lips. After that report from Bård we've got absolutely no choice.'

'The cops have no proof.'

Borkenhagen asks if the police nowadays need a pile of proof if there is enough circumstantial evidence. He asks Lipinski if he wants to be locked up until long after retirement age.

'If only Kykke'd had the nous to burn the bike after the boy'd crashed,' he says with a deep sigh. 'I bet Kykke's prints are all over the Ninja. They'll put out a search for him. Unlikely to be today though because the cops don't do anything serious until Kripos have carried out a forensic examination. But it'll be tomorrow.'

Borkenhagen throws a mobile to Lipinski, tells him to do something useful and ring a garage and hire a car with a trailer for heavy motorbikes.

9

Terje Kykkelsrud has turned off the E18 in Karlstad, heading south through the town to the island of Hammerö. On the far side, where a sign says it is a nature reserve, he parks his bike and finds a pine to lean back against while the sun scorches down and makes Lake Vänern glitter as far as the misty horizon in the distant south.

The pine is in a grove that reminds him of the clump of trees in Vilhelm Thygesen's garden. They sat there once in better times, Thygesen, Borken and he, round a garden table with wine glasses on. They were three losers sipping the gnat's piss that Thygesen called redcurrant wine.

Thygesen had been kicked out of the legal profession, Borken had gone bankrupt and been disqualified from running a company again and he himself had been sent ashore from a North Sea rig for agitator activities.

Thygesen moaned about how old he had become and how hard he had lived.

To which Borken said: 'You're the same age as Jack Nicholson and I doubt you've had more bloody women and booze than him.'

The three of them didn't talk about anything criminal. The conversation round the table focused on surviving in a hard world, by honest means. For Thygesen it was a question of getting himself into gear, away from the void created by useless alcoholic inactivity. For Borken the aim was to return as a trader of motorbikes and parts. Borken was right that the market would pick up again in the nineties. The trouble was he never had a share of the boom.

Kykkelsrud wanted to start up a state-authorised motorbike workshop. He viewed the little hiccough the Seven Samurai had had with the council as a temporary obstacle they would overcome. And the middle-class biddy of a mayor as a poseur, swollen with a self-importance it would be easy to deflate.

He had felt he could trust Thygesen when he rang him during the strike on the North Sea Star and asked what they could do about the company's bugging of cabins and meeting rooms. The strikers had found the listening equipment and had technical evidence. Thygesen was in charge when the strike committee brought the case to court in Stavanger. He got hold of a more recognised lawyer, someone called Hydle, to run the case. But Thygesen did a masterful job initially. Losing the bugging case and the strike itself was a different matter – a taste of capitalism's bitter chalice.

When the fight for The Middle of Nowhere began Kykkelsrud let Jens Petter Sundin establish contact with Thygesen because Sundin had a relative, someone who had been a friend of Thygesen's and had been killed. He wanted to test the young hanger-on to see if he was up to anything except giving lip.

He was. For a short while. When the club went down the tube Sundin started to show another side of himself. He emerged as a little rat, an informer. Shame it hadn't been necessary to do away with him rather than Strand the dreamer.

A single sailing boat crosses the lake's immense surface slowly in the light breeze that barely ripples the sea.

If he were in that boat the world would appear different to him.

We're all in the same boat, that is what people say, and they are talking rubbish.

We are all in separate boats. Only in dreams do we sail

on Lake Vänern with someone, in a boat with white sails, in the sun and summer wind.

Kykke takes out the Dictaphone, rewinds to the beginning of the tape, turns up the volume and hears himself say: 'What kind of society, Beach Boy?'

His voice is higher than he thought, and clearer, not so much of the growl that he hears when he speaks.

The boy he has killed answers: 'The society for a fair distribution of goods.'

Kykke looks across the biggest inland lake in Scandinavia while the dead boy talks to him from the Dictaphone.

He answers Beach Boy with a salvo of questions: 'But for God's sake, where have you got that from? Is it the social welfare officer at Trøgstad? It sounds like that Socialist Kristin Halvorsen on TV. What did Ryland say to the prison shrink's waffle? That he would immediately fork out a million in the name of social justice and socialism?'

'He didn't say anything at all,' the boy says in an offended voice. 'I thought Ryland would feel very threatened by my letter. Regardless of who the dead woman was, whether she was a drugs mule, prostitute or just a normal secretary, it wouldn't be healthy for a director in charge of millions of petrol kroner to be connected with a murdered woman.'

'All right, you've got a point. What about the cops?'

'I'm getting to that, Kykke. As this Ryland bastard didn't answer my first letter, I wrote a second and sharpened the tone. I said if he didn't contact me so that we could agree on how the demands would be met I'd get the police to put a picture of the woman in the papers. If he didn't contact me then I would go to the tabloids. The rag that paid best for the story. I wrote that even if he wasn't the normal type of millionaire who appeared in the papers – buying a palace in Holmenkollen and a Ferrari or going to balls with the starlets from *Hotel Cæsar*, things the rich like to do – he would be splashed over the front page anyway as the MD who knew the dead woman.'

'There's a certain sick logic to your plan.'

A bumble bee buzzes between the sea thrift in front of the pine trees. It is a real giant of a bee.

Kykkelsrud follows its flight. He imagines he *is* the bee. It is a pleasant thought.

Poor bloody bee if *it* had to think it was *him*, a confused murdering bee which didn't dare rely on its friends.

'What made a little shit like you think the cops would really print a picture of the murdered woman?'

'It started as something we joked about in clink. Of course all of Trøgstad was following the Orderud triple murder case when it came to court over Easter. It's the kind of case that makes a small-time crook feel like an innocent lamb. An old boy who was in for only some minor offence, but who had done time in Botsen for safe-cracking, laughed so much about the sock business that he almost cut off his arm with a crosscut saw. He said "The good old Murder Commission would have known". The Murder Commission was the forerunner of Kripos. The old boy thought the Murder Commission would never have tolerated being told to go out and search for the Orderud sock for the umpteenth time.'

'Here's to clever safe-crackers,' Kykkelsrud hears himself say.

He swallows a mouthful of Farris water from a bottle. It tastes of chlorine. He took it from the tap at a petrol station. When he checked his account in an ATM in Karlstad it was in the red. The money Borken promised he would pay in was overdue.

The boy drones the way people on speed do: 'The old man started talking about the woman who'd been found dead at Thygesen's. He said he was absolutely sure Thygesen was involved. He really hated Thygesen because, when he was a cop in Notodden, he'd arrested him after a break-in at Hydro. "The Murder Commission would never have stopped until they had Thygesen nailed for the murder," he said. "But nowadays the idle Kripos lot allow themselves to be sidetracked and controlled by the papers in Akersgata. They have nothing else on their minds but the Orderud case and have completely forgotten the murdered woman at Thygesen's. It's a scandal." Everything he said gave me an idea, so I rang Kripos.'

'You rang Kripos from Trøgstad Prison?'

'Yep. It's not difficult. You just have to scrape together some coins, queue by the welfare-building phone and dial the number when it's your turn. You're thinking Kripos will want to know who's calling them. How will they actually find out it was me? There are eighty men locked up. Finding the one individual who rang requires a lot of filtering and sorting. I spoke English to confuse Kripos, to make them think I was black. I got an A in my English oral at Kirkeparken. No problem. I got through to Kripos and said I had some info about the Thygesen woman, asked for Stribolt, the detective whose name was in the paper. But I got a crabby bitch, someone called Vaage. She said she was dealing with the case and I had to talk to her. So I did.'

'You're a weird'un, Beach Boy. And what tales did you tell Kripos?'

A small blue tanker sets a course south-west across Lake Vänern. Even though it is sailing in fresh water the little boat floats like a cork. Probably in ballast from Kristinhamn. Oil is transported right to the heart of Sweden from the reserves in the North Sea.

'I didn't tell any tales,' says the boy's voice on the tape. 'Can I have a little swig of your beer before I die of thirst?'

'If you don't touch the metal with your lips. I'm not sure we have the same bacteria.'

The boy drinks, burps out loud and, encouraged by his

oratory talents, continues: 'First, I repeated to this Vaage all the safecracker had said about the Murder Commission. Then I said that the whole case of the forgotten murdered woman would open – I said open like a lotus flower the way you do when you're pissed – if a picture appeared in the press. And I said I had specific information that could tie the murder to one of Norway's most powerful men, and to a bikers' club in Østfold.'

'You said *that*? A bikers' club in Østfold?'

'Yes, I did. A bikers' club in Eastfold.'

'Jesus Christ.'

Resounding silence on the tape.

Then the boy speaks, out of breath: 'Don't look at me like that. I wanted to kill two birds with one stone. That was the whole point. To flush the rich guy out and at the same time create panic in the Kamikaze gang. That was my big plan. Getting a million for the club by grabbing Ryland by the balls and breaking the back of the Kamikazes so that they never show their gibbon faces again.'

On the machine there is the sound of beer squirting out of a can as it is crushed.

'You've destroyed the Carlsberg can, Kykke,' the boy's voice says.

'Oh, yes? So I have. Have you considered how your words might sound if I tell you the Kamikazes didn't operate from the shack in Aspedammen – *we* did?'

'But Bård said the Kamikazes did…'

'Bård's a creep, and you've behaved like a third-rate half-wit. I'm sweating like a pig. I'll have to cool down in the stream.'

There is a click as the Dictaphone is switched off.

Kykkelsrud hears his own footsteps in the gravel and a voice from afar, which is his own, shouts: 'Don't mess about with the machine. If you've turned it on, turn it off.'

Silence. Suddenly there is Beach Boy's voice, loud and

shrill. He is singing, it must be a song by Aretha Franklin: 'Let's kick the ballistics. Let's kick the ballistics. Let's kick the ballistics.' Then there are a few hiccoughs, unclear words, and loud and clear: 'Borken. Hello, Borken! When you hear this and some shit has happened to me, you should know that… There was a song my father loved, but the priest refused to play it at the funeral. Writing love letters in the sand. Sung by Pat Boone. Can you hear me? Love letters in the sand. I've written a letter in the sand, you might say. Perhaps it isn't a love letter. Do you know what I mean? A letter telling the truth. Now I have to switch off and pretend I've been whittling some bits of wood. Kykke's coming out of the forest washed and clean. He looks like Old Nick himself.'

10

'DO YOU KNOW THIS voice?' asks Vanja Vaage, the duty officer at Kripos.

Local Police Chief Harald Herføll is sitting in his office listening on the phone to Vaage playing the tape. What he hears is the voice of someone ringing in; all calls are routinely recorded at the Kriminalpolitisentral in Oslo.

He is fairly sure he knows the voice. But he doesn't want to appear too sure. Over-confident sheriffs out here in the bush are not popular in the capital.

So he hesitates and answers in the negative.

'Have you heard this voice before?' Vaage asks.

'He's speaking English.'

'Yes sir, he's speaking English.'

'Let me hear a little more.'

'Here we go.'

'... that the woman was killed because of a drug operation that went wrong,' the boy says on the Kripos tape. 'And that if you publish her picture, things will explode and some motorbikers in Eastfold will be very sorry, and a bigshot, the name of which I have, will come out in the open... and sorry, no more coins for the telephone machine. My name is Banzai Boy, and I call you from a wood factory in the forest, and will call you again. Do you at the Crime Police Centre accept collect calls, *noteringsoverføring* in Norwegian?'

In Herføll's estimation, this is pretty good school English, the kind someone like Øystein Strand would speak.

Is he sure?

'Banzai Boy was a nickname Øystein Strand used,' Herføll says. 'Apparently in Japanese *banzai* means "Charge, attack".'

'I see,' Vaage says. 'Can you identify the voice?'

Herføll lights what is for him a very rare cigarette, a Petterøes from the packet of twenty in his drawer. He immediately has the taste of death in his mouth. But also the taste of life. The life he dreamed about when he became a policeman, an action-filled life hanging around in more exciting bars than The Bait and The Summer House in Moss and arresting gangsters.

'I'm not a hundred per cent sure,' he says while a little cheapskate in his brain calculated how much he could claim in petrol allowance if he drove to Oslo to listen to the Kripos recording. To many recordings, if he has understood Strand the chatterbox correctly.

'Do I hear a provincial taximeter ticking?' Vaage asks.

Can the witch read my thoughts?

'I'm ninety-nine per cent sure the voice you've played me belongs to the deceased, Øystein Strand,' Herføll says.

'Ninety-nine is good enough for us. For your information, this is one of many recordings of a hitherto anonymous caller from a line we've traced back to the coin-operated machines inmates use in Trøgstad Prison. We haven't had the resources to investigate who the caller was. You've been a great help, Herføll,' Vaage says.

'Pleasure.'

'You've given us a case. And it'll be even stronger if you can tell us where *herr* Kykkelsrud, *herr* Borkenhagen and *herr* Lipinski are at present.'

Herføll doesn't want to throw in his hand now. He would like to bid three hearts. The problem is he doesn't know. From early February the activity of the Seven Samurai at The Middle of Nowhere has been zero.

Kykkelsrud has been to the site and removed all the tools and equipment, which he sold using an ex-club member at Værven, in Moss, as a middleman. These deals were done by two fallen working-class heroes, in broad daylight, with no chance for the little undercover network they have in Moss to prove so much as a hint of fencing.

Borkenhagen has been sunning himself in Crete. Herføll knows that because a cousin of his was on the same package tour and said so when she came home. Lipinski has been at home in Skredderåsen and actually stood as a prosecution witness in a trial about some unpleasant cat murders in his suburb of Moss.

Selling tools on the quayside, a trip to the Med, witness in a cat murder case – are these small-town activities of any interest to Kripos?

'You're holding back information,' says the mind reader from the sulphur mine in Helgeland who has become a super-cop in Oslo.

'Not at all,' Herføll replies. 'I've just got so very little to give you. I know almost nothing about the movements of the three Samurai since early February.'

'Glad you're being honest. Tell me what you know.'

Herføll tells her the little he knows.

'Any idea who Mr Bigshot could be?' Vaage asks.

'If he's a local the only bigshot we have in the Moss region is Ari Behn,' Herføll says.

'I think we can leave him to Princess Märtha to worry about,' Vaage says. 'We have some info from Follo Police District. A person called Lips has been named by a pusher in Drøbak as an amphetamine dealer. Does that tally with what you know of him in Våler?'

'It tallies with rumours we've heard from Sundin, our insider. Borkenhagen wanted to turn the Samurai into a drugs outfit,' Herføll answers.

'Our pusher says he thought the drugs he got from this

Lips came via the Baltic, to be precise Tallinn. Does that ring a bell?'

Herføll says no. Vaage tells him not to hesitate to call her if he hears about anything else. She informs him that a forensics officer is on his way to Moss to examine the motorbike that Øystein Strand was riding. Herføll makes a note of the officer's name: Gunvald Larsson.

*

Terje Kykkelsrud removes the little cassette from the Dictaphone, places it on a pine root and smashes it with a rock. Then he sets fire to it. The smoke from the burning plastic makes him feel sick. He has to move away. The pine needles at the foot of the tree catch fire. Cursing, he stamps out the fire.

Was it necessary to destroy the tape? Of course it was. There was evidence on it that could have had him behind bars for life. That possibility still existed. Borken would have to survive without the tape.

Kykkelsrud visualises being stopped at a checkpoint and the police finding the cassette with Strand's voice on.

He has to face the facts.

Because it was murder, regardless of whether Strand realised the brakes were fixed and chose to go hell for leather into the forest.

He cannot allow himself to regret not withdrawing from the Seven Samurai a long time ago when it was obvious he would not get permission to build a garage in The Middle of Nowhere. He cannot allow himself to become sentimental. Even if he is not attracted by the prospect of becoming a brothel director in Tallinn, he is attracted by the big bucks Borken and Lips say they can earn there. What they have earned from a couple of successful amphetamine ops is peanuts in reality. They will earn, according to Lips, this money multiplied by a hundred in Tallinn. As the mafia in Estonia has spread into Finland and Sweden and the rich pastures there, a vacuum has been created in their homeland. Finnish bandits have begun to migrate across the Gulf of Finland and establish themselves in Estonia. There should be opportunities for Norwegians too, with a bit of start-up capital and efficient organisation.

The blue tanker on Lake Vänern disappears into the mist on the horizon.

Kykkelsrud mounts his bike.

His sole satisfaction is that he gave Beach Boy a sermon about eternity before he was despatched there.

He rummages for Beach Boy's CD player with the Laurie Anderson disc he hasn't heard before. There is a track called 'Love Among the Sailors'. He puts in the earplugs, dons the helmet and gazes across the lake as the woman sings. There isn't much of a tune and she hasn't got much of a voice either. She sings:

There is a hot wind blowing
It moves across the oceans and into every port.
A plague. A black plague.
There's danger everywhere.
And you've been sailing.
And you're alone on an island now tuning in.

*

Vilhelm Thygesen hears a cry, slings his mattock and looks up at the May sky arching over Oslo, as blue as the faded denim shirt he is wearing. Two large birds, they must be crows, fly slowly above the treetops in Bestum, where he has lived for most of his life, where he owns the plot that has become his universe. Where he is planning to hold on tight and live to his dying day, irrespective of any tempting offers Bruun & Spydevold, the estate agents, make him.

Although the two birds in flight look like crows he doesn't think they are because they seem to have a much greater wing span. They must be herons, grey herons, and one cries again, a hoarse, harsh kaark kaark. Quickly, a reflex action, Thygesen grabs the birdwatching binoculars he has placed on the garden bench, focuses on the birds and confirms that he is right: it is a pair of herons with their characteristic black outer wing feathers, yellow beaks and yellow feet. They fly as they always do, heavily, with the neck bent back so that only the head protrudes in front of the wings.

The herons are blown upwards and manage to fly for a while with the wind, towards Bestum Bay where they probably have their nests. They look like two planes against the sky. Another croaked cry. It hits a nerve in Thygesen.

Ever since he saw the sketch of the murdered woman in the morning edition of the *Aftenposten* he has been out of sorts. She, the dead, frozen stiff Picea has haunted his conscious mind and dreams. The newspaper picture edged her closer to him again.

Thygesen takes the spade from the wheelbarrow and shovels away the top layer of the ground he has hacked at in the corner of the garden where he found Picea at the beginning of February. He doesn't understand why it is only now, almost in the middle of May, that Kripos are publishing a picture of her. He feels no need to understand.

Ever since the snow disappeared early in April he has been thinking about planting a guelder rose by the spruce tree where Picea lay.

Last year, in the hawthorn hedge that borders his plot to the west, he discovered an alien presence. A thornless bush had grown there. At first he thought it was an elder, a red-berried elder. The yellowish bark on the thin stem made him doubt his judgement, and when he cut off a branch and found no brown, porous marrow he realised it couldn't possibly be an elder. It had to be a guelder-rose, an example of *Viburnum opulus*, which grows wild in Norway and spreads into gardens and hedges. He has a magnificent specimen of the genus in his mixed hedge facing Lütken's land to the south. The main branches grow at an angle of forty-five degrees on the stem, causing the bush to resemble a cross. Hence the name *krossved* in Norwegian.

In Vestre Crematorium Alf Rolfsen has painted a tree that looks like a cross.

The tree reminds Thygesen of the guelder rose.

The hole is deep enough now. He picks up the clump of earth with the little bush and places it carefully into the hole, stamps the soil around it and soaks it thoroughly with water from a can. Takes a rollie from the windcheater he hung on the spruce, lights a match, studies his workmanship and has a few sips from a bottle of water. It is still hot. At its peak, on this the first day of summer in Østland, the temperature must have been around twenty-five degrees.

His shirt is drenched with sweat. A job he has been thinking of doing for ages is done. It feels good that the unknown woman has a botanical memorial erected in the place where he found her.

Thygesen puts on his jacket and strolls over to the post box on the gate to see if the evening edition of *Aftenposten* has come. There are no papers in the box. What he sees is a large, unfranked envelope with his name written on the outside. He opens the envelope and takes out a sheet of paper. There are pictures stuck to the sheet. One is the identikit picture of Picea, to which has been added a sketch of her naked body. Another is an old black-and-white newspaper photo of himself, in one of his beardless phases. A body has been sketched underneath, and in his hand he is holding a knife. Which is stuck into Picea's stomach.

From her stomach oozes what might be her intestines, but it looks more like small loaves, baguettes. The third and lowest picture is a grainy colour photo of Picea.

Thygesen feels a chill run down his sweaty back.

He closes the post box lid. Saunters down the drive. The shingle crunches under his trainers. In the hall he forgets to kick off his shoes and takes clods of soil in with him.

It is cool inside the house. He pours himself a mug of tar-like coffee from the jug, sits down at the work table in the sitting room, rolls himself a smoke and puts on his reading glasses. Studies the sheet with the pictures stuck on. Lights the roll-up, which goes out without him noticing.

The colour photo of Picea was taken while she was still alive. She is with other people, whose faces are blurred. It must have been taken on board a plane or a train, or a bus. Picea was sitting in a dark green seat and leaning forward. She is wearing the same light-coloured blouse she was wearing when he found her dead. Her face is quite sharp, in contrast to her arms which are out of focus, probably because she moved them at the crucial moment. Her eyes are wide open. The flash has made her pupils go red. Her mouth is open too, as though she is saying or shouting something, most likely to the photographer.

Her facial expression is one of anger. Or it can be interpreted that way, as though she is livid. The people in the row of seats behind her are shadowy figures. Behind Picea's head there is something white. It is a head cover of the type placed on the top of plane or car seats. In the olden days such cloths were called antimacassars because they were meant to protect furniture against hair pomades made of greasy, aromatic oil from Macassar in the East Indies. There are letters visible on the white material, but they are unreadable.

Thygesen takes out a magnifying glass from the desk

drawer. He examines the letters. It says: www.nsb.no.

Picea was on a train, a Norwegian train.

Thygesen grabs the mobile phone on the charger. No doubt about what he has to do. Ring Stribolt at Kripos.

Between his hands he holds a piece of paper which is evidence in the case Stribolt hasn't managed to solve. During the conversations Stribolt had with him Thygesen realised that the investigation had hit a brick wall.

Now he has something to help Stribolt, the Finnmark man with the dolphin smile. The problem is that he has no idea where the pictures came from or who put the anonymous letter in his post box. Anonymous?

Thygesen turns over the paper. On the back there is a drawing of two paws with claws. Between the paws there is what looks like an American football. Underneath, written in a fine felt-tip pen, it says: Give us Speed and Service, Mr Lawyer! PP Productions is offering you a role in a documentary, Vilhelm Thygesen. They will contact you. But if you want to be a star you'll have to share the stardust you found inside the dead woman when you sliced her up. See Wilhelmsen Line's old slogan: 'For Speed and Service'. You probably haven't used up all the shit yourself because we've been keeping an eye on you, and you've looked pretty clean since you finally came home to Norway. If you've sold it you're smarter than we took you for. No one at Ullern VG admits to having bought any. According to our calculations you're sitting on amphetamine (we think it's amphetamine and hope it isn't heroin) worth five million kroner. Respectful greetings, Dr Papaya and Captain Paw-Paw. PS We're multi-artists armed with live ammo and desperation. DS.'

Adolescent pranks. This was just an adolescent prank. Childish scribbles. School leavers' jape! Isn't this the time kids finish their secondary schooling? He hasn't seen many kids in red overalls this year, and he hasn't missed them. It is around this time, leading up to 17 May, Independence Day, as always, isn't it?

Ullern VG must be Ullern *Videregående*, a selective school for sixteen to nineteen-year-olds, upper secondary, as it is called in bureaucrat-speak nowadays, all in the name of equality. If it is an Ullern student who posted this envelope they will soon be here in their cars singing the post-pubertal mating song 'Oggy-oggy-oggy, oi-oi-oi, here comes an Ullern boy.'

Bloody hell. Where's the gun?

If they have live ammo, his ammo is more live.

Dr Papaya and Captain Paw-Paw! And the old Wilhelmsen slogan. That was right; 'For Speed and Service' was the slogan of Wilhelmsen Lines, the proud liners of their day.

How did they find the slogan? And how on earth did the bloody clowns get the crazy idea that he cut drugs worth five million kroner out of Picea's stomach? They call themselves multi-artists, but *that* is not an artistic idea, in his humble opinion. It is an idea that should have the bearer despatched post-haste to Vinderen Psychiatric Clinic for Adolescents.

Thygesen's house is full of voices, of old sounds, as all hundred-year-old timber houses are by their very nature. Here people have talked, sung, laughed and cried since before the dissolution of the union with Sweden in 1905, through two world wars and a long post-war period. If science develops a method for monitoring sounds from logs in timber walls his house has a lot to say. It is not unlikely that a method will be developed.

The sound waves must, as they hit molecules in the woodwork, trigger microscopic changes, which modern computer technology ought to be able to monitor and recode into comprehensible acoustic trails.

When he moved back to his house he decided to

turn a deaf ear to the sounds. He didn't wish the past to talk to him. He wanted to look to the future. Instead he contemplated his navel and the tips of his shoes. But that is another story. By and large he has succeeded in keeping the history of the house at arm's length.

Now a voice is talking to him, a loud and unpleasantly sharp, stressed voice. It is his mother's. 'It's really funny, Steffa,' she says. Actually she is talking to her sister, Aunt Steffa. Tea cups clink on a silver tray. 'The English in Kenya are so snobbish that they can't say papaya – they call the fruit paw-paw.'

Aunt Steffa had fled back home from her job as a governess in Kenya because of an uprising in a village in the British colony. She gave 'the little savage' – he was fifteen in 1952 – a sola topee and a zebra's tail as a present. He wore the helmet at a fancy dress ball at school. He wondered if he could use the zebra's tail in sadomasochistic activities he had read about in a magazine his sister Vigdis said he shouldn't have been reading.

'The English can't pronounce papaya,' says his mother, and she follows up this declaration with a laugh that for once sounds free and unrestrained.

His father, the judge, immediately counters with a gruff retort: 'If you despise the English so, do you perhaps side with the Mau Mau?'

Aunt Steffa heaves a sigh. The brutality of the Mau Mau uprising.

His mother says nothing.

The voices fall silent.

As far as he can remember eighty to ninety white farmers were killed in attacks while the British eliminated more than ten thousand rebels.

This memory of a conversation enables Thygesen to decode a rebus the letter writer, or letter writers, presumably didn't think he would be able to crack. The two paws, in

English, make up paw-paw. What he took to be an American football is in fact not a ball but a papaya fruit.

So what?

Have Picea's murderers contacted him via an anonymous letter? Or is it someone who was robbed of a body they thought contained dope?

The author of the letter has a colour photo of Picea, of Picea alive and well. Where did they get that from? What does it mean that it exists and has been sent to him in an unfranked envelope?

What should he do? What action should he respond with to a letter like that?

Could the letter be a police provocation?

His contact with Kripos since the discovery of Picea's body has been limited. Stribolt rang him a couple of times while he was in Sarajevo visiting Vera Alam, and Vaage called him on his mobile. Stribolt rang him again when he stopped off in Paris to do some stamp deals on the way back.

The ostensible reason for Stribolt's call was to check Vera's health. It could have been worse. Cancer had been diagnosed, but it hadn't spread. She was determined to carry on her work in Bosnia and didn't want to return home. Vaage rang to ask a great number of far-fetched questions about the possibility of Vera having had contact with the murdered woman. In fact, she also asked whether Bernhard Levin might have known Picea.

It was only when Thygesen asked if he or Levin were under suspicion of having run a prostitution ring that Vaage shut up.

He personally had rung Kripos once since he came home at the end of March to enquire whether the cops were spying on him and, if so, why. There was some guy in a leather coat wandering up and down Skogveien peering into his property.

Could this suspicious leather-coat guy have been

Dr Papaya or Captain Paw-Paw? Were the letter writers keeping an eye on him?

The odds of the letter being police provocation or the police running surveillance from the shrubberies of Bestum are so small they are as good as zero. If there ever were officers in the old Murder Commission who would have done anything to hang Vilhelm Thygesen's scalp from their belt, they are either dead or they retired ages ago. These old boys bore a special grudge against him as he was a disgraced police officer. But now their boots were hung up, if not placed in boxes with the rest of them. There are new, young brooms sweeping clean at the present Kripos. They have no inherent hatred of old Thygesen; he is not the enemy incarnate.

If Vaage and Stribolt *really* suspected him of murder or of being an accessory to murder they would have put him under more duress, tried to squeeze him, expose him to mental torture during the interviews. He rang Kripos about the leather-coat guy, though more to check the state of play and hear if they had found any more leads.

He looked at the drawing of Picea's body. Of course they weren't baguettes coming out of her stomach – they are supposed to be drugs packed in plastic bags which she had swallowed.

He is convinced Picea was not a drugs courier. The times he has imagined what she was like she hasn't come across as a mule. She is no Mother Teresa either, but somewhere between a gangster and a saint. Or between a whore and a Madonna? No, neither a whore nor a Madonna.

He sits with the collage that brands him as a disemboweller. Will it have any further impact on Kripos? What has he got to lose by telling the truth about the letter he has received? Police logic is a special kind of logic: the person who knows something is suspect.

Naively and innocently, you report a find you assume

could be important and immediately you are trapped like a fly in a spider's web.

Despite these doubts, there is only one rational solution to the dilemma.

Thygesen lifts the mobile off the charger, dials 22 07 70 00, presses the blue call button and gets the switchboard at Kripos. He asks to be put through to Chief Inspector Arve Stribolt.

A few seconds pass. The switchboard voice tells him that Stribolt has recently left town and will not be available until 14 May.

He should ask to be put through to Vanja Vaage. But his courage deserts him at the thought of the dragon and he presses *off*. He calls Stribolt's mobile number and reaches voicemail.

Thygesen switches off without leaving a message.

*

The switchboard message that Stribolt was out of town was a little white lie. He is on his way to Halden to question a witness, but has got no further than his desk, where he is talking to Vaage. She is reading a printout of an email Stribolt has received from a student in Halden by the name of Hege Dorothy Rønningen.

Rønningen writes: 'I hereby volunteer myself as a witness in a murder case. I recognise the woman whose picture was in the newspaper today, 11.05.01. I'm sure I saw this woman on the train between Göteborg and Oslo on Sunday 28 Jan. If you are interested, I can be contacted by email or on 916 202 77.'

'Cool email address,' Vaage says. Rønningen is a hotmail account holder and her address is *d.ronningen*, which, without the full stop, is Norwegian for queen. 'Did she have anything to add when you phoned?'

'A lot,' Stribolt answers. 'She seems great. I have no doubt it'd be worth going down to visit her. She noticed one important detail that doesn't appear on the drawing. Picea had a deformed ear.'

'Good. Looks like she has her own homepage. You've checked the net of course, haven't you?'

'I have,' Stribolt says with a blush.

Rønningen's website is www. dotti-de-la-motti.no.

'You're a dirty old *snuskhummer*,' Vanja Vaage says, lapsing into Swedish with a laugh. She has spent a few frisky weekends in a cabin on the Koster Islands with a hot fireman from Strømstad and has picked up quite a number of Swedish expressions.

'And you're a wanton hussy,' Arve Stribolt answers.

'Let's see about this Miss Dotti de la Motti then,' Vaage says. 'You'll see how fast I am on the net. I'm greased lightning.'

'Rønningen's not a porn model if that's what you think,' Stribolt says.

'I don't think anything. I'm just checking the evidence in a case and you blushed like a boiled *snuskhummer*.'

Vaage clicks. On screen comes a text: INLINES ONLINE. Welcome to the homepage of Dotti de la Motti. SITE FOR GOOD BUYS ONLINE OF CHEAP LATVIAN INLINES.

Beneath the text a pile of blonde curls appears, and slowly but surely a light-skinned forehead and two black eyebrows.

'She sells inline skates,' Stribolt says. 'From Latvia.'

'Let's have a look, shall we. If this is a sales site why isn't it called com or dot com?'

'How the hell should I know why it's not Dotti dot com?'

'The question is whether there's more to Dotti than dots,' Vaage says. 'She certainly uses enough kohl.'

'Kohl?'

'Eyeliner.'

Suddenly the complete picture pops up on the screen. A full-length young woman. She is the type we used, in the very old days, to call robust.

'She's absolutely starkers!' Vaage bursts out in triumph.

'Rubbish,' Stribolt answers. 'She's wearing a flesh-coloured bikini, roller skates and elbow and knee protectors. It's certainly the right gear if you're selling a modern, youthful sports product. In fact, she's also wearing round glasses, as you can see. John Lennon glasses.'

'She's got very modest boobs, but big hips.'

'I can't do anything about that,' Stribolt says.

'Have you checked the references of this potential crown witness?' Vaage asks.

'I've called a teacher at the college in Østfold where she studies. He confirmed that she was observant and reliable.'

'Are you going by car to Halden?'

'Too hot to drive. I'll catch the train. Unless you detain me any further I can catch the four o'clock.'

'Have a good trip,' Vaage says, giving her colleague a pat on the highest point of his body when he bends down to pick arctic berries on the marshes in Skaidi.

*

Vilhelm Thygesen has drunk two drams of ice-cold Calvados from the bottle he keeps in the fridge since he returned from Paris and has promised himself he will save.

With the taste of burnt apples on his tongue he calls the Kripos number again. He asks for Vaage and he gets her.

She appears to be in an unusually good mood.

Thygesen tells her about the anonymous letter he has received and the picture of Picea which was taken while she was still alive.

He hears Vaage tapping on the keyboard while asking

him short, precise questions, which he tries to answer succinctly.

'May I come and see you after I clock off at four?' Vaage asks.

Thygesen hesitates and searches for an excuse to avoid a visitation from Kripos. He fails. Having said A, he will have to say B.

'OK,' he says.

'Where are you?'

'Home. Where else?'

'You're ringing from a mobile. It could be absolutely anywhere in the western world.'

'Right now my mobile's in Bestum.'

II

Unknown to the boss, the employees of Statens Nasjonale Oljeinvesteringsfond, SNOIF for short, have sneaked out of their offices on the top floor into Tordenskjoldsgate on this boiling hot Friday afternoon to get the earliest weekend possible.

Only MD Gerhard Ryland's anteroom is manned as the clock approaches four and knocking-off time. John Olsen sits there sweating and scratching his walrus moustache, musing glumly whether Ryland has hanged himself behind a locked door.

His boss has been even more absent-minded and reticent than usual all day. After lunch he cancelled a meeting with two reps from Norpaper, Helsinki, holed himself up in his office and said he wasn't taking any calls.

Olsen notices that Ryland has rung a couple of times from his mobile after going into hiding. The electro-magnetic waves from his phone make the computer in the anteroom flicker slightly. Otherwise everything has been quiet. He put through one call, from a man who refused to give his name but said it was a matter of life and death. Other incoming messages for his boss he has noted down on his jotter.

It is now 15.50. Olsen has other plans for this Friday than sitting and waiting for a signal from the social-democratic sphinx. It is definitely time for a beer on the quay in Aker Brygge. He dials 01 on the intercom. It rings and rings. Eventually Ryland answers.

'I was wondering whether I could call it a day,' Olsen says.

'Not just yet,' Ryland answers. 'Pop in before you leave. I'll be with you in five minutes.'

Olsen hears his boss's door being unlocked. He leans out of the window and waits. The heat rises from the tarmac on the street seven floors down. He can see straight down the low-cut dresses of two winter-pale girls from the Employment Office who are standing on the pavement smoking. Summer has arrived in a single day. A sweet perfume mingles with the stench of exhaust fumes rising upwards. Could it be from the maple trees? Or from the cherry trees in full flower all over this heat-shimmering city?

The wall clock shows 15.55. Olsen does up the top button of his shirt, knocks and enters Ryland's office. The room stinks of tobacco in the semi-gloom. Not a single window is open. The curtains closest to Ryland's desk are drawn. His boss is nowhere to be seen.

The windows are shut, so at least he hasn't jumped out, Olsen thinks.

He must be in the toilet.

The only luxury Ryland allowed himself when Bondevik's government set up the Oil Fund was that he had a private toilet attached to his otherwise spartan office. Ryland also instituted a deal with Health & Safety that the smoking law would not apply to the MD.

After he was employed to work for Ryland, John Olsen began to doubt the truth of the old proverb that the sum of all vices is constant. In his experience his boss has only one vice and that is his bloody pipe-smoking.

Stalin is in the ashtray reeking of burnt nuns, as though there were witches' trials going on in Ryland's office.

Olsen doesn't know whether Ryland knows that his employees call his favourite pipe Stalin or if his boss knows how much they dislike the aroma of Three Nuns tobacco. Whereas the other offices are copiously decorated with lithographs from the state's stock of visual art Ryland has no adornment on his walls other than a drawing in framed glass. It is a puzzle he tries out on all his new staff. Olsen was given advance warning by the chief accountant and therefore managed to think on his feet: the cigarette holder symbolises USA's President Franklyn D Roosevelt, the cigar Britain's wartime Prime Minister Winston Churchill and the crooked pipe Joseph Stalin.

There are equals signs between these symbols of smoking, and the equation concludes with a V, which stands for victory, for victory in the Second World War.

Ryland is almost morbidly preoccupied by the history of war and especially the Russians fighting on the Eastern Front. But being a spy for the Russians in his youth is probably just one of those malicious rumours that hound every boss of a certain heft.

And Ryland has heft, despite his peculiarities and his extremely withdrawn personality, all his decency and virtue. He has cleverly manoeuvred SNOIF through the tainted waters of the Norwegian financial world. Stood up against the capital moguls when necessary, ducked when it was prudent. The return for the fund has been as good as in the best share funds. The boss's integrity is undisputed. He hasn't allowed himself to be led by his crooked nose, his hawk beak.

A wallpapered door that merges indistinguishably with the rest of the dark blue office wall opens. Out comes the tall, skinny Gerhard Henry Ryland, his hair dripping with water. He is wearing his light grey suit, and the jacket and garish tie – a present from the Norwegian Union of Municipal and General Employees – are stained with dark patches.

'You have to comb your hair,' Ryland says, wiping his colourless face with a paper towel. He has combed his dark hair back and parted it at the side. A perennial discussion amongst his staff is whether it is dyed or not. Olsen thinks his hair colour is natural. 'Now that summer's here it's best with water. Would you like a coffee, John?'

Olsen looks at the steel coffee flask on the pedestal by the suite of sofas. It is the one he brings in every lunch time. He declines the offer.

'You put a call through to me,' Ryland says, taking his place in his chair behind the desk and offering Olsen a chair in front.

'Yes, sorry, but he was insistent.'

'It was a threat,' Ryland says.

'From the bloody Finns?'

'No, this was about something else.'

Is that a smile his boss is putting on? If so, it is extremely suspicious.

'We log and record all calls digitally, don't we?' Ryland asks.

'In accordance with your orders after you felt threatened by Kingo, and there hasn't been any change to my knowledge.'

'And the machine connected to the switchboard records on the HD and a diskette?'

Olsen nods. It is a mystery to him why his boss always asks him about things he already knows and never asks about things he *doesn't* know.

'I'd like you to bring me today's diskette.'

'Now?'

'Yes, this minute,' Ryland says. 'ASAP, as they say.'

Olsen takes the diskette from the switchboard computer. He places it on his boss's desk. Ryland doesn't look up; he is studying a couple of letters in front of him. They are brown around the edges, scorched, as if someone had tried to set fire to them.

'Is that a map of Treasure Island you've got there?' Olsen asks to break the silence.

'Not at all,' Ryland replies, looking up. His gaze couldn't be more distant. The moisture on his forehead is sweat, not water. 'We, that is I, I personally… am in a bit of a spot. So I'd like you to do me a couple more favours. Firstly, I'd like you to drive me to a meeting in Østfold this evening, to a place called Bærøe estate. I'm in no shape to drive myself.'

'Actually, that's a little inconvenient, Gerhard.'

'You'll get paid double the overtime rate.'

'Triple,' Olsen says. He doesn't head the Union of Commerce and Office section of SNOIF for nothing.

'Let's say triple then. Before we leave you'll have to pick up Natasha from home in Røa. You take me to Bærøe. I'll make my own way once the dinner and meeting are over. You drive straight to my cabin by Skjeberg Bay and stay there until Monday with Natasha. She's fairly balanced at the moment, so there'll be no problems if you guard the medicine cupboard and the bar like a dragon.'

'That's my weekend gone for a burton,' Olsen says. 'In fact, I did have other plans.'

'No surprises there,' Ryland answers drily. 'You will be well rewarded.'

'Triple overtime rate?'

'Plus some.'

Ryland pulls out a drawer from his desk, locates a pile of share certificates and fans them out in front of his secretary. There is an elephant printed on the certificates. Its legs are designed in such a way that they form the word 'Moss'.

'This is ten shares in the Peterson Group,' Ryland says. 'The one that owns Cellulosen in Moss and much more. They're yours if you do me the favours I've asked you about.'

'You're trying to bribe me,' Olsen says, dumbfounded. 'This is tantamount to corruption!'

'Every good firm has to have a bit of corruption,' Ryland answers wearily.

After union leader John Olsen has calmed down and stashed the Peterson shares in his sporty rucksack, he is ordered to make his way to the quay at Akerbrygge and relax. He is also instructed not to drink anything stronger than a Clausthaler, or alternatively a Norwegian Munkholm.

Ryland sits in the stale air of his office studying the two letters scorched at the edges. He thinks he understands the purpose of the scorched letters. It is to give them a sense of being documents from fantasy literature, a touch of *The Hobbit* or something like that.

The first letter he received is entitled 'The Forest' and reads as follows: '*Herr* Gerhard Ryland, Oil Investment Fund. I, a warrior, hereby demand one million kroner for a biker clubhouse. Place the money in the old camo-painted, or camouflage-hued as snobs like you might say, warehouses by the Bærøe road in Hobøl, which were formerly used by the Våler rocket battery. You will find the precise location by consulting the Directorate for Civil Protection. It was people like you who made sure the battery was closed down and who destroyed great plans in connection with another place in the forest. Labour Party big shots! Traitors of the people! I know storage space was builded in the mountain at the Våler battery so as to be able to take American nuclear warheads that could be fired by Nike rockets. Not big weapons, tactical ones. If we get the warehouse the club will then expand and take over several of the buildings and make a nuclear missile museum in Våler. I assume you will be a key sponsor. Initially, I want only one million of all the kroner you administer. I will tell you how the money is to be handed over after you have replied to this letter. Send your response to Reidar Isachsen, Aspedammen 112, 1766 Halden. Then I will get it. Do not try to contact Reidar Isachsen. This is, by the way, impossible. He is a zombie. If you don't reply, the following will happen: your connection with the unidentified woman who was found murdered in Vilhelm Thygesen's garden in Oslo last winter will be revealed to the whole world. I know that a piece of paper with your name and private address on – Anton Tschudis vei 30, 1344 Haslum – was found in the woman's bag. How will you explain that when tabloid journalists start ringing you up, Ryland? You have a problem. Which can be solved by paying me a little money, on behalf of the club. The problem will get bigger if you don't bother to answer or contact the police. I am in constant contact with the police, you see. If you don't reply, I will make sure the police put a picture of the murdered woman in the papers. That will almost certainly cause an outcry and total panic. Best regards, Banzai Boy.'

When Ryland received this clumsy blackmail letter at the beginning of April he didn't place any importance on it. He put the letter in the drawer for begging letters and strange enquiries addressed to the MD of SNOIF. It was, and is, a full drawer. As a matter of form, he checked the national register to see if there was a Reidar Isachsen with a postal address in Aspedammen. He speculated where this Banzai Boy had got his private address from and concluded the boy – judging by the handwriting it had to be a young boy – had also used the national register.

What slightly concerned him was that it wasn't beyond the realm of possibility that a piece of paper or a card bearing his name and address had actually been found on or near the dead woman, by the person or persons who killed her or found her. All over Europe there were potential female victims to whom in an unguarded moment Natasha might have given his name, followed by assurances that if he was contacted on the arrival of said poverty-stricken or persecuted woman in Norway, the gates of the kingdom's heavens would open.

Natasha has a heart that is greater than her common sense.

Ryland casts a glance at the photo of his wife which he keeps under his transparent plastic blotter. The picture is only a couple of years old. She took it herself, with the self-timing release, on a sea-smoothed rock by their cabin. She is holding an armful of summery flowers and beaming to the world. But the eyes with the raven-black, endlessly long lashes are closed because she doesn't want to see a world that is too evil for her.

He has loved Natasha ever since he met her in Leningrad, as the town was called in those days, during a study tour arranged by the Norway-Soviet Friendship Association in 1966. He was twenty-five at that time. She was twenty-three. An orphaned child from a besieged town where a million people, including Natasha's parents and two eldest sisters, starved to death during the war. A child, yes, an eternal child who had no wish to be an adult.

'I still love you,' Ryland says, trying to light his pipe, a Danish Stanwell, which his employees have dubbed Stalin. They should have known the model was called a Rhodesian. He has carefully filed off the brand name as he doesn't think it seemly for a man in his position to have a pipe which is engraved with a clear reference to a former colonial power.

He skims the second letter, which is entitled 'The Strand'. It is even crazier than the first: MD RYLAND! You didn't answer my letter about the million. Either you are a coward or too dumb to see the seriousness of the matter. I want a good upbringing for children and teenagers. A fair distribution of goods! A fight against capitalist powers. Let the rich foot the bill! Let the oil money be used for the good of the people instead of making the rich even richer. I am angry. I want my demands met NOW. You know what you got to do. Otherwise you will be "blown away" as criminals say and I am, as I'm sure you have realised, a criminal who can do a variety of dangerous things if I have to. The big danger for you is that your name was found near the woman who was murdered. You can't wriggle out of that. When the papers discover that, they will think she was your little whore, won't they? They might get it into their heads that YOU were the person who killed her, in cold blood. That won't be very good for you or for your fund. A million from your chest is just a crumb from the rich man's table. I reckon you will pay when you see the picture of her in the papers. The police is interested. Check out Chief Inspector Stribolt in Kripos. I have just spoken to him. I have examined my heart and racked my brains and concluded that nothing will be as OK as the club getting one million kroner from YOU via the fund. Unfortunately at the moment I can't win a million on Big Brother or any reality series, although I would be a clear candidate to win the TV jackpot. But in my present situation that is not possible, unfortunately. No way! Fucking impossible, Mr Scrooge Ryland!!! And when everything is sorted with the clubhouse I will fly round the globe to all the great beaches like a Beach Boy. Why shouldn't I? Why should I graft away in the forest in the freezing cold when the sun is shining in the tropics? Think about it. Treat Beach Boy to a trip to Bali, Barbados, the Bahamas, Brazil, Copacabana, Ipanema and you got no more problems. I will be as silent as a coral reefer, ha ha. Get the joke? Coral reefER? As quiet as the Pacific in a conch shell. As mute as a coconut. Kripos is getting more and more interested. The night is falling around me but I have taken a little pill, so that's fine, the net is closing in on you. Answer me NOW and I will arrange a drop-off place for the bag of cash worth 1 MILLION KRONER in unmarked one-hundred, two-hundred and five-hundred notes. Impatiently yours, best regards, Beach Boy alias Banzai Boy. COUGH UP! JUST DO IT! Nike Boy is using his FORCE.'

Ryland reckoned he could safely file these infantile

letters under 'I' for idiots, along with begging letters and enquiries about state money for the construction of castles in the air. But now events have begun to run away with him, on this, the first real day of summer. He is under pressure over the issue of the Norpaper merger, and then there is this private strain on top of everything else.

The boy who, in his own amateur way, has been trying to blackmail him *has* unbelievably, somehow or other, managed to get the police to publish an identikit drawing of the murdered woman. It is in *Aftenposten* and the tabloids, which Ryland doesn't usually read. Only when *Verdens Gang* runs a new story in its continuing vendetta against him and the oil fund, only then does he bother to read *VG*.

Does he recognise the woman in the drawing? He has his doubts. He really isn't sure. And if there is one thing he hates it is doubt.

On every occasion that offers itself he takes Natasha with him on his travels in Europe, on shorter or longer holidays. Travelling quells her restlessness, acts as a cure for her neuroses. She is never as happy as when she can sit in a pavement café in a city watching people walk by and confirming that most are well nourished, that the world is populated by living creatures who look as if they get enough food and not just Biafran and Ethiopian children and slum kids from Manila, Bucharest and Novosibirsk, the kind Natasha sees on TV.

When Natasha is all light and joy about being among the living, the sated millions, she is also unusually open, affectionate and chatty. She can speak a little in most major European languages and finds it easy to make contact with foreign women. Among them there is always one or more she feels sorry for and thinks they deserve a better, safer life in Norway.

The portrait the police have drawn could be one of these women. She is dark-haired and lean – or was, she is dead of course – and is reminiscent of the Natasha he met in Leningrad. Natasha before she imagined she was suffering from fibromyalgia and began to go to seed and put on weight.

The problem is that the woman – if he may formulate himself so brutally, and he can, in his mind – is the type there are thirteen to the dozen of in European capitals. She could have been a waitress in Rome with a dubious work permit in Italy, an immigrant street girl in Marseille selling flowers in the afternoon and her body in the evening, or a gypsy beggar in Prague.

If a woman like her tells Natasha she is being persecuted, Natasha will say she has to come to the safe haven that is Norway, and deftly, under the table, pass over his name and address so that she has a contact person in paradise. Many such women find it easy to say, in good faith, that they are being harassed or persecuted for the simple reason that they *are*. They have trouble with greedy employers, pimps, people smugglers and immigration bureaucracy.

This woman, badly drawn and stylised, reminds him vaguely of a hairdresser at Holywell Hotel in Athens. There was a minor drama in the salon because Natasha wasn't happy with the haircut she had received and thought her hair had been cut too short, by an unprofessional person. Besides, she had asked for a perm with waves and had curls instead. The coiffeuse lifted her own hair to console Natasha and demonstrated that the customer could have very short hair because she didn't have a deformed ear to hide.

The scene ended in a tearful reconciliation. He was so ill at ease that he retreated to a bar and knocked back a rare whiskey. On his return one of the other girls in the deserted basement salon was taking photos of Natasha and her new friend, the coiffeuse. From what he could gather the woman was Greek and not a persecuted refugee from

Faroffistan or a prostitute from Moldova. That is how easy it is to make mistakes. He can speak just as little Greek as Natasha, a few words from a phrasebook. A woman who lives illegally in a country will try to seem even more normal and native than the country's legal inhabitants. If, for example, she is a hairdresser during the day and forced into prostitution after the salon closes, she will try to hide the latter fact with all the means a woman has at her disposal.

He isn't getting anywhere with thinking like this. He will have to go through Natasha's chaotic collection of holiday snaps.

In one of the blackmail letters the writer mentioned nuclear warehouses in Våler. It appeared to be nonsense, completely contrary to official Norwegian policy on foreign bases. However, it seems there are some grounds to the claim. *Aftenposten* has just reviewed a new historical book which proves that nuclear warheads were built in Våler and at other batteries. How could someone so young know that?

Who was the caller who was put through and said that a man by the name of Beach Boy was dead and demanded Gerhard Ryland's total silence, unless he wished another murder to be committed?

The person who rang Gerhard Ryland and threatened to kill him was no kid on some crazy quest for a million kroner. This was an adult man, and he articulated what he had to say in brief, clear sentences: if Ryland didn't keep his mouth shut about Beach Boy's attempted blackmail, Ryland would be next on the list after the boy. The voice demanded no money, only silence. Before ringing off he warned Ryland in no uncertain terms that he was not to contact the police.

Ryland smokes Stalin cold and bites so hard that a piece of the mouthpiece breaks off.

Who could the caller have been? The man spoke normal Norwegian, Østland dialect, maybe an Østfolder. He expressed himself the way Ryland imagines a heavy would.

Could it have been one of Kingo's men?

Kingo the arriviste, the prince of wood pellets, the son of the hymn-writer's grandson, haunts Norway's wood-processing industry. As far as the Norpaper merger is concerned, Kingo and SNOIF are on a collision course. Kingo has learned his business methods in the new capitalist Russia. Initially it seems highly unlikely that he should also haunt a murder case.

But you have to be open to all eventualities.

The anonymous caller's warning about going to the police is the type of threat no sensible, rational person should heed of course.

If only you could be confident that there weren't any leaks inside the police. If only it were as simple as picking up a phone, calling the police and presenting your case.

The problem is that there are leaks inside the police. The organisation leaked like a sieve to the newspaper houses in Akersgata during the massive Orderud case. A civil servant who wants to earn himself some easy money can tell the unscrupulous hacks at *Verdens Gang* that the tabloid's arch-enemy, the MD of the oil fund, is involved in an unsolved murder case. *VG* is bound to throw all caution to the wind and just think of sex and sales. The name of a man *VG* doesn't like, because he is an old fogey who sees it as his duty to prevent the destruction of Norwegian industry, is found on a murdered woman. Accordingly, this man, the enemy in journalistic logic, has had a sexual encounter with this woman and then killed her or got someone else to do so, to hide his trail of depravity.

Such patent nonsense won't do long-term damage as it doesn't have a scrap of truth in it. But it will do irreparable harm short-term. Kingo will be able to use the scandal for all it is worth to discredit an opponent in a situation where there is a lot at stake.

'Shit sticks,' Ryland says, spitting out a bit of the mouthpiece. He notices that he doesn't spit it into the waste-paper basket but on to the carpet.

If he goes to the police and there is a leak, vital national interests could be compromised. If he doesn't go to the police, he is behaving improperly and not doing his civic duty. The best policy is to go to the police, but the best policy can be the enemy of a good policy.

This is his dilemma. He has never been confronted by a dilemma that didn't have a logical solution. Often the solution has been to take the middle path, to find a balance in the middle. The greatest threat he faces personally is death. Hmmm. He can live with that for the time being. It is only him. In the bigger picture – the one that concerns more important interests than his own skin – the worst that can happen is that he, and thus his cause, is attacked in the media as the result of a scandal. His mission, quite irrespective of what politicians might think, is to use oil funds in such a way that Kingo cannot merge with Borregaard, Peterson and the SBF paper plant.

Kingo makes it known that a merger of this kind between the three heavyweights in Østfold's wood-processing industry would be beneficial to Norway and he would like a long-term ownership in the interests of the nation. In his argument he claims that Peterson was extremely close to selling up to the new Finnish conglomerate Nordic Paper Mills, abbreviated to Norpaper, and that Borregaard, after using the raw might of shareholders to liberate Sarpsborg from the Orkla concern, is open to foreign buy-outs if it stays on its own. The same applies to the SBF plant in Halden. This bluff has won over Norwegian authorities and the media. What they don't know is that Kingo is pulling the wool over their eyes. He wants to increase his company's total value through a merger and then sell on the whole caboodle to Canada. As he has kept the Canadian card close to his chest this secret plan cannot be documented.

SNO – which is what Ryland chooses to call the institution he heads, because Kjell Magne Bondevik's abbreviation SNOIF sounds like the name of a third-division football team from the ex-Prime Minister's home region – has to try to block the merger plan by buying up the minority in Borregaard and Peterson. As this won't be enough, the Finns have to come in with a restricted equity interest. The difficulty with this is that whoever gives Finland, powered by the Nokia locomotive, an inch could end up losing much more. Peterson's position is unclear and ambivalent. There is a sense that Peterson still wants to sell majority ownership to Norpaper. Then the national anti-merger argument will fail.

Kingo made a fortune importing cheap pulp from Russia, with its base in Arkhangelsk. Afterwards it was logs, big time. He has used all his power in the public arena and all his warped charm trying to thwart SNO investment in Østfold. In the background he has used the coarsest of threats. So far he hasn't succeeded. A scandal is exactly what he needs, especially one which he himself hasn't caused but which will fall like a luscious ripe peach into his diamond-studded millionaire's lap.

There has to be a middle way. There has to be cover for his back.

Ryland dials the number of the only person he trusts in the Norwegian media, Ernst Filtvedt at *Dagens Næringsliv*, from his own mobile.

Filtvedt has been in the game since *DN* was the *Sjøfartstidende*. He is one of the few veterans who can still keep up in the hunt alongside distempered newspaper bloodhounds. And even though he has enough to leak he can also be very tight-lipped.

Filtvedt answers, as rusty as a ship ready for the scrapheap.

'I've got something for you,' Ryland says. 'It's very off-the-record.'

'I'm very off the record myself. I'm at the Fridtjof in the middle of my third pint. Or it could be the fourth. If it's any more of your Kingo-Kongo stuff it's going to be bloody late before I cast off from here.'

'Kingo-Kongo?'

'Kingkong Kingo. I can't listen to any more of your fantasies about Kingo. Give me one single bit of proof that the Canadians are the big, bad wolf and I'll listen.'

'This is about something quite different. It's personal and serious.'

'Jesus, I didn't know that a paragon of virtue like you did personal.'

'Can we meet where the ladies have the biggest…'

'The biggest tits in town. I can be there in five minutes.'

*

'Why do you use a chainsaw on those small bushes?' Vanja Vaage asks. 'Is it to show you use a sledgehammer to crack nuts?'

Vilhelm Thygesen stops the chainsaw that he has put on a rock in idle mode. He straightens his back and takes off his white protective gloves and opens the mesh visor of his helmet.

'The chainsaw needs some exercise,' he says, 'and so do I. You don't need a sauna when you've got a chainsaw. There's no job that makes you sweat as much as using a chainsaw in full protective gear.'

'You look trendy. The complete Alaska look.'

'If I'd known you were coming I'd have taken off all the lumberjack stuff.'

Thygesen flicks off his heavy leather boots and strips off the black protective trousers without any further ado. He is wearing shorts underneath, jeans with the legs cut off. They match the drenched denim shirt. He grabs a towel hanging from the branch of a small pine he hasn't mown down yet and wipes the sweat off his face and arms.

'You don't look bad yourself,' he says. 'Is that the full Riviera look?'

'Latest fashion from Cubus.'

The latest fashion from Cubus, if Vaage is telling the truth, must be baggy khaki shorts which leave a lot to the imagination and a tight-fitting, turquoise top, which doesn't.

Vaage asks if it isn't dangerous to have a ponytail when you are working with a chainsaw. Couldn't it get caught in the chain and cause the user to cut off his own head? No, Thygesen answers. Only idiots use a chainsaw behind their backs.

'You damage small, innocent trees,' she says.

'*Innocent?* It's a mystery to me why these pines died over the winter. Now I've solved the death riddle and I feel like testing it out on others. You're the first person to appear. So you tell me why.'

'Exhaust fumes?'

'Nonsense. Environmental nonsense.'

'If I answer the greenhouse effect, is that environmental nonsense as well?'

Thygesen nods. He takes off his shirt and wipes down his lean, grey-haired chest. It is clear he has been outdoors a lot, but not uncovered. His body is pale, apart from a tanned wedge down from his neck and lower down on his chest where the spring sun sneaked in. He isn't muscular and he has no six-pack. He is an ascetic, not an athlete.

In an era of history notable for plentiful living which has given most western men a paunch, Thygesen hasn't got one.

'Fungus', he says. 'The wet autumn has led to fungal attacks on all small pines in Østland. Haven't you noticed all the brown pines?'

'No,' Vaage answers. 'Oh, I did see some on the road here. I thought it was caused by salt.'

'We live in the so-called age of information. But neither TV nor the papers can be bothered to tell us why millions of pines in Norway have died in a veritable epidemic over the winter, and the danger of infection is still acute. I had to ring experts at the Agricultural High School in Ås to get a sensible answer to the riddle. The answer was the damn *Lophodermium seditiosum*. It attacks small trees from the ground and up to a height of around two metres, as you can see.'

Thygesen holds the top of a pine at his own height and shakes the brown needles off.

'What's really bad is that the fungus paves the way for other fungi which can attack big and small pines alike. *Gremmeniella abietina*. I cut down the small dry pines so that these fungi won't spread to the whole clump of grown pines.'

He points to the clump of pines by the door and carries on talking in a dramatic voice. A large-scale fungal attack can, according to what he has been told, put paid to the most magnificent pines. If they survive it may have damaged the trees so badly that they can become a breeding ground for the feared pine shoot beetle, alias the bark beetle.

'Then you've had it,' Thygesen says. 'Then the elm disease which ravaged Oslo in the 1980s is just small fry. We can wave goodbye to half of Nordmarken. And there's not one bugger in Norwegian public services who cares.'

'Interesting,' Vaage says. 'Actually it was another riddle that brought me here.'

'Naturally,' Thygesen says, rubbing his body energetically. 'Just hear me out before we get to the point. When you're as old as me, and I'm almost twice as old as you, you will probably also have given up trying to understand "the riddle that is yourself". For most of us it is completely unsolvable. If you're as bright as you appear you'll also have given up trying to solve the riddle of the universe. You'll concentrate on nature's greater and smaller challenges. That's healthy. It's balm to the soul. Especially for lonely souls. By the way, do you originate from the Italian or Spanish pirates who drifted on to Nordland's shores?'

'Not as far as I know,' Vaage answers. 'My great-great-grandfather was a Sami from Tysfjord. That's the most exotic element in our family. Why do you ask?'

'Because you're quite dark. A sort of Anna Hofstad type.'

'Are you trying to flirt with me?'

'Who knows what can get in the head of a recluse now the summer is upon us and women are throwing off their winter coats and circulating hormones.'

Vanja Vaage and Vilhelm Thygesen wander into the latter's cool house, where he puts on a fleece jacket and she takes out a light cotton cardigan from the bag she is carrying. She slips into it to cover her bare shoulders, and her chest.

Thygesen puts on some coffee.

12

GERHARD RYLAND TAKES THE lift down from the sixth floor. It stops on the fourth and four men in Boss and Armani suits enter and fill the space. They know very well who Ryland is, but they don't deign to say hello to one of the state's money-moving lackeys. Because they are private money-movers, they represent the free movement of capital. They have set up the institution Ermine Funds, and when Ryland discovered what ermine was in Norwegian, *hermelin*, he dubbed the gang on the fourth floor 'The Hermelins', also the name of a Swedish noble family.

In Swedish there is an expression 'a cat among ermine' and Ryland is the cat.

That suits him fine, a shaggy, grey street cat, a decent Social Democrat among all the smarty pants who think money creates money and don't understand it is work that creates capital, productive work.

The Hermelins have, in the hearing of SNO employees, called him 'an anachronistic fool', a man from the past, a man who doesn't understand that industrial capital must lose to financial capital, these are new times and the Labour Party's narrative as the industry party is on the wane.

Ryland lets the four men get out first. They disappear in a cloud of exorbitant aftershave. He goes out into Tordenskiolds gate, which is now in shade from the Town Hall. The carillon in the eastern tower plays a folk melody. He can never remember which one it is; he doesn't have an ear for it. But the fragile sound of the bells high above the town makes him think of the poet Rudolf Nilsen's poem

'In the Middle of the Town', even if the bells that made Nilsen's heart swing with joy were not the Town Hall's but the Post Office's.

Long, too long, my heart was without song.
But now I live in the middle of the city where I used to belong,
and my heart leaps with joy to hear the Post House gong!

The city, ah always the city, until I should pass away.
Like an electric lamp when its filament has had its day.
Can I lighten the town to make the mood less grey?

You've got to have ice in your guts, you have to bide your time, Ryland thinks as he hums the verses walking through the sweaty crowd on the pavement and crossing the street called after another naval hero, one who saw more ice than most Norwegians, the great Arctic explorer, Otto Sverdrup.

Ryland buys an ice cream at the kiosk on the corner of the Town Hall square. People call it a krone ice cream, but of course it doesn't cost a krone any more, it costs fifteen. However, the fact that it doesn't cost more is a sign that the mixed economy model is still keeping inflation in check. Which shows that it is possible to steer an economy despite globalisation. He is a central piece in the game to ensure that kind of control. He cannot let covert threats sweep such a piece off the table.

He walks into the burning sun in the finest square in Oslo, which now really is magnificent. In his time on the city council he fought to convert the magnificent Town Hall square from being a motorway into becoming a living, traffic-free market place. The project was ratified. Where ten thousand cars a day used to whizz past there is now a single tram. Ingratitude being the reward in this world, as soon as the Town Hall project was complete, the Labour Party was voted out of office.

Fountains cool the square. The fjord glitters like rippling filigree silver outside Honnør wharf.

Ernst Filtvedt is sitting as arranged on a bench in the shadow of 'the ladies with the biggest tits in town' – sculptor Emil Lie's colossal bronze women. If you hadn't known Filtvedt was one of the country's most experienced journalists, you wouldn't think he was a gentleman of the press but a tramp. A tousle-haired man who always reminds Ryland of the old radio tune 'There's Nothing Up Top, It's All Round About', wearing a navy blue blazer which looks as if it was washed in salt water, and shiny Terylene trousers. In the sixties when Filtvedt came ashore for good and began to write about the launching of ships in *Sjøfarten* he was well dressed, like a chief officer on shore leave. When *Sjøfarten* became *Dagens Næringsliv*, a business newspaper, and the house gradually filled with Bolsheviks in corduroy suits and leather ties, Filtvedt thought he had to show it was he who, despite his liberal opinions, came from the genuine working class; Tofte in Hurum, to be precise. He adopted the vagrant look that deceived many a finance director into thinking he was a half-wit.

It is claimed about Filtvedt that when *Dagens Næringsliv* editor Kåre Valebrokk made his famous remark that a journalist should smell of beer after lunch, Filtvedt said at a morning meeting that all journalists who don't smell of beer before breakfast are wimps, unworthy of such a noble profession.

Ryland thinks he has seen through Filtvedt's masquerade. He knows that the shabby outfit is a façade and the man never touches a drop – except perhaps for an extremely light wine – until the working day is over.

He sits down on the bench beside Filtvedt and is immediately enveloped in a cloud of beer vapour. He bolts down the ice cream. They are both surprised when he accepts the cigarette that Filtvedt offers him.

'You have to be in deep shit if you accept a Camel,' Filtvedt says. 'It's not like you to eat ice cream or land in personal trouble. Tell me more.'

'I've been receiving blackmail letters and death threats.'

'Not bad. And now you think Kingo really wants to destroy you with any means at his disposal?'

'The few antennae I have tell me Kingo's not behind this. Not even Kingo would involve a lady in this to discredit me.'

'Lady? You're not running about with women, are you?'

'On top of which she's dead.'

'This just gets better and better,' Filtvedt says, scratching the hair on his neck. 'News to me that you were a necrophiliac, Gerry Ryland.'

'It's the woman who was found murdered in Bestum last winter. In Thygesen's garden. The ne'er-do-well, you know, who used to be a lawyer.'

'Now this is beginning to look like a story.'

Filtvedt hauls a bedraggled notebook from his jacket pocket and, after a great deal of effort, also a biro that works.

His effort is in vain.

'No notes, thank you,' Ryland says in a brusque MD-voice. 'Everything said here stays between us. Deal?'

'Rotten deal, but OK. If anything has to leak, I want to be the channel. Who dropped the dead woman in your lap?'

'You'll find out the little I know and understand. First, flick through these.'

Ryland opens his briefcase and gives Filtvedt copies of the two blackmail letters.

A negress – at least that was what they were called

when Ryland was a student in sixties London and saw dark-skinned women from every corner of the empire – walks past, straight-backed. Although she is swathed in textiles even he, who normally doesn't care about such matters, can sense the rotation of her hips.

'Right, you *have* started looking at women, haven't you?' Filtvedt says without glancing up from the letters.

Ryland doesn't answer.

'She's from Somalia. They're all as tall and crabby as Naomi Campbell. And a bodyguard comes hard on their heels.'

A crowd of unusually loud, chattering Africans walks past the bench. Filtvedt says he thinks the Somalis shriek and shout in such an annoying way because they are used to the desert wind drowning out their voices.

Ryland makes no comment.

Filtvedt passes him the letters and says: 'This blackmailer must be a cross between a left-wing politico on the make and the Karate Kid. Nothing to take seriously, Gerry, my son.'

Ryland gives Filtvedt this morning's *Verdens Gang* and tells him to open it at page five. Filtvedt studies the sketch of the murdered woman and the short text. He asks a few questions, which Ryland answers in the negative.

'All right, Mr Clean,' Filtvedt says. 'If you're not absolutely sure who she is, but you're absolutely sure you haven't laid a finger on her, how did your name end up in her possession?'

Ryland presents his hypothesis.

'If it hadn't been you,' Filtvedt says, 'I'd say you were feeding me pure, unmitigated bullshit. But as it *is* you, the man who is more decent than any bishop, and I know about Natasha's passion for the world's persecuted, I'll endeavour to believe you. How does Thygesen come into the picture, by the way? As she was dumped on him, he couldn't possibly be without taint. Thygesen not being involved is as likely as Deutsche Bank selling Morgan Grenfell for a dime.'

'No idea about Thygesen,' Ryland says. 'He's never been my concern.'

'*Been my concern*? I mean to say. You can't afford to be such a stuffed shirt now, Gerry. Get it out of your system!'

'I know so little. A man sounding very serious rang me today to tell me the blackmailer's dead and it'll be my turn next if I breathe a word about the blackmail.'

'Did the caller say who the blackmailer was or when and how he'd been killed? Or, most importantly, why?'

'No. It was a very short conversation, the kind where you feel no desire to confront or question.'

Ryland lights another rare cigarette and puffs at it remorselessly as Filtvedt asks what the envelopes the letters came in looked like. Had he kept them? So that the police could check for fingerprints and test the stamps for saliva, which can reveal the sender's DNA profile. He emphasises that Reidar Isachsen is the obvious lead to follow and insists that if the million was to go to this address there must be some connection with the blackmailer or blackmailers.

His conclusion is clear: 'You've got only one option, Gerry, and that's to tell the cops. That's what everyone subjected to blackmail should do.'

'I'm afraid of leaks.'

'You have a point. Nevertheless, I believe the risk of that in a case which has received so little publicity is minimal. It's the big ones where the police, the prosecution and the defence leak as if on a payroll. The police must have a pecuniary or a prestige reason for leaking. I can't see any reason for them to do so in this business.'

'Isn't it good enough to have spoken to you this time round?'

'No,' replies Filtvedt. 'I can't be a substitute for the police.'

'Will you take care of the letters for me?'

Filtvedt nods.

'I've also got a digital log of today's incoming calls,' Ryland says, holding up a diskette. 'We just record the phone numbers, not the conversations themselves. On this diskette there is the number of the threatening call. It came in at about half past twelve.'

Ryland passes it to Filtvedt, who at first refuses to take it on the basis that he prefers not to hold original evidence. He allows himself to be persuaded when he is reassured again that he will be the first to know if Ryland decides to go public.

'We're two old-school, honourable pashas,' Filtvedt says, casting a longing glance up at the bronze breasts behind the bench where the two men are sitting. 'We're grateful for small mercies. We're still alive. School leavers haven't painted the nipples on Lie's sculptures red and the bloody taggers have kept away.'

'I regret I'm alive now and not in the thirties,' Ryland says.

'You would've liked to be a planned economist under Stalin?'

'I would've liked to be around to create the New Deal under *him*.'

Ryland points east to the granite statue of Franklin Delano Roosevelt hidden in a clump of trees on the slope up towards the plain north of Akershus Fortress.

'The council has placed a box for used syringes at Roosevelt's feet,' Filtvedt says. 'That's how far your bloody welfare state has gone. Are you going to be able to stop the biggest merger in Norwegian history, by the way?'

'I've got a meeting with Peterson and the Finns this evening, in Bærøe in Hobøl.'

'Give me a buzz when the meeting's over. And go to the police for Christ's sake when you're back in town.'

'I'm sending Natasha to the cabin so that I can spend the weekend going through her stuff to see if I can find a clue there.'

'You've heard my advice. Go to the police right away, otherwise you'll regret it.'

13

'I'VE EXPLAINED MYSELF AS carefully and truthfully as I can,' Vilhelm Thygesen says. 'Yet I still have a sneaking sensation you suspect *me* of taking this photo.'

He points to the photo of Picea lying on the blue wax cloth with the windmill motif that covers his kitchen table.

Vaage drinks the last, lukewarm drop of coffee and studies her notes.

'I'm absolutely fed up with your suspicions,' Thygesen continues. 'There's no logical reason for them. If I'd taken a photo of Picea while she was alive I'd have been the world's biggest numbskull to give it to Kripos and try to make them think someone else had taken it and planted it on me. Why the hell would I go to that trouble?'

'Fine,' Vaage answers. 'Fair enough.'

Thygesen wipes the sweat off his forehead with kitchen roll. He sits zipping his fleece up and down, gets to his feet, goes into the hall and changes his jacket for a red and black checked flannel shirt.

'Are you going to send an undercover cop here to nab Dr Papaya and Captain Paw-Paw, should the phantom or phantoms materialise?' he asks.

'I'm going to suggest it,' Vaage answers. 'I'll see what I can do.'

'I've given you lot photographic proof that should be of some use. So perhaps we've finished now, have we?'

'Not quite. Are you aware of the recent movements of one Terje Kykkelsrud?'

'The movements of *who*?'

'Terje Kykkelsrud. One of the leaders of a biker gang in Østfold.'

'Oh, you mean Kykke. The one-eyed giant who rides a Kawasaki named after one of the Cyclops in ancient Greece. Brontosaurus? No, that's a dinosaur. His machine's called Brontes. It's aeons since I've had anything to do with his crowd.'

'One man's aeon,' Vaage says. 'We're talking the first half of the nineties.'

'I've repressed any thoughts about them. I screwed up a case I was doing for them because I missed an appeal date to the court of enforcement.'

'When did you last have any contact with Kykkelsrud or any of the other self-dubbed Seven Samurai?'

'None since the case went belly up. That is, Kykke rang me a couple of times when he was pissed and threatened to run me over with studded tyres and flay me alive. Only little civilities like that. I considered him a harmless soul behind an intimidating façade. Any real malice there is in Kykke lies very, very deep. If you know anything about such a working-class hero it's impossible to believe that he would stoop so low as to use Dr Papaya or Captain Paw-Paw as aliases.'

'I don't believe anything, I'm just asking. Besides I don't have the honour of being acquainted with *herr* Kykkelsrud.'

'But you must have a reason for asking. If you tell me the reason perhaps I can give you a better answer.'

'At the present...' Vaage says, and pauses.

'I'm glad you didn't say "at the present juncture in the investigation". You would've fallen five notches in my respect, and probably a couple more in your own.'

'Your wall clock can't possibly be right, Thygesen, can it?

'Wall clock?'

'Do you *have* to answer half my questions with

questions,' Vaage says, pointing to a round instrument encased in brass with glass in front of a white face with two hands.

Thygesen laughs in a way she finds particularly unpleasant. Wolf-like laughter from a mouth with brown, stained teeth.

'That's not a clock,' he guffaws. 'That's a barometer.'

'Sorry,' Vaage replies. 'I left my contact lenses at work.'

Thygesen gets up and taps the barometer glass. The black pressure hand moves from "change" to "fair". He adjusts the brass hand until it is over the black one.

He says with a laugh: 'You can console yourself with the thought that this isn't your biggest blunder, Vanja Vaage. Looks like there'll be high pressure and nice weather tomorrow as well, even if the weather forecast says high winds over the mountains to the east.'

The laughter is contagious, and Vaage has to laugh too. It is liberating, if not unbridled.

Thygesen, playing the role of cheery, gallant gentleman, looks at his watch, announces that it is ten to six, stands up and puts on a fresh pot of coffee. Vaage says she has to go to the car to get her glasses and her watch, and there is a phone call she has to make.

She slides into the overheated car, which is her private Escort – not an open-top unfortunately – and casts a glance at another Ford parked in Thygesen's drive, a rust-heap of a Fiesta. It belongs to Vera Alam, and for a few brief moments she wonders how cancer-afflicted Alam in Sarajevo is progressing, whether the relationship between Alam and Thygesen was really as platonic as he suggests. Surely even a single man of sixty-four must have some kind of sex life? Thygesen calls himself a pensioner, on a disability pension, but he doesn't seem to have laid anchor to the boat of life and put his erotic years behind him.

Vaage dismisses these thoughts. She does it physically,

by smacking her temples, first on the right, then on the left. She never remembers which half of the brain your sexual thoughts are supposed to be lodged.

Quickly she taps in Stribolt's number, rings and receives an immediate answer.

'Have you started the interview?' Vaage asks.

'No, I'm standing on the platform in Halden. Just got off the train. The Østfold line can't be as crazy as everyone says. NSB runs a very strict timetable.'

'I've got some important info for you before you tackle Dotti. There is material evidence showing Picea while she was still alive. This strengthens Rønningen's claim that she saw Picea on board a train.'

'What sort of material evidence?'

'A colour photo. The person is unquestionably Picea.'

'How did you get your mitts on that?'

'From Thygesen,' Vaage answers.

It all goes quiet in Halden.

'I'm at Thygesen's now, questioning him,' Vaage says.

'Well, I'm buggered. Wow. Explain to a sweaty detective what happened.'

Vaage explains.

'I have only one question,' Stribolt says. 'Are you sure Thygesen *received* the photo and he didn't take it himself?'

'Pretty sure. My gut feeling tells me he's speaking the truth. He must be irrational, bordering on psychotic, if he's taken photos of Picea and voluntarily told us about it.'

Stribolt asks Vaage to ring him at once if Thygesen says anything else he ought to know.

Vaage puts on her glasses and walks back into the house, which for some strange reason reminds her of the house on the prairie, even though it looks like every other tarred Norwegian log house from around the previous turn of the century.

After all the coffee she has poured down her she needs the toilet again. It is located next to the hall, she remembers from her previous visit in February. She has read somewhere, perhaps it was in *Dagbladet*'s Saturday magazine, that you can learn about single menfolk by studying the standards of their toilets. If this is correct, Thygesen is normal, indeed, almost disappointingly ordinary. The toilet is well equipped with paper and all sorts: brush, soap, which is where it should be on the small basin with hot and cold taps, old newspapers in a bamboo rack. The door can be closed from the inside with a hook; she puts it through the eye, sits down on the seat, which is wooden and very comfortable for the behind, and flips through the papers. *Newsweek*, *National Geographic*. No porn, not even a solitary *Vi Menn*. Oddly enough, an ancient copy of *Tique* fashion magazine.

The only thing of note she finds is a framed photographic portrait of the legendary Apache Chief Geronimo on the toilet wall. Must be one of his heroes.

What is missing is a mirror. But only effete men have a mirror over the basin.

In the kitchen she finds Thygesen pulling a cork from a wine bottle.

'Don't worry,' he says, 'this isn't my home-grown redcurrant plonk.'

'Thank you, but I'm driving,' Vaage says, turning the glass placed by her seat upside down.

'Not from Bestum but Bordeaux,' Thygesen says, smelling the cork, filling a glass and putting it next to Vaage. 'Tax-free from Paris.'

'Are you deaf?'

'In this kind of situation I can be terribly hard of hearing. You mentioned Kykkelsrud. So I assume that he's involved in some way or other. I know a good deal about him from way back before the Seven Samurai and quite different gangs. You don't have to screw up your face like that. Would you like to see a photo of Kykke taken exactly twenty-five years ago?'

Thygesen slides a newspaper cutting across the table. It is a whole page, dominated by a line of men. In the foreground there is a glimpse of shadowy figures which are obviously police officers.

'Found it in my archive,' Thygesen says. 'I was a kind of adviser to Kykke during a strike in the North Sea. But this picture is of another, earlier strike. At a rail freight company in 1976. An illegal strike. A wildcat strike, as employers and the Labour Party called it. The man towering up from the others in the line is Terje Kykkelsrud. We had something in common in those days, he and I, although we didn't know each other. We were part of the atmosphere around the Workers' Communist Party. Sympathisers, as they used to say.'

Vaage lifts the yellowing cutting.

'Has to be *Klassekampen*,' she says, expelling a puff of air.

'Doesn't *have* to be, though in fact it is. All the newspapers devoted huge spreads to the strike. It was thought it presaged the famous armed revolution. If you'd like to hear about male collectives and political collectives that have marked both Kykke and me, be my guest. We can discuss interesting splintering tendencies and the effect they had on individuals like Kykke. If not, you can bugger off back home to the mountain known as the Hamarøy Dick.'

Vaage pauses for effect before countering: 'To the mountain known as the Træn Pole then, for my taste. It's the tallest one beneath the Arctic Circle, in the archipelago of my childhood.'

'You're not going to spit in the glass if you don't have shop-bought wine on the table, are you?'

'Idiot,' Vaage says, grabbing the glass Thygesen shoves over towards her.

'You're driving,' Thygesen says, wagging his forefinger.

'As you know, one can leave the car in the drive.'

14

From Halden railway station Arve Stribolt wanders along the Tista towards the police department, which is in a red-brick building by the river. He has been there several times before, the last was when Kripos asked him to assist in the investigation of a bank robbery in which two Nazis were involved.

Although the distance between the two towns is so immense and the topography is so different and the housing stock in Halden doesn't date from the reconstruction period after the Second World War, it still reminds him of his own town, Hammerfest. It must be the provinciality, the activity in the town; it is a place for normal people, where ostentatious wealth barely exists. Stribolt likes to go to small Norwegian towns and he likes getting away again when his job is done.

He is met by a friendly soul at the department and is given an office on the first floor, along with kind instructions to help himself to as much coffee as he wants from the machine in the corridor. Plus strict instructions not to smoke in the office, on pain of death, as the Haldeners say.

As there is an ashtray on the desk he takes the risk and lights up. If he gets a bullet in his carcass he won't be the first. From the office window he has a view of the scene where the biggest crime mystery in the history of Scandinavia took place.

Stribolt makes himself comfortable in the chair and is soon lost in reverie. He imagines he is a king waiting for a queen. No one can deny a serving policeman the sweet anticipation of interviewing a young woman with d.ronningen as her email address and Dotti de la Motti as her internet name.

He has summoned Hege Dorothy Rønningen to appear at 18.30. From what he had been led to believe about the Østfold railway he had genuinely assumed the train wouldn't be on time and arrive in Halden at 17.52, but it did. So he had half an hour to kill.

Stribolt stares out of the window at Frederiksten Fortress where the swallowtail flag flutters crisply in a southerly breeze that has picked up over the border town. Up there was where Karl XII was shot and killed one winter's day in 1718. According to the old calendar, on 30 November; according to the modern one, 11 December, which some consider to be the Devil's birthday. Straight after the Swedish king was killed a rumour spread like wildfire through Norway and Sweden that he had been assassinated by his own men. The motive for the murder was said to be the Swedish officer class's war weariness. The hero king after the victory in the battle against the Russians at Narva in 1700 had become a zero king after the defeat to Peter the Great's forces at Poltava during the Winter War in 1709. Karl XII lost all the Swedes' foreign possessions and in so doing destroyed Sweden as a great power. To regain his popularity he tried to conquer Norway from the Danes. Not even he could manage that at the first attempt in 1716. Then he did, two years later; another attempt which didn't look as if it were going to succeed either.

In one of the trenches the Swedish invaders had dug to attack Gyldenløve Fort, Karl XII fell to a bullet that hit him in the temple and went right through his head.

Stribolt logs into the office computer with the password he received from the duty officer. He gets into the police's word-processing software and clicks through to a standard interview form. As the country's police stations are not yet linked via intranet there is no way of getting into his own files at Kripos and picking up documents from the Picea case. So instead he surfs the web, to a discussion forum on the net called *Who killed Karl XII?*

It had gone quiet after the Swedish neo-Nazis got tired of debating. So far in 2001 there hasn't been much traffic on the site. Stribolt clicks on to one of his own contributions. Under the pseudonym of Thundershield he discusses the motive and draws the conclusion that the Norwegians had the strongest reason to kill the king. In his piece, which he was quite happy with, he writes that the assassination rumour grew because the Swedish officers were trying, in vain, to keep the king's death a secret. Thus the rank and file soldiers suspected the officers' secrecy was because they had shot the king in a cowardly ambush.

Stribolt clicks back to the first piece he wrote on the forum. It is a lightly edited school essay he wrote in his first year at upper secondary. Entitled 'The ultimate proof that we Norwegians killed Karl XII', it is an imaginative account of how an extremely proficient detective by the name of Evar Boltirs finds a hidden letter behind the wallpaper at a manor house by Kongsvinger. In the letter the former owner of the manor confesses that it was he who fired the shot from Gyldenløve and killed the king. Fearing reprisals from the Swedes, the gunman made his colleagues promise to maintain their silence. On the parchment there is a map and a cryptic code. Boltirs cracks the code and finds, first, the bullet hidden in a well in Skåne that he has to dive down into, and second, on a hush-hush journey across Russia, shadowed by the KGB, the gun the farmer from Kongsvinger sold to a Russian count who wanted the murder weapon as a souvenir. Metallurgic tests show that the specially cast bullet is exactly the same kind of brass as that which is used to make buttons for Norwegian uniforms and the pattern on the bullet reveals it was fired by the gun in the Russian count's possession.

The text is illustrated with the famous photograph taken in 1917 of the king's mummified cranium with a fist-size hole in it. The essay opens with a quotation from Volume 7 of *Norway's History* in which Professor Knut Mykland writes: 'Despite thorough analyses of the written material and repeated analyses of Karl XII's cranium it has not been possible to give a certain answer to whether it was a Norwegian or a Swedish assassin who killed the king, and this question is certain to remain unanswered in the future.'

The conclusion of the essay is the engraving on the Danish commemorative medal: 'The Swedish lion fell at the feet of the Norwegian lion. There it lost its life and its last heroic blood.'

There is a tap on the office door. Stribolt closes the screen showing the skull, takes out his comb and runs it through his hair. He would have liked to have a bit more hair. Soon he will be as old as Karl XII was when he died, thirty-six, and his hair is thinning, as the Swedish king's was. Unfortunately he doesn't have the fine curls flowing down his neck that Karl has in all the paintings.

The Dotti who enters has the same elegant curls in reality that she has on her internet photo. But the girl Stribolt is observing now is only a pale reflection of the dynamic roller-skater on the internet. Perhaps Dotti has two personalities: one she reveals on the net and one which studies 'commercial German and international trade' at the college in Østfold. At the police station she definitely looks like a serious student. She is wearing the same round glasses as on the net. But no make-up apart from brownish lipstick smudged in one corner.

She is a little shorter than he had imagined. Despite the heat she is wearing a thick, woollen, grey polo-neck jumper and trousers with side-pockets on both thighs.

They shake hands. Her grip is loose and clammy. She doesn't introduce herself as Dotti but with her Christian name.

She takes off a tiny rucksack, fishes out a mobile phone and switches it off.

'Are you allowed to smoke here?' she asks with an eye on the ashtray.

'Not really. But feel free,' Stribolt answers, thinking he has read something about how many different roles today's young people play. How they can shift roles faster than a policeman changes his light blue uniform shirt.

'I'm really nervous,' she says. 'I've never had anything to do with the police before.'

While Rønningen smokes a Prince cigarette Stribolt fills in the interview form with personal details. The information comes thick and fast. She is twenty-three years old. She has been studying in Halden for a year and is actually from Elverum. The only question that causes her any concern is the one about marital status. She mounts a weak smile and says it is so uncertain she had better say single or whatever it is called.

Stribolt asks if she would like some coffee and she accepts.

He pops in to see the duty officer and asks if there are any faxes from Oslo. Vaage was supposed to fax over Picea's photo as soon as she was back at HQ in Bryn. No faxes have arrived, says the duty officer, who doesn't seem to have the scepticism Kripos officers often encounter in their provincial colleagues: don't take our cases, don't mix in our circles.

Stribolt brings a coffee from the machine in the corridor.

He reminds Rønningen, in somewhat stilted terms it seems to him, about a witness's duty to make a truthful statement. She sips her coffee.

'Let's begin with when and where you caught the train,' he says.

'I got on the train in Öxnered. It was the one from Göteborg to Oslo. Or it might've even come from Copenhagen. Sunday 28 January, and it was late. Should've been in Öxnered at half past six, but it didn't arrive until seven.'

'Are we talking about the evening train?'

'Yes. It was dark and unpleasant on the deserted station, and bitingly cold.'

'What had you been doing in Öxnered?'

'Nothing. I'd visited my bloke in Uddevalla. He drove me to Öxnered, which is the closest railway station, but couldn't be bothered to wait until the train came. We'd been arguing a lot all weekend. The train was pretty full when it did finally arrive. And unfortunately I got a seat in a compartment with a bloody pest.'

'A pest?'

'Yes, some crazy guy taking pictures of the other passengers. It was only when I objected to being photographed that I noticed the woman whose picture is in the paper. The one who's been killed.'

Stribolt asks if the woman had any special characteristics.

'There was something funny about one ear,' Rønningen says, holding her right ear with her thumb and first finger. 'When this guy's harassment got to her she brushed her hair to one side and I saw there was something strange about her ear, as if it were torn. I thought it was so sad for a woman who was otherwise so beautiful. Beautiful in a kind of Mediterranean way.'

'Did you have an impression of where she might be from? Nationality?'

'It's hard to say. She spoke English with a very strong accent, a bit like Russians do. But I only heard a few words. She told the guy taking photos to "go away, go away". And then he sat down beside her and she changed places and sat beside me. Asked me if that was OK. "OK I sit here?" I must have looked pretty sullen. I was boiling with anger about all the mess with Kalle.'

'Kalle?'

'My bloke, who dumped me at the station.'

'You didn't speak to the foreign woman?'

'Couple of words. She asked when the train would arrive in Oslo. She had a ticket with a timetable attached. The train was due to arrive at 21.45. I told her we were a good thirty minutes late and it might be more the way things were going. She asked if I knew whether it was difficult to find a hotel room in Oslo and whether I could recommend somewhere. I answered that it was easy in the middle of winter, though I didn't know anywhere cheap. She would have to ask at Oslo station. The idiot taking photos had moved up the train. The woman took a book from her bag and started reading.'

'You've got a keen eye and a good memory,' Stribolt says. 'Do you remember which book?'

'Yes, I do. I noticed because at first I thought it was some kind of terrorist stuff. The book was in English and entitled *Memed, My Hawk*, written by someone called Yaşar something or other. A hawk's a military rocket, isn't it, and I thought the author might be Arafat. But when she moved her fingers off the cover, where the author's name was, I could see it was Kemal. Then I remembered I'd read the book in Norwegian when I was at school. I come from a family where the kids are fed all kinds of books about poor people who become rebels and heroes. Kind of radical.'

'I do too, in fact,' Stribolt says. 'My father was a pool supervisor at Isbjørnhallen in Hammerfest and a hardened communist.'

Rønningen doesn't find this information wildly peripheral; she smiles almost like on the net and says: '*My* father's probably the only major in the army who's stood for the Socialist Left Party at the elections.'

'Do you remember the Norwegian title of the book?' Stribolt asks.

'*Sultne Memed?*'

'*Magre Memed*, unless I'm much mistaken. Romantic thing about a Turkish village. The hero, Memed, fights the landowners and wins the princess and half the kingdom.'

'Did he rebel because the girl he loved was killed by a nobleman, Aga?' asks Rønningen, who has a glint in her blue eyes behind the glasses.

'Yes, think that's how it was,' Stribolt answers. 'Have you heard that the writer, Kemal, risks going to prison in Turkey because he supports the Kurds?'

'No, I've got more than enough to do with reading the books on the syllabus and I haven't kept up with international politics.'

'If it's OK with you, I'd like to adjourn the interview and check something online.'

Rønningen nods.

Stribolt uses his favourite search engine, Google, to look for Yaşer Kemal and immediately finds a plethora of information confirming what he thought, that the Turkish author Yaşar – or Yasir as he is called in Norwegian – Kemal has committed himself to the Kurdish cause. Kemal has written books, pamphlets and articles in which he argues for the Kurds' right to have their own language and their own culture. From being the Turkish candidate for the Nobel Prize in literature he has become a candidate for prison.

On the interview form Stribolt writes: 'Draft. Hypothesis: Kurdish trail. Was Picea really a Kurd? Based on statement from Rønningen that she was reading Kemal on the train. Kemal is an active, committed intellectual who is taking risks in his old age. Picea reads a seditious novel written by a writer supporting the fight for Kurdish rights. But why is she reading the Memed novel in English? Perhaps because she, as a Kurd, doesn't want to read the book in the original Turkish. Or simply because she wants to learn English by reading a story where she knows the context in which the plot is played out.

'I roll back my mind to the autopsy. How thin we thought Picea was, lying on the stretcher in the Pathology Institute. I saw and still see her as a rebellious spirit from the mountains on the Turkish peninsula. I am aware this might be a romanticisation. And as I have imagined her as a Kurd from the very start I have to be careful about pursuing this idea, this view, too far.'

Stribolt saves what he has written, apologises to Rønningen by saying that he has a tendency to lose himself in detail when he finds new leads.

'I got so excited I forgot to ask you to give me a precise description of Picea,' he says.

'Picea?'

'That's a codename we've given her as we haven't identified her yet.'

Rønningen says she is a hundred per cent sure that the woman was wearing a white blouse and had a dark padded coat with her, but was unsure whether she had a skirt or trousers on.

'I might remember if you can tell me where the toilet is.'

Stribolt gives her directions. He doesn't understand why Rønningen is so tense. He is reminded of the Olaf Palme investigator Hans Holmér, who put all his efforts into searching among the Kurds in Sweden at the start of his endeavours to identify the Swedish Prime Minister's killer. At that time in 1986, when young Stribolt decided to stifle his prejudices about the police, defy his father's deep aversion to the bourgeois forces of law and order and apply for a place at Police College, journalist Jan Guillou's public derision of Holmér's Kurdish trail left an indelible mark on him. If a leading Swedish detective could make such a cardinal error as to invest all his and his staff's energy in pursuing one lead there should be hope for a hobby detective from Hammerfest to become a passable officer, not to say a *better* detective. Sadly, there is no sign that that has indeed come about. Then again he hasn't had the main responsibility for solving any real crime mysteries until the Picea riddle was dropped in his lap in February of 2001.

If he succeeds in solving it, he will be able to leave Kripos walking tall. He has been on the way out for a long time. He has bad chemistry with his boss, Arne Huuse. Stribolt drafted one of his many letters of resignation in March when Huuse said on the TV news that ninety-five per cent of all the heroin smuggling in Norway was undertaken by Kosovo-Albanians. Not one single person in the media reacted to this initiative. What made the hairs on Stribolt's neck stand up wasn't that Huuse was spreading disinformation. His boss had proof for what he said. But he didn't *need* to release all the force's knowledge about heroin seizures and the Albanian mafia.

Especially not in a situation where there was public debate about the sending of Kosovo refugees to Norway. This was going to criminalise and stigmatise a whole ethnic group.

Another officer incapable of understanding that it is better to keep your mouth tightly buttoned is one Ola Thune. The private detective has bad-mouthed the police during almost every major case over the last few years. If there is anything in the rumours that Huuse is thinking of employing Thune as the Head of the Investigation Department and calling it the Homicide Commission, Thune, on his way in, will meet Stribolt on his way out.

Rønningen returns with her lipstick adjusted and says apologetically that she cannot remember any more about the woman's clothes. What she does remember is that she wore no make-up, at least none that was obvious, and she wasn't carrying much. Only a suitcase, the type you can take on a plane as hand luggage, and a bag.

Stribolt notices that Rønningen looked straight at him when she mentioned the suitcase, but glanced away when she mentioned the bag.

'It doesn't matter about her clothes,' he says. 'I'd like to know more about the pest.'

'He was definitely Norwegian,' Rønningen says. 'From Oslo West I would guess. Judging by his accent. A motormouth as he waltzed around with his camera taking photos and annoying people. He said he wanted to document life on board the world's most boring train. Words to that effect. Those who objected were told they were enemies of art.'

'Age and appearance?'

'Around twenty-five. Tall and strong. Bit flabby. Dark hair. Most was hidden under a captain's hat, a sailor's hat, whatever they are. The bit that was visible was quite long and looked dirty. Greasy. And he was wearing a leather coat which he didn't take off even though it was suffocatingly hot in the compartment. Leather boots. Don't remember his trousers.'

The description of the pest on the train doesn't tally with the one Stribolt was given of young Øystein Strand who was killed in a possible rigged accident in Østfold. On the other hand, the captain's hat and the leather coat suggest the person using the alias Captain Paw-Paw, who sent the photo of Picea alive to Thygesen and which he passed on to Vaage.

'Was he high?' Stribolt asks.

'Not on alcohol, maybe on drugs. I remember thinking he was as high as his girl was low.'

'Girl? Was someone with him?'

'Yes, I forgot to say that. She didn't stand out. She was asleep from the moment I got on the train to the moment I got off in Halden. It went through my mind that she must have taken something that knocked her out. I remember a big head of tousled hair with red stripes in and a face so white you could say she was as white as a sheet. I couldn't see any more of her because she was wrapped in a blanket.'

'You said drugs. Any idea what kind?'

'I'm no expert on drugs,' Rønningen says, trying without much success to roll her eyes coquettishly. 'He was pretty hyper and wild-eyed, but kept his feet even though the train was swaying all over the place. That's how people get when they take amphetamines or drink a very strong cocktail with what the Swedes call party poppers.'

'The camera?' Stribolt asks, adding the keyword to the screen.

'Small, shiny. Nothing special. But when he came back to my compartment as we were going through the wasteland before Ed he took out a big, old-fashioned video camera and started filming the passengers. One guy jumped to his feet to fetch the conductor. And she, the woman who was later killed, was so fed up with having a camera thrust up her nose she began to cry. She went and hid in the toilet. Then there was another woman, also foreign, who was so angry she tried to knock the camera out of the guy's hands. When we arrived at Ed the whole train was invaded by Norwegian customs officials doing a cattle check.'

'A foot-and-mouth disease control,' Stribolt says.

'Exactly. I hate the expression, foot-and-mouth disease, it sounds so revolting. There was quite a commotion when the customs officials got on. The guy was filming total chaos, and didn't stop. The woman who'd tried to snatch his camera saw the officials and ran off the train without taking her suitcase.'

'Interesting. Was she arrested?'

'Not as far as I could see.'

'Was she very similar in appearance to the woman we call Picea?'

'She was dark-haired too. But fatter. And she spoke German. At least she could swear in German, because she shouted *Scheisskerl* when she hit him.'

'What did Picea do during the check?'

'She returned from the toilet after we left Ed. I didn't see her being checked. She didn't look like a meat smuggler.'

'And the passport control?' Stribolt asks.

'They didn't seem very interested in anyone's passports except the poor couple with the packet of salami,' Rønningen says. 'In the end the conductor came and stopped the guy using the camera. But the pest made a drawing which he showed everyone. Pornographic. The woman you call Picea… said "crazy man, dangerous man" and asked if there were cheap hotels in Halden. I said the best for her would be the Grand in the square outside the station.

'She said she had been travelling for a long time and rubbed her eyes as if to show she was worn out. She gave the finger to the film guy although he didn't see it and then we both got off in Halden.'

'She got off in Halden?'

'Yes, despite having a ticket for Oslo.'

'You're sure she didn't get back on the train?'

'Absolutely sure. We both lit up a cigarette. You couldn't smoke on the train. I pointed to the Grand. The train chugged off.'

'The photo freak, did he get off in Halden too?'

'I don't think so. If he did, I didn't see him.'

'Are you sure?'

'Pretty sure. I was so relieved that we'd got away from any more hassle with the nutter. No, if he'd got off I'd have noticed. We notice unpleasant things much faster than nice things.'

Stribolt goes for a coffee refill. In the corridor he curses: 'Shit, this is a clear murderer type, but he gets off at the wrong station, or at least he doesn't get off at the same station as the victim.'

Back in the interview room, he asks for a little break, adds the new information and notes down some more questions.

'So she got off in Halden unexpectedly. Did you see anyone meet her or walk towards her?' he asks.

'No, I hurried to my car, which was in the NSB car park. It's a crappy little car, a Fiat Ritmo, and I was worried it wouldn't start in the cold.'

'Did it?'

'Almost,' Rønningen says, imitating the sound of an unwilling starter motor driven by a frozen battery: 'Oonk, oonk, oonk. I gave up and went to find a taxi, at great expense.'

'Did you see any more of Picea around the station or nearby?'

'No, I thought she'd gone to the Grand. It's not far, just across the street from the station.'

'You mentioned another woman. The one who ran off in Ed and left a suitcase on the train. Did Picea take the suitcase?'

'No, she had her own.'

'And a bag,' Stribolt adds. 'I've got here that she had a bag. Was there anything special about it?'

'Only that it was more expensive and elegant than her other stuff. Crocodile skin. Probably fake, but it looked authentic enough.'

'Did she have the bag when she got off the train?'

'Yes, I think so.'

'But you're not sure?'

'Odd question,' Rønningen says. She blushes lightly but becomingly. 'Do you think there might have been dope in it and she was supposed to take it to Oslo where it would be collected?'

'I have no idea.'

'I'm sure she took her bag. That was where she had her cigarettes and her dictionary.'

'Dictionary?'

'Yes, I forgot to say. While she was reading the Memed book she was using a small English dictionary, a Collins.'

'What was the other language?'

'Russian.'

'Russian?'

'Is that so strange? I'm positive there were Cyrillic letters on the cover.'

'Hell,' Stribolt says.

'Did I say something wrong?' asks Hege Dorothy Rønningen.

'No, no, no. My hypothesis has just been sunk, that's all. Let's call it a day now. I'm waiting for photographic evidence from Kripos in Oslo which I'd like you to see. Can we meet again, preferably early tomorrow?'

Rønningen says that is fine. She doesn't have any lectures until eleven. Stribolt feels an immense desire to invite her out for a beer, but stops himself and, after she has left, growls: 'Long live professionalism. Death to professionalism.'

15

In the light spring evening on the Scandinavian peninsula, a Kawasaki motorbike is roaring through the Swedish countryside of Södermanland, a Toyota Landcruiser is motoring through the forest in the Norwegian county of Østfold and an ancient, recently stolen, Datsun is heading towards Aspedammen outside Halden by the Swedish border. The three men, with three very different Japanese vehicles, also have very distinct intentions as regards their journeys.

Kykkelsrud, behind the handlebars of the bike he calls Brontes, is fleeing from a murder he has committed. Before him lies a future in a country that until recently was a part of the Soviet Union, but is now open to any capital, legal or otherwise. But he isn't sure that the partners in the gang he still belongs to are trustworthy. So he has taken precautions. When the light evening turns into golden night he will meet his partners, Borken and Lips, in Stockholm. He doesn't take the main road through Västmanland and Uppland, as most Norwegians do. Kykke has chosen to take the road south around Lake Mälaren, for no other reason than that he, as a biker, prefers that route.

Bård Isachsen, known to his friends as Bård the Board, is driving towards Aspedammen where he has a job to do. He is going to burn down the abandoned shack his uncle owns so that any evidence of the crime committed there is destroyed. Bård the Board thinks the crime that took place in his uncle's house was drug smuggling, and it is true that the house was used a drugs warehouse. What he doesn't know is that a murder was also committed there, a murder that in the eyes of the law has to be viewed as premeditated.

Bård the Board assumes he is in with Borken after his smart disguise and having given such a precise report on how Beach Boy died. When Uncle Reidar's house has been burned down his star will be even higher with the gang. And he will get a stack of cash, which he sorely needs after dropping out of school and being unemployed for eighteen months. To start the fire he has brought a five-litre can of petrol. He took it from Øystein's mother's place when he popped in to say how sorry he was that her son had died in an accident. She has only a small lawn outside her house in Tistedalen and she hardly ever cuts it. So she won't notice the petrol can for her mower has gone.

Gerhard Ryland is sitting behind the wheel in his private Landcruiser. The big car is one of the few luxuries he allows himself. Beside him in the passenger seat sits his secretary John Olsen, who has doubled as his trusty sidekick on a few occasions. Fru Ryland, Natasha, is lying on the back seat in a foetal position, asleep, covered with her coat. Ryland is on the way to a decisive dinner on the Bærøe estate. There he will meet the top management of the Peterson concern and the negotiators from the Finnish Norpaper company. What they will decide is whether the wood-processing industry in Østfold will broadly speaking still be in Norwegian hands. The worst scenario for the negotiations over dinner is that Peterson refuses to sell to the Finns and prefers to merge with the financial tightrope walker Kingo, with the sole intention of selling up lock, stock and barrel to Canada.

Ryland has other things on his mind too. He is pondering his decision not to go to the police and report the blackmail attempt. He still thinks the risk of a police leak to the media is so great that it isn't an option.

'Left here,' says Olsen, the map reader.

They have driven down the E6 south from Oslo, turned on to the R121 by Såner Church and are now coming on to the R120 between Moss and Elvestad.

'Now it's straight for five or six kilometres, then there's a signpost to Bærøe,' Olsen says.

After a couple of minutes he speaks up again: 'There must have been an accident here.'

He points to the police cordon alongside the road.

'Someone must have misjudged the bend,' Ryland says. 'People drive like bats out of hell.'

'And die like flies.'

*

In Halden, Arve Stribolt, the Kripos detective, goes to the Grand Hotel. He spends an hour plying between the guest books and the staff. His conclusion is that no single woman answering to Picea's description registered at the Grand on the evening of 28 January or any of the subsequent days.

'It's all too rare for stylish, single women to be guests here,' the receptionist sighed.

Stribolt has invited the receptionist to a beer so that he can hear a little about what goes on in the area around Halden station in the evenings. From what Stribolt has been told, there is no life at all. The hot rods – of which there are many in Halden – don't burn rubber around the station. If Halden had open prostitution in the streets there might have been a red-light area between the station and the harbour, but it doesn't.

'No, there's nothing here at night,' the receptionist says. 'It's just so quiet.'

They both listen to the silence in Halden until the rising wind catches an empty beer can and rattles it down the street outside the hotel window.

*

The wind in Aspedammen Forest is gusting hard. The spruce trees move like trolls swaying in the pitch darkness. Bård Isachsen has parked the stolen rust-bucket out of sight from the drunkard who is Reidar's neighbour and lives in a timber hovel that is almost as tumbledown as his uncle's. There is light in the kitchen window, but the old soak is nowhere to be seen.

The last time he was here the guy came out pissed and started talking with Øystein, Beach Boy, who had been in Reidar's house looking for dope. Øystein, the dickhead, thought the house was let to the Kamikaze gang.

He never knew it was his own gang, the Seven Samurai, who were renting the house. When Øystein finally got into his car he was annoyed that he hadn't found any dope, only a ladies bag.

'I reckon they've been having orgies in there,' Øystein said at the time. 'And it must've been a pretty wild affair because there's menstrual blood over the walls.'

He was told to sling the bag and when he drove down into town Øystein said he would throw it into the Tista.

Perhaps Borken and Lips had raped someone in Reidar's house and wanted any evidence of that burned, as well as whatever drugs could be found? No point thinking about that now. Just do the job and get the hell out of it.

Quickly Bård the Board sprinkles petrol over the woodwork of his uncle's house. He rolls up a newspaper he brought with him into a little ball, lights a corner and throws it against the wall.

It bursts into flames with even more intensity than he thought it would. Bård the Board runs across a field, which is fallow, almost falls head-first into a ditch, reaches his car and drives off. Not back to Halden where he came from, but inland to the forest roads towards the Anker mountains. Mountain after mountain, there are only forest-clad ridges, about three hundred metres high. But it is wonderful terrain to hide a car, and he knows where the key is in a cabin by a lake called Mørte.

In the rear-view mirror he can see the flames towering from the burning house and sparks flying, a shower of sparks. He passes a bend and then all there is to see is black forest.

The house, a stone's throw from Isachsen's, is the old farmhouse on what used to be a smallholding. Bjørn Riiser is inside sleeping on a hard bed in the kitchen, as he often does, at all times of the day and night. Beside him, on the floor, is a bottle of Polish vodka, which a friend of his bought on board one of the boats that transport magazine paper from the SBF paper plant to Germany.

Riiser is woken up by the smell of smoke. He opens his eyes and looks around. Fortunately he can see. So it wasn't methanol in the vodka but proper alcohol. Did he forget to stub out his cigarette and set fire to the rag rug again? No, there isn't any smoke in the kitchen. What he can smell is only smoke and it is very strong. He struggles to his feet and peeks out of the window.

The whole of Isachsen's abandoned glory is ablaze. Sparks shoot up from this inferno of flames, right up to the heavens, but the wind scatters some here, there and everywhere.

Riiser looks down along his house wall. He thinks he can see a strange light there. It takes him seconds to realise that his wall is alight. His house is burning too. He will have to run up to the bedroom on the first floor to get his wallet, which is all the money he owns.

He arrives, finds the leather wallet where it should be, in his jacket, dives back down the stairs and into the porch. By the front door he almost chokes in the thick, fetid smoke; it must be the roofing felt which is burning like a torch.

The kitchen is smoke-free. He lifts the clasps on the

window and tries to push it open. It hasn't been opened for many years and is stuck fast.

Riiser knows what to do. He might have done little else but drink for the last ten to twelve years, but he is an old sea dog and he has done the odd fire drill. He wraps a kitchen towel round his right hand, remembers he used to have a decent right hook in his earlier days and punches the window until the glass shatters.

He clambers up and squeezes through the window frame. A sharp stabbing pain in his stomach. There must have been some shards left that have pierced the flesh. He tries to stand up, doesn't have the strength and loses his grip. The pain spreads across his stomach like the fires of hell. Feels with his hand, looks at it. Covered with blood. It is pumping out of him.

'Oh, Lord God,' groans Bjørn Riiser. It isn't a cry for salvation, for he doesn't believe in such. It is his last and he has one final hope. He hopes life will manage to ebb out of him before he becomes prey to the flames.

*

Stribolt is sitting in his room at the Grand and working on the notes he made after the interviews with Rønningen and the receptionist. He hears sirens. He gets up, looks through the window and sees one fire engine, and then another, they are heading south. A fire must have broken out somewhere along Iddefjord.

Stribolt rings Vaage's mobile.

She is still at Vilhelm Thygesen's and her voice sounds thick. Stribolt briefs her on the interview with the excellent witness, Rønningen, and allows himself a comment: she doesn't look as stylish in reality as on the net.

'Thygesen's telling me about the demise of the modern man,' Vaage says.

'Is it interesting?'

'Yes.'

'Is it relevant to our case?'

'Not in the slightest.'

'Watch yourself with that slimy buttock-groper,' Stribolt says. 'He's supposed to have had quite a reputation as a seducer in his time.'

'He won't seduce me.'

'I thought it was a stupid idea to fax over the photo of Picea. The quality won't be good enough. Can you scan it and send it electronically to our friends at Halden police station?'

'No problem.'

'Early tomorrow morning. Preferably at nine on the dot.'

'Jawohl.'

*

'We have a problem, Kykke,' Borken says. 'Lips's contact here in Sweden who we were relying on to exchange our Norwegian kroner for German marks hasn't shown up.'

'The marks we need for Tallinn,' Lips explains.

The three of them are standing on the pavement outside Sjøfartshotellet in Stockholm, where Kykke has parked his bike.

'There are banks in Stockholm, aren't there?' Kykke says.

'Too much dough to change,' Lips answers with a smile which is no more than a thin line. 'Too risky. That's why we've got to go and do the exchange with new guys we've found.'

'I've had a long journey here,' Kykke says. 'What I fancy now is a hot shower and a cold beer. Can't you boys fix the transaction?'

'These guys live in Västerås,' Borken says. 'They're Yugos.'

'Yugos?' Kykke repeats.

'Yugoslavs,' Lips says.

'I'm not going to fuckin' Västerås to deal with a gang of bloody Yugoslavs,' Kykke says. 'You go and sort out the shit.'

'My bike's in Tallinn,' Lips answers.

'And I've put mine in a shed on the ferry quay because this hotel doesn't have a garage and there's so much theft in Stockholm,' Borken says. 'You don't have to go all the way back to Västerås. We've struck a compromise. They meet us halfway. Place called Bro. Lips can ride pillion with you, as the map reader. He'll sort everything with the Yugos. You don't have to think about a thing, Kykke. You've done your bit in Norway. Just one little job left and we're ready for Estonia.'

'*Niet*,' Kykke says. 'As we're so bloody rich, Lips can take a taxi to the meeting place.'

'You never know what kind of driver you get,' Lips says. 'It might be a blabber.'

'The Yugos are going to clear off if we arrive in a taxi,' Borken says. 'Honestly, Kykke. We've just got the time. The boat sails at dawn.'

'Norwegian money's worth nothing in Tallinn,' Lips says.

'All it's good for is wiping your arse,' Borken adds with a hollow guffaw.

Kykke flings up his arms and says fine, OK. Lips puts on his helmet, shows the map he is holding and points to Bro, which is in a bay called Brofjärden by the northern bank of Lake Mälaren, halfway between Stockholm and Enköping. He shoves the map into his leather jacket and jumps on to the back of Brontes with a briefcase in his lap.

'Let's kick the ballistics,' Kykke says.

16

KYKKE SEES A SIGN saying Bro, feels a tap on his right shoulder and turns off the motorway between Stockholm and Enköping. He goes through a tunnel under the motorway and slows as he enters the tiny town of Bro. A tap on his left shoulder and he turns on to a narrow country road that runs across cultivated land and forests of deciduous trees. Passes a little church that shines white in the night that has become surprisingly dark. According to the road sign this must be Låssa Church.

The road leads down a steep hill to a tarmacked turnaround on a headland by a fjord coming out of Lake Mälaren. From there a path goes down to the lake, probably to a beach or a pontoon. There are no houses here. But there is a sign warning people not to dump rubbish. Someone must have disobeyed the sign because there is an old stove on the edge of a ditch. It is tilted in such a way that the top is level with the ground.

The black hotplates, two large ones beside each other and a little one underneath, remind Kykke of the eyes and mouth of a death mask.

Kykke shudders at the sight. Can a dumped stove in a Swedish ditch be an omen of death? He doesn't believe in omens. But he can feel in his bones that he is right in his suspicion that close friends can become bitter enemies. If he had been Socrates, friends would have had the poisoned chalice ready for him now.

Lips dismounts and goes for a walk around the area. Kykke doesn't move from Brontes and keeps the engine running and the headlamps switched on. He takes off his helmet. Immediately there is the buzz of mosquitoes. The clearing is surrounded on almost all sides by alder thicket. The shrubs keep the dampness in the air under a sky which has become overcast.

Kykke rolls a cigarette and lights it to keep the mosquitoes at bay and his brain sharp. He switches off the lights, kills the engine.

'The Yugos have chosen a bloody mozzie nest,' says Lips, who has returned to the bike after his recce. He has also lit up. The cigarette glow looks like a laser beam in the darkness.

'You've been here before,' Kykke says. 'Otherwise you'd never have found it.'

Lips nods. His head sways like a rice-paper lamp above his body.

'Yeah, I know this place. Kykke, we've always worked on a need-to-know basis. So we never told you who was delivering the goods that we've earned our dough on. I doubt I'll be saying too much if I tell you it was the Yugos and this is one place we've used for the handover.'

Kykke listens to the lapping of the waves from Lake Mälaren, to the distant drone of traffic on the motorway, to the rustling in the scrub, caused by the wind or maybe a small animal.

'How long are we going to wait here?' he asks.

'They're coming,' Lips says. 'They've got further to come than we had.'

A sound like the blast of a muted trumpet causes Lips to swivel round. More blasts from down by the lake.

'Eurasian bittern,' Kykke says.

'Eh?'

'It's a bittern. A bird. A wading bird. Lives in the reeds. Rare in Norway, but one spring a bittern landed in the mere by my cabin in the Finnish Forest. That's how I know.'

'Oh, yeah,' Lips answers, unnecessarily trampling his cigarette end flat.

'There's a car coming.'

A big, white van rolls down the slope to the turnaround.

'VW van,' Lips says. 'That's our guys.'

The van halts as soon as it enters the tarmac, thirty metres away from Brontes, facing it with the headlamps on full.

'Haven't they heard about dipping lights?' Kykke mutters.

'Wait here,' Lips says. 'I'll go over and do the business.'

Kykke gets off the bike and stands with it between him and Lips and the van.

Lips saunters. He has taken only seven to eight steps, then he stops. Kykke hears the clicks as Lips opens the locks on the briefcase. Kykke undoes the straps round the toolbox. Lips throws the briefcase down and turns with a gun in his hand.

Kykke crouches behind Brontes. A shot is fired. Lead hits a harder metal. The ricochet whines through the air.

'Run for it, Lips!' Kykke yells. 'I've got live hand grenades.'

Another shot, which hits something soft. Must have been a tree trunk.

'I'm gonna chuck a grenade!'

'You're bluffing.'

'And you can't hit a bloody barn door.'

Kykke takes the grenade. On his knees, hidden behind the bike, he holds up the grenade in his right hand.

Lips shoots for the third time. The shot seems to lose itself in thin air, probably where the bittern is flying off now, far from the battle of the flightless bipeds.

'I'm taking out the pin!' Kykke shouts.

Trembling hands fumble and the pin is caught in the cotton, but he manages to pull it out. Through the spikes of the front wheel he sees Lips turn and set off at a run.

Kykke can't remember how many he has to count before he throws. It is several lives since he was in the army. He counts to three and tosses it to a point between Lips and the van Lips is making for, hears the grenade land on the tarmac and then he rolls away from the bike in case a hot splinter hits the petrol tank.

Nothing happens.

An immense flash of light, followed by a sharp, but not deafening, explosion, splinters whizz through air, a gurgled scream. Silence. Kykke lies stock-still, flat on his stomach. Behind him, in the scrub, an animal leaps through the dry undergrowth. In front of him he hears what sounds like an angry snake hissing. He knows what it is. A splinter must have punctured a tyre. He hopes it isn't one of Brontes'.

The lights on the van come closer. They seem to be tilted. One of the VW's front wheels must be holed.

Kykke keeps rolling, away from the open area, down into the ditch where the stove is, stinging himself on the nettles. The van reverses and wobbles from side to side. He sees it is towing a trailer with Statoil written on the side. It is a rented vehicle. The Yugoslavian mafia does not drive rental vehicles. There is a scream of metal on metal. The steel rim is destroying the rubber.

'You won't get far, Borken,' Kykke whispers. He swallows the taste of blood. 'You used to be my best pal.' He tries to curb the red madness roaming his brain in an attempt to leave through his eyes, putting immense pressure on his eyeballs. He closes his eyes and sees a burning monk on each retina. The monks sit in the lotus position and allow the flames to rise. No one can stand such a vision, so Kykke opens his eyes again.

The van veers to one side, turns towards the steep slope, starts moving, now all he can see is the rear lights. Kykke crawls out of the ditch on all fours, past Brontes, to a dark figure strewn across the tarmac. There is blood, a pool of blood. The gun is in the pool.

Kykke runs back, starts Brontes, there is no smell of petrol, the tank must be intact. He loads the gun and slips it behind his belt. Heads up the slope in no great haste. Sees the white van and trailer bumping along the road. There is a smell of burnt rubber and metal.

Kykke approaches until he is ten metres behind the van, which has no speed left in it. Kykke brakes and stops. Plants his feet on the ground. Raises the gun with both hands as he has seen in films, aims at the rear window and fires. The shot smashes the window to pieces. But the van continues to limp on.

Kykke gets closer, stops and aims again. Left of the hole where the window was. Squeezes the trigger. The flame from the muzzle blinds him. The van comes to a sudden halt and he almost crashes into the trailer.

He waits, sitting on his bike. The van must be in gear, otherwise it would have rolled back. His ears are ringing. His nose smarts with the smell of gunpowder. He is breathing heavily, like a beached whale, in gasps, then he hyperventilates. He kicks out the stand for Brontes. Creeps along the left side of the van with his gun raised. If Lips had a shooter, Borken may have one too. Borken is a slippery customer; he may well be playing possum.

Was a slippery customer.

Borken is slumped over the wheel with a gaping wound in the back of his head.

Kykke takes a deep breath, leans inside and switches off the ignition. The lights die. There isn't a sound to be heard anywhere along the deserted road. The boys chose a good place to carry out the liquidation. Give them that. Their own fault they underestimated him. There is nothing new in this world. He takes another deep breath and pulls the wallet from Borken's jacket pocket. The dead man will have to fund the living man on his further travels. On the dashboard is Borken's favourite knife, a Rambo job with a jungle-green shaft. Kykke takes the knife. It might come in handy when he has to cut dwarf birch on the northern plateaus.

He motors back to the turnaround to pick up his helmet, and then Kykke roars off, eases the throttle through Bro, finds a turning to Sigtuna, stops where the road crosses a bridge, goes down to the river, slings the gun in and washes the blood off his hands. Washes his face. Puts the leather rag in his pocket.

What now? *Now* Lapland is waiting.

He has read in a magazine about a recluse who pans for gold on the Anarjohka on the Finnmark Plateau. There has to be room for another recluse up in Norway's most deserted wilderness.

*

Gerhard Ryland leaves the dinner in Bærøe, sated and full of distinguished cognac, business unfinished. Both the Finns and Peterson are playing hard poker, keeping their cards close to their chests. He asks the taxi driver he ordered to drive to Haslum.

The driver from Moss doesn't know where Haslum is. He receives an explanation and grunts with satisfaction at the long trip ahead.

'Have you got enough money on you or on your card?' the driver asks.

'Money's the only thing I have enough of,' Ryland answers.

Vanja Vaage can't say the same as she leaves Thygesen's place in a taxi. She has counted her loose change and hopes two hundred and thirty-five kroner will get her back home to Hellerud late on a Friday evening.

She has listened to Thygesen. He gave a lecture that could have been entitled 'From near-Marxist to total misanthrope'. If what he said can be considered pieces in the puzzle the Picea case is becoming, the pieces will have to swirl around loose in her subconscious. She is too tired to think and falls asleep on the back seat.

*

By Lake Mørte in the Anker mountains, Bård Isachsen is standing in front of a mirror in the bedroom of the cabin he has gone to. He has lit a candle to be able to see his own face. As soon as he arrived there he crept under all the duvets with a torch to drive away his fear of the darkness. He woke up from a terrible nightmare, and by then the batteries were flat. He had dreamed about maggots. White maggots, like those under the bark of old trees. Crawling over his face and eating it.

Now he has woken up, he can see his face is intact. 'Nice and regular', as a girl once said, 'but a bit bland, kind of.' Perhaps he should have let his hair grow a little longer. With it cut short, his head looks like a ball, a furry tennis ball. It is not his fault he seems so *ordinary*. It is his parents' fault; they gave him the genes he has. But it wasn't them who gave him the talent he has for skateboarding. He has developed this talent himself through hard training. You don't get board-artistry genes from a father who grafts in Kakken and a mother who works in a shoe shop.

A talent, the only one you have in the world, has to be nurtured covertly and displayed on the street or in a half-pipe. Show it off, man! She had to admire him up in Hemsedal when he swept away from her on the black piste, the same girl who said he looked an idiot. Because what she really meant was that he was an idiot. A zero, as Uncle Reidar is always saying.

Reidar has loads of loot and pulls loads of women. He hasn't earned any money working but by smuggling booze and gambling at Momarken. Now he can live the life of Riley on Lanzarote without doing a stroke except for eating, drinking and bedding single women on package tours.

Willing women. He would have liked a woman here, in this solitude, in this darkness. For lack of anything better, a picture of a woman.

Bård goes with the flickering candle to the sitting room. There is a table with magazines in front of the fireplace. Just standard weeklies and clothes catalogues. In one of the catalogues there is a lingerie section. One in a tanga will do the job.

Party time, man.

17

A BIG MOTORBIKE TURNS into a 24-hour service station in Borlänge, in the Swedish Dales. The man who dismounts is as large as his bike. In the neon lights by the pumps he surveys the contents of a thick wallet. Most of the notes are German marks, more than five thousand Deutschmark. In Swedish money that is one thousand eight hundred kronor. He also finds a driving licence, the kind Borken got from Drammen that time there were plenty of them in circulation. The licence is made out to a man by the name of Henrik Lindberg. The photo shows a plump, beardless guy of his age. If he is stopped at a checkpoint he can say his name is Lindberg and he has grown a beard since the photo was taken.

He goes into the kiosk and buys a packet of plasters, a map of Sweden, a little torch, a steel Thermos which he asks to be filled up with coffee, a couple of bottles of Ramlösa mineral water and a sumptuous smörgåsbord, spread with liver paste. They have Petterøes tobacco, so he buys a five-pack and cigarette papers.

In the toilet he washes thoroughly and at great length. He feels empty rather than tired, but his eyelids are heavy. When he took a bend around Lake Mälaren he managed to graze a knee. He washes it and applies a plaster. He has also got a terrible backache. It is forcing him to lean too far forward on the bike.

He sits on a bench on the edge of the service station, gobbles down the sandwich and studies the map in the torchlight. The terrain ahead of him on his journey north is not new to him. There is hardly a section of the road in central Sweden he hasn't been on at some time or other.

The further north he goes, the more deserted the countryside. He has always loved these Swedish wilds. Wild forest kilometre after kilometre. The ride might fill the vacuum in his soul with the redemption the long haul in Sweden has always given him.

Terje Kykkelsrud takes the driving licence from his slim wallet, cuts the plastic card into pieces with Borken's knife and stamps the bits into the soil beside the bench. The plastic sleeve where he has kept the vehicle registration card for Brontes receives the same treatment. He throws his empty wallet into the bushes.

He plans the route north alongside Lake Siljan to Mora and Orsa. From Orsa it is one hundred and twenty-five kilometres of forest and even more forest to Sveg. Then he crosses Orsa Finnmark, where unlike his own Finnish Forest in Norway there are still Finnish names: Noppikoski and Våssinjärvi. With the little he knows about the Finnish language he can say *koski* means waterfall and *järvi* lake. There are also Swedish names in Finnmark. Helvetsfallet, descent to hell, is the name of a gorge where the Norrland railway runs, marked on the map with a line as thin as a pubic hair. On a bad day, or at least a dark night, one might be tempted to go there to finish with this life and pass into a new one. Into hell.

A little place east of the R45 has the name Rosentorp, a rose farm. In the next life he could settle there as a crofter, with or without rosebuds. Hunting and fishing, and if there was a woman in the picture, bringing up a bunch of kids. But the road from Rosentorp to Helvetsfallet is not long.

'I never promised you a rose garden,' Terje Kykkelsrud hums.

A man who in peacetime has killed three men in one day can hardly expect a rose garden.

From the pannier he takes out the Swedish plate from the Ninja that he stole for Beach Boy, unscrews the Norwegian plate on his bike and replaces it with the Swedish one. He throws the plate in the same direction as the wallet and feels a little stab in his soul. The plate has been on Brontes ever since he bought it new fifteen years ago.

If he is stopped by the cops on the country road he will say that he borrowed the bike off a Swedish friend. They might believe him.

He puts in the earplugs, leaves Borlänge and listens to the CD on Beach Boy's player. The special lady, Laurie Anderson, sings to him alone all the way to Leksand. It may not be beautiful, but it is true.

Did you think this was the way
Your world would end?
Hombres. Sailors. Comrades.

There is no pure land now.

When was the truth beautiful? Terje Kykkelsrud thinks as he shifts down and passes slowly through Rättvik. The lights from the small town reflect in Lake Siljan. This is beautiful, but in a minute or two the lights are behind him and no longer exist.

After Orsa he gives it full throttle on the road that goes north through the immense forest. He plays the Anderson CD again and pushes Brontes as fast as he can to stay awake. Because of the ache in his back he lies so flat on the bike that his chin is almost touching the headlamp. There isn't much to watch out for on the deserted country road.

And we stand here on the pier
Watching you drown.
Love among the sailors.

Love among the sailors.
There is a hot wind blowing
Plague drifts across the oceans.
And if this is the work of an angry god
I want to look into his angry face.
There is no pure land now. No safe place.
Come with us into the mountains.
Hombres. Sailors. Comrades.

Oh, the loneliness kilometre after kilometre.

Soon he will have a lake on his left. It is called Fågelsjön. Bird Lake. He is flying like a bird himself through the night. Speed is all he has. Speed is his only quality.

Far ahead he sees a red light. Could it be a signal lamp where the Norrland railway crosses the R road?

No, the light is too small and too low to be a railway signal.

It must be the rear light of a parked juggernaut.

Just hurtle past.

It is a one-eyed bandit.

A timber lorry. The pile of logs is as high as a house.

The vehicle has only one red eye, like a brother Cyclops on the road.

Kykke tries to twist Brontes to the side, but his reactions are too slow.

The bike skids out of control and slides away from underneath him. He is thrown sidelong into the logs.

*

It is the morning of Saturday 12 May. Maybritt Strand is sitting in a little house in Tistedalen and trying to swallow a mouthful of coffee. It won't go down. She finds a bottle of three stars in the kitchen cupboard and pours a dram of cognac into her coffee cup. It helps. She has had a sleepless night sitting in the living room armchair, staring at nothing, and her eyes are bloodshot, like the eyes of a redfish dragged up from the depths of the ocean.

She kept away from the tempting Rohypnol all night. In a very short time, the blink of an eye, she has lost her ex-husband and her son. If she is going to come through this crisis she will have to try to stay clean, off pills anyway.

On the first floor her sister is asleep. She has come from Dokka to console and help her and all that that entails. Although she is a Christian she had a bottle of homebrew with her. A 69-year-old man has been found dead after a fire in an old detached house near Aspedammen. The fire broke out in a neighbour's house. Because of the strong wind sparks set fire to the house where the man was living. The police in Halden suspect arson.

Cognac on an empty stomach makes Maybritt Strand feel dizzy. She leans back in the armchair and falls asleep at once.

*

An hour and a half later Stribolt is woken by the call he had requested. He starts working while he sits in the breakfast room at the Grand. He rings NSB to find out who the conductor was on the evening train to Oslo on 28 January. After being passed from pillar to post he is told the crew was Swedish. He rings the central station in Göteborg and there too he is sent from one person to another, backwards and forwards, until he finds an intelligent soul who can give him an answer. The crew on the relevant train consisted of three members of staff: Hernandez, Njutånger and Ställberg. Stribolt has to argue for a while until he is given their private telephone numbers.

He doesn't ring them in alphabetical order. For some

reason he calculates that the person he is least likely to find at home is Hernandez.

Njutånger is a woman with an extremely pleasant voice, judging by the message on her answering machine.

'Helena Njutånger,' Stribolt whispers and takes a sip of coffee, which is not at all bad considering it is the hotel variety. 'What a name. A Swedish combination of beauty, enjoyment and regret.'

Ställberg is at work, a grumpy man informs him. A son or a partner maybe.

Hernandez answers at once. He has loud music on and puts down his phone to lower the volume. He is over the moon to receive a call from Norway and asks if the Norwegian officer can hear what he was playing.

Stribolt knows as little about music as a former national football coach, Egil 'Drillo' Olsen. Pass, he says.

Hernandez reacts with mild shock and tells him the piece of music was Edvard Grieg's Violin Sonata in G Major. He must come from the far south of Sweden because he talks with a very strong Skanian accent.

Once he is in the picture regarding the incident on board the train on the last Sunday in January, Hernandez remembers the young man who was harassing the other passengers by photographing or filming them.

'My most important question is whether he stayed on the train to Oslo,' Stribolt says.

Hernandez is sure he did. On their arrival at Oslo station it turned out the young woman who was his travelling companion had fallen unconscious. An ambulance had to be called. From what Hernandez could see, the paramedics managed to revive the woman.

'Thank you very much,' Stribolt says, even though in fact there was little to thank him for.

He walks to the police station and is there for nine on the dot. The normal Halden silence is replaced by considerable activity. The Halden police have to deal with what might be a case of arson and murder. An elderly man, a retired seaman, has died in a fire in a house in Aspedammen. The fire started in a neighbour's house, which was empty, and spread to the unfortunate man's timber shack. He was found hanging from a window he had tried to escape through, completely charred.

Vaage hasn't emailed through a photo of Picea. Stribolt wonders whether to ring HQ, but decides to wait until half past nine when he has a meeting with Hege Dorothy Rønningen. He enquires after Gunvald Larsson to check whether a forensic analysis has been done on Øystein Strand's motorbike.

Larsson is out on a job, but in Oslo, not Moss. Stribolt phones him.

'Weren't you doing a bike assignment in Moss, Larsson?'

'We sent Lein instead. I'm on a stakeout. Half the staff at Kripos are off sick after all the efforts to find the Orderud sock.'

'Where are you then?'

'I'm sitting in a plumber's van where Bestumveien and Skogveien meet, hoping to catch some nutter who's threatened Thygesen.'

'Who sent you there?'

'Vaage, backed up by the highest authority.'

'I suppose we should have communicated via police channels, but I'm in Halden and I have some info you need right now,' Stribolt says.

He gives Larsson a description of the train pest.

'Is he violent?' Larsson asks. 'Armed?'

'His behaviour on the train suggests he does what suits him and he takes no account of anyone else. People like that tend to be aggressive when they meet resistance. Remember, Larsson, you're a lightweight and you have no training in arrests.'

'I'm a terrier,' Larsson says.

'OK, but you're no bloody pitbull,' Stribolt says. 'Over and out.'

*

Maybritt Strand is woken by her sister, who immediately talks about the fire in Aspedammen. Her sister, Gretelill, was upset by all the sirens wailing on Friday night. Gretelill has got it into her head that Halden is a dangerous place which could blow up at any moment and where murderers lurk around every house corner. She justifies these fears by alluding to the ravages of the triple murderer in Tistedal at the beginning of the 1990s, and harping on about there being a nuclear reactor in the middle of town.

'He was sweet, the boy who came to offer his condolences yesterday,' Gretelill says. 'Reminded me a bit of my own Kjellemann.'

'Bård? Bård the Board? He's a sack of shite.'

'You shouldn't use such vulgar expressions about people.'

'He's a spoilt brat who's never done a stroke of work in his life. A conceited *artist*.'

'Oh, my goodness,' says Gretelill. 'If he's as bad as you say, why did you lend him your petrol can then?'

'I haven't lent anyone a petrol can. Have I got a petrol can?'

'The green one. For the lawn mower.'

'Oh, yes. What about it?'

'He walked off with it. Boys are always after petrol for their mopeds and so on, you know.'

'Did Bård Isachsen steal my petrol can? Is *that* what you're trying to tell me? And there was an arson attack in Aspedammen! Great heavens. I'll have to ring the police.'

'Your landline's been cut off and your card's run out, do you remember?'

'Whoops, I almost said shit. I'd better cycle to the kiosk.'

'You've been drinking, Maybritt. I can smell it on your breath.'

'Lend me some money for a taxi, will you?'

*

At a quarter past nine Kripos forensics officer Lein calls Stribolt's mobile phone.

'The brakes on the Ninja were fixed,' Lein says. 'The guys at the garage in Moss and I are a hundred per cent certain. Whoever disconnected the brakes did an expert job. The boy riding the bike didn't have a hope in hell.'

Stribolt thinks a hope in hell was exactly what Øystein Strand did have, but doesn't say as much. They discuss the fingerprints on the bike.

Vaage rings and says the photo of Picea is being sent, but they have to solve a problem with the scanner first. She has also heard the latest news from Moss.

'We've discussed that here,' Vaage says. 'In my opinion we have enough material to put out a search for Terje Kykkelsrud. Nationally and via Interpol.'

'You do that,' Stribolt answers.

18

AT NINE TWENTY-FIVE THE duty officer at Halden police station receives the photograph of Picea by email. He contacts the Kripos officer they have banging about the building.

The sight of Picea alive has such an impact on Stribolt that he has to sit down.

So that was how she looked. More attractive alive, of course, than frozen and dead in Thygesen's garden or kept cool in the mortuary.

Why did this woman have to die by a murderer's hand?

Here in the provinces of Norway from Russia. If she really was Russian.

He has a vague theory as to why she was murdered. But more important than all theory is practice now.

In the photo you can glimpse the top of a crocodile-skin bag in Picea's lap.

At half past nine Rønningen, the witness, arrives. She is even paler now than at the first interview. Stribolt accompanies her to the interview room. He pushes a copy of the photo across the table.

'Yes, that's her, the woman on the train,' Rønningen says. 'It's so awful what happened to her.'

'We'll come back to the photo,' Stribolt says, putting on the sternest tone he had in his repertoire. 'Let me get straight to the point with another question. About her bag and what you know about it.'

'There's been a fire in Aspedammen,' Rønningen says, chewing her lip. She has given the brown lipstick a miss today. Stribolt thinks she looks better now au naturel, but to be frank she has also lost her appeal.

'I see,' Stribolt says, leaning back in his chair expectantly.

'I don't feel well. I might be running a bit of a temperature. I'll take my jacket off,' Rønningen says. She is wearing a standard denim jacket, no special features. She removes it and hangs it over the back of the chair. Under her jacket she is wearing a T-shirt with a picture of a tug and a line of writing beneath in German: *Schlepper – kein Mensch ist illegal.* The motif and the words attract Stribolt's attention to such an extent that Rønningen becomes aware of it.

'I got the T-shirt in Hamburg,' she says. 'We went there on a course with the school, college, that is. I was given it by some politically committed guy in a pub. Had to wash it three times to get it clean. The tug was bringing refugees to Germany.'

'Are you interested in the refugee issue? Asylum seekers?'

'A bit, all in the name of decency. Perhaps more than other students. I'd like to join Amnesty or something like that. But I haven't got any time. My studies are swallowing me up.'

'As far as I know the writing says – I'm no great shakes at German – that no human is illegal. That must mean that whoever made the T-shirts thinks illegal immigrants are not actually illegal.'

'I suppose it does, theoretically,' Rønningen answers hesitantly.

'Could you imagine smuggling an illegal immigrant into Norway?'

Rønningen takes off her glasses, blows on the lenses and wipes them with a handkerchief. Puts her glasses back on and eyes Stribolt sternly.

'Why do you ask me that? Am I suspected of people smuggling?'

'Not at all,' Stribolt replies, offering her a cigarette from the packet of Prince he remembered to buy at the station kiosk. 'It was just a random thought. Forget it.'

'I have lots of T-shirts with all sorts of slogans,' Rønningen says, accepting a cigarette and a light. 'I collect them. Wearing them doesn't necessarily mean I fully support the slogan.'

'Of course, of course. If everyone who wore a Che Guavara T-shirt really was a revolutionary, a world revolution would be right round the corner.'

'For example, I have one that says *Golfers do it with clubs.* But I'm no fan of golf or a high swing.'

Rønningen blushes. Stribolt can feel that he is blushing too.

'I think we've covered the theme of refugees and T-shirts now,' Stribolt says, making a note on a pad. He decides not to use the computer, where he has the internet on the screen, in order to make the interview feel less formal. 'You mentioned a fire.'

Rønningen coughs and blows a cloud of smoke.

'I don't mean to keep anything back from the police,' she says. 'On the other hand, I find myself in a moral dilemma. How far does being a witness actually go? I've thought about it half the night. I've given you my statement about the woman on the train. I think I've done my duty. What do you call it? My civic duty. But what more can and should I say without bringing innocent parties into the case or creating problems for friends?'

'You have not only a duty,' Stribolt says. 'You also have a *right*, no, two rights. First of all, the right to stay silent. Secondly, the right to unburden yourself of whatever pains you.'

'Sorry, but that sounds a bit saccharine and pseudo-philosophical.'

Rønningen asks if she can draw the curtains. She has

the sun in her eyes. Stribolt nods, and she walks over.

He presses a few keys on the computer to get up the word-processing program. In some mysterious way the holed cranium of Karl XII flickers across the screen and he gives an involuntary gasp.

Rønningen, by the window, looks at the image.

'Jeez, what a creepy skull,' she exclaims.

'Evidence in another case I'm busy with,' Stribolt says, removing the Swedish king with a click, and asks Rønningen to tell him what she would like to say about the fire.

'The house that burned down was haunted. The empty house, that is, the one that burned down first. In the town there were rumours that a gang of boys was holding parties there with a steady supply of booze and dope. I think that was an exaggeration, the kind of thing that boys say to show off. Because I do a bit of roller-skating I know some of the boys…'

'Carry on, Dotti,' Stribolt says, blushing.

'For a woman in my position,' Rønningen says with a quick smile, the first in this session, 'most of these boys are uncouth snot-nosed kids, way beneath my dignity. But business is business, and I try to flog them the cheap skates I import.'

'From Latvia,' Stribolt lets slip.

'How do you know that?'

'Perhaps we can come back to that.'

'One of the boys I connect with the house in Aspedammen – I won't mention any names, at least not for now – came to see me in Remmen. In the block where I live, that is. Well, he didn't come to see me but a girl he knows who lives with me. We, she and I, were having a cuba libre together. He burst in and showed me something I'd seen before.'

'Something?'

'A bag. A ladies handbag. You see what I mean?'

'Not quite,' Stribolt says.

'I'm positive it was the bag that belonged to the woman on the train. The one you called Picea.'

'This could be a vital piece of information. Where did the boy say he found it?'

'He said he'd found it in a bin by the station. The railway station. I didn't believe him for a second, it was just lies. Because he didn't say that until I'd told him I'd seen that same bag on the train not so long ago. And then I said he should watch out he isn't arrested for theft.'

'How did he react?'

'He just grinned, in a kind of stupid, sheepish way, and then he left.'

Stribolt decides to shoot from the hip: 'Did that boy have a Christian name starting with Ø?'

Not a flicker on Rønningen's face.

'A nickname beginning with B?'

She opens her mouth, closes it again, opens it and says: 'Now you're pushing me further than I find acceptable.'

'I apologise,' Stribolt says, 'but in fact I am leading a murder inquiry.'

'Can I have some coffee and a break?'

'No.'

Stribolt opens his briefcase and removes a pile of documents. He flicks through them and finds the one he is looking for, a note from the police department in Våler. 'If the boy was Øystein Strand, alias Beach Boy or Banzai Boy, reporting him won't affect you in the slightest.'

'Why not?'

'Because he's dead,' Stribolt says.

'You're kidding.'

'No, he *is* dead.'

'If you're bluffing I find that totally unacceptable.'

Stribolt tells her about Strand's motorbike accident.

'We suspect murder,' he says finally. 'Premeditated murder.'

'Good God, who would want to murder him? He was just a boy. A messed-up boy, but nevertheless.'

'I can't reveal the name of the suspect at this moment,' Stribolt says. 'However, we have established that you knew Øystein Strand.'

'Not so much knew as knew *about*. Halden's a tiny little dump. Everyone knows everyone. If you've been to a rock concert, you're on nodding terms with half the town the day after.'

'I conclude it was Strand who showed you the bag?'

Rønningen nods.

'You thought he was lying when he said he'd found it in an NSB bin. Did you have any idea how or where he could have got hold of it?'

'Basically, no. But Anita did.'

'Anita?'

'The girl I was having a drink with when he came.'

'I need her full name.'

'Is that absolutely necessary?'

'Absolutely.'

'Anita Jæger Johannesen.'

'Is she a student too?'

'She was then, last winter. She has more imagination than me and conjured up this scene of sexual slavery in the deserted house in the forest. She followed the boy, Øystein Strand, when he left our block. He'd tried to check her out before, but she was less than medium-interested. When she came back she said she'd seen another guy outside in a car she was sure wasn't his. A guy who in some way was related to the house in Aspedammen. Don't ask me who he was because I have no idea. I told Anita about the woman on the train. Anita began to fantasise that she'd been kidnapped and held as a sex slave in the isolated house. She's got a thing about sex. I wonder how she'll get on in Ayia Napa. The following day…'

'Hang on a moment. I have to take notes. Coffee?'

Stribolt walks off whistling to get coffee from the machine in the corridor. It must be Halden's answer to the widow of Zarephath's jug, as it always seems to be full.

Two uniformed officers are in front of him in the queue. They tell him they have a suspect for the arson in Aspedammen. Stribolt asks if he is local and is informed he is a young man from Halden and they will soon make an arrest.

'Let me know as soon as you've got him,' Stribolt says.

Rønningen then says that she, albeit reluctantly, drove her friend Anita up to the house in Aspedammen the day after the bag incident.

'Even though it was the middle of the day the place still seemed sinister. Fortunately the house was locked so we didn't have to go in. By the way, it looked as if there had been a break-in because the door frame was splintered. Anita found a bit of wood and ran around banging on the walls and the cellar door and listening for responses. We managed to peer in through the kitchen window and what we saw was enough to make you spew up.'

'Oh, yes?'

'The gang of boys had made a dreadful mess in the kitchen. We thought they must have been throwing ketchup at each other because it was all over the walls. Unless they were playing paintball.'

Stribolt decides not to comment.

'When we were about to go, up came this cross-eyed old pig… well, I suppose it must have been the unfortunate man who died in the fire last night because he came from the shit-heap next door. He asked Anita and me if we'd like to join him in a Bermuda Triangle. I said the Bermuda Triangle was a disaster area and Anita said *he* looked like a wandering disaster area, and so on. Perhaps we were a bit tough on him. He said we should watch out because he reckoned a woman had been killed in the house we'd been snooping round. A gypsy woman, he drivelled on, a lot better-looking than us. Than Anita and me, I mean. We put our arses in gear, if you'll pardon the expression, and left as quickly as we could. The following week Anita was offered a job as a tour guide in Cyprus and that was when she dropped out of her studies. I didn't think any more about what we'd been talking about until I saw the picture of Picea and contacted you at Kripos.'

Stribolt winds up the interview with Hege Dorothy Rønningen. 'Your statement has been of enormous value,' he says. 'The case has moved along nicely. I'll probably need to talk to you again when we have further information.'

'I feel I've been put under unreasonable stress,' Rønningen says on her way out of the door.

'You have not. Hey, you forgot your jacket.'

Stribolt helps her on with her denim jacket, in cavalier fashion. He has the perfume of a woman in his nostrils, but it is drowned by the scent of a solution to a murder case that has stymied him from the beginning of February to the middle of May.

'Where can you get a good lunch in this town?' he asks.

'If you like pasta there's a new place that's popular with students. It's called 25 September Plassen and is in Repslagergata. Cross the bridge over the Tista, follow Storgata and take the third turning on the left.'

*

Gunvald Larsson provided Vilhelm Thygesen with a walkie-talkie. Then the squat oddball from Kripos ordered Thygesen to stay indoors 'while I wait in the surveillance car for my prey'.

Thygesen refused point-blank to obey. He explained to Larsson that he had important things to do outdoors, it was life or death.

When Larsson heard that the lives he was going to save were those of some pine trees he burst into laughter. Thygesen tried to get the man to understand that trees might be more important for the future of the planet than the human race and gave him a little lecture about the winter's death-bringing fungal attacks on the pines in Bestum and the rest of Østland. He placed the aluminium ladder against a fungus-affected tree and motioned that he was going to climb to the top.

Thygesen calmed Larsson down by telling him that he would have a good vantage point from the top of the tree. Larsson responded by giving him a brief review of yesterday's news from the interview front in Halden. Thygesen sensed that the forensics officer was straying beyond his remit when he told him about the train pest, but he was grateful for the information.

A walkie-talkie is a nuisance when you are working at the top of a ladder placed against the round, slippery upper trunk of a pine tree. Thygesen has managed to attach the device to his belt. He has also ordered Larsson not to blather unnecessarily.

In total radio silence Thygesen, sweating profusely, manages to cut off two branches with brown needles by the gate. There are two branches left. One is so high that he can barely reach it with the long-handled pruner. The other is at the back of the tree in an awkward position.

During the night the wind had strengthened. It shook the treetops, which is what made Thygesen aware that the fungal plague had also affected one of his big trees. The wind is picking up again and makes the whole tree sway. Thygesen embraces the trunk as if it were a woman.

The walkie-talkie crackles. Thygesen steps down two

rungs on the ladder before answering.

'Is this our man?' Larsson asks.

'I can't see anyone.'

'By the gate, a bit further up the street than yours. He's got a hand in the post box.'

'For Christ's sake, that's Svendsby, my neighbour. You can't nab him. He's perfectly harmless.'

'OK.'

Larsson has taken up a position in a plumbing contractor's van, which he claims belongs to his brother-in-law. And there he waits, with an immense pipe wrench at the ready.

*

Stribolt doesn't make it to 25 September Plassen. A skinny, fair-haired officer, who according to his name plate is called Håkenby, stops him on the way out.

'The arson suspect has been arrested and is in the interview room,' Håkenby announces, not without some pride.

'Wow, that was efficient.'

'He made it very easy for us. He cycled home to the house where his parents live. In Kjærlighetsstien.'

'What did he say?'

'He's trying to stay silent and tough it out. He's threatened to sue us because he's got a cheap ticket to Ibiza which runs out today.'

'ID?' Stribolt asks.

'Name's Bård Isachsen. Twenty-three years old. Unemployed school dropout. Known locally as a good skateboarder. Known to us as a small-time crook on the lowest rung. Has a couple of conditional convictions and a fistful of fines. Car theft, drunk in a public place, possession of hash. The usual. We think the bike he came on was stolen, by the way. Boys like him don't normally use a DBS Alivio with thin tyres.'

'Have we got enough proof to keep him in custody?'

'We have a strong witness statement. Woman saw him steal a petrol can, which he probably used to set light to the house. We found the can at the scene. Trouble is the plastic has partly melted due to the heat. But we don't need to tell him that. We can say we're checking the can for prints, and in principle that's true, even if we don't expect to find any.'

'Does he know a man died in the fire?'

'Unlikely. He says he has an alibi. He spent the evening and night in a cabin with a woman, and early in the morning he cycled straight to town from the cabin near Lake Mørte. We assume he legged it after the fire and hid in the forest.'

'What do you think could be his motive for setting fire to the house?'

'We haven't got that far yet. We thought, having you from Kripos, we could use you to break the wall of silence. You would be present at the interview. I'm the nice local guy and you're the menacing stranger who can quote the letter of the law.'

'Fine by me.' Stribolt answers. 'Where is he?'

'In with me.'

Håkenby opens the door to his office. Inside is a young female officer with a boy dressed in a grey track suit with the hood of his jacket up. His eyes are blueberry-blue and meet Stribolt's searching gaze straight-on.

'You can go now, Rita,' Håkenby says.

The young officer leaves the room.

Stribolt takes the chair where she had been sitting and places it by the wall furthest from the boy. He decides to remain standing. Places his briefcase on the chair and opens it so that the pile of papers can be seen.

'This is Chief Inspector Stribolt from the Kriminal-politisentral in Oslo,' Håkenby says. 'He's come here because of you. So perhaps you can understand how important this is?'

The boy licks his lips, but doesn't lower his eyes.

'We have a very reliable witness who says she saw you steal a petrol can from an outhouse in Tistedal,' Håkenby says. 'Green plastic can, made in Sweden. Identical to the one we found at the crime scene in Aspedammen. Remarkable, don't you think?'

Bård Isachsen doesn't answer.

'Indeed. The witness is Maybritt Strand, mother of the deceased Øystein Strand. He was a friend of yours, wasn't he?'

'I knew him.'

'Fru Strand told us that on mature reflection it struck her as strange that you should drop by to offer your condolences *before* the police had gone public with the name of the motorbike accident victim. Any comment?'

'I'd heard about it.'

'From whom?'

'Don't remember. In town. When one of the boys snuffs it like that it's not long before all Halden knows.'

Stribolt raises an open palm to stop the interview. He takes his time and makes careful notes. Because the information is interesting and because he wants to keep young Isachsen on tenterhooks.

Håkenby continues: 'You won't say who you were with on this alleged cabin trip and who could give you an alibi. Give me a reason for the secrecy.'

'She lives with another guy who's put her up the duff,' Isachsen says, suddenly lowering his hood. 'There are traces of me all over the cabin. My semen is everywhere and you can do one of those DNA tests if you want.'

Stribolt coughs, and asks a question: 'Håkenby, what was the name of the man who died?'

'Riiser. Bjørn Riiser.'

'Name mean anything to you, Isachsen?' Stribolt asks.

The boy shakes his head.

'Why did you kill him then?'

'I haven't bloody killed anyone!'

'Easy now,' Håkenby says. 'And sit down. Otherwise we'll have to handcuff you. Just to refresh your memory, Riiser is the man who lived next door to your uncle. When you set fire to your uncle's house the fire spread to Riiser's. He died and in fact his body wasn't a very pleasant sight.'

'I know nothing about that,' Isachsen says, trying to keep the mask. He has turned very pale.

Stribolt goes to the bookcase in the office and pulls out *Norway's Laws*. He flicks through to the Criminal Code and assumes a very formal tone: 'The thing is this, Isachsen. You're likely to be charged with one count of arson and one count of murder, according to clause 148. Whosoever causes a fire, etc. The minimum sentence is five years if someone dies in an arson attack. But if arson is assumed to cover another serious crime then we're talking the strictest punishment the law can apply. Sadly, that's exactly what we think your mission was. To set fire to a house to destroy traces of an earlier crime. Personally, I think this crime was murder. In which case, you're in dire straits, son.'

'I want a lawyer,' Isachsen says.

'He wants a lawyer,' Stribolt says, turning to Håkenby. 'I think we should advise him against that.'

'A lawyer will only make it worse for you now,' Håkenby says. 'I believe Chief Inspector Stribolt has something up his sleeve which might be better for you.'

'Exactly,' Stribolt says. 'If you're co-operative we might be able to lower the charge using clause 151, concerning negligence. The punishment for this is only "fines or imprisonment for up to three years". This presupposes you come clean with us.'

'I set fire to the house because Uncle Reidar wanted the

insurance money,' Isachsen says. 'I didn't mean to set fire to another house. That shit goes up like straw.'

Stribolt decides to try a subterfuge: 'An insurance swindle sounds plausible. However, one prerequisite is that the house is indeed insured. At Kripos we check most things, so we did a round of insurance companies as well. Your uncle didn't have any insurance on the old shack. You might just as well have lit a bonfire for the insurance money.'

'He *has* got insurance,' Isachsen retorts. 'The house was massively over-insured and he was always banging on about how he hoped lightning would strike.'

'OK, OK,' Stribolt says. 'Let me take another tack. Do you know a bikers' club called the Seven Samurai?'

'I've heard of them. But they aren't round here. They're in the forests by Moss.'

'I'm going to read you a list of the three names of the leaders in the Seven Samurai. We at Kripos understand completely that no one wants to grass on their friends. So you don't need to say a word. I just want you to give me a little nod if the name seems familiar.'

Håkenby has to turn away so as not to smile at the trickery in progress.

'Terje Kykkelsrud, known as Kykke,' Stribolt reads.

Isachsen nods.

'Richard Lipinski.'

No reaction.

'Known as Lips.'

A nod.

'Leif André Borkenhagen.'

The nod is so low that Bård Isachsen's forehead is close to touching the table in front of him. He doesn't lift his head again. A liquid is dripping on to the table.

'You fucking know everything anyway,' Isachsen says in a tearful voice.

'We just have to fill in one or two details,' Stribolt says. 'I need to know which of them gave you the order to burn the house down. Kykkelsrud, Lipinski or Borkenhagen?'

'Borken. It was Borken.'

'Do you know where he is at present?'

'He's supposed to be going to one of the Baltic countries.'

'How did you communicate?'

'By mobile phone.'

'Were you aware that what you were destroying was clues in a murder case?' Stribolt asks.

'I haven't killed anyone!'

'No one's saying you killed the woman in question.'

'What woman? I've never heard anything about any dead woman. Borken rented Uncle Reidar's house off me to use it as a depot for smuggled goods.'

'What sort?'

'Booze and cigarettes.'

'You're not doing your cause any good by lying again. Let's says drugs, shall we? Amphetamines. Cocaine?'

'All I know is that it was dope.'

'Håkenby, can you note down that we have a preliminary confession and we're taking a break,' Stribolt says.

19

TRIUMPHANT, STRIBOLT WALKS BACK to the office in Halden he regards as his own and rings Vaage.

'We've got a witness statement which allows us to nail a couple more guys as well as Kykkelsrud. You can now officially search for Leif André Borkenhagen and you can have Richard Lipinski into the bargain.'

'Sorry,' Vaage says. 'No point.'

'*No point?*'

'These boys are no longer with us, Arve.'

'Vanja. Don't talk in tongues like some Sami sorceress.'

'The Swedish police have just contacted us because two men identified as the Norwegian citizens Borkenhagen and Lipinski have been found dead in Sweden. To be precise, in Låssa parish in Stockholm province.'

'I couldn't care less which parish they're in. *How* did they die?'

'Our Scandinavian brothers believe they were killed in what seems to have been a gang showdown. Lipinski was blown up by a bomb or a grenade, Borkenhagen was shot through the back of the head.'

'Oh, sweet Jesus.'

'Yes, you can say that again.'

'When were they killed?'

'Probably last night. The Swedes will give us more precise info when they've finished the forensics.'

'Have the Swedes got any leads?'

'They've just started the investigation. Our two Samurai were found in a hidden area by Lake Mälaren. There are no witnesses, at least not so far, who saw or heard anything. The bodies were found by an ornithologist. A birdwatcher.'

'Are we sending officers over to help?' Stribolt asks.

'Not for the moment. The Swedes are more experienced at handling gang murders than we are.'

'Kykkelsrud?'

'No results from the search in yet. He might have been part of the massacre, only he hasn't been found yet. Might be at the bottom of Lake Mälaren.'

'Do you want to hear what I discovered in Halden, in all modesty?'

'Come on then.'

Stribolt tells her about Rønningen's statement, the arson and murder in Aspedammen, the arrest of Bård Isachsen and the links between him, Øystein Strand and the three leaders of the bikers' club.

'And where does this take us?' Vaage asks.

'I've come up with the following hypothesis: As regards Picea, I think she was the victim of a tragic mix-up. Rønningen told me that a dark-haired woman panicked and left the train in Ed on the Swedish side of the border. Her panic was triggered by an invasion of Norwegian customs officials carrying out a foot-and-mouth check. Let's say this woman, the one who got off in Ed, was a drugs courier. She was supposed to meet a gang in Halden, but never got that far because she fled in haste without telling the gang. Picea got off in Halden because she was being harassed by the idiot who took photos of her and threatened Thygesen. Picea might have left the train in Halden although her ticket was for Oslo because she was exhausted after a long journey. Or quite simply because she thought she'd find a cheaper hotel room in a provincial town than exorbitant Oslo.'

'So far, so good.'

'So Picea gets off in Halden. Waiting for her is a sombre

welcoming committee consisting of one or more Samurai. They assume she's the mule they're expecting. Dark-haired foreigner, right? The station's unlit. All cats are grey in the dark. The bastards, in my opinion there must have been more than one, bundle her into the car they have nearby. She protests and resists, perhaps violently. From Rønningen's description of her on the train we know Picea had a temper and wasn't the type to let herself be pushed around. The Samurai don't understand why she's so stubborn. They tie her up, I suppose, and drive her to this remote house in Aspedammen which they're still using as a base. There, they search her, in an extremely brutal way, I reckon. They don't find what they're looking for: amphetamines in bags stuck to her body. I'm ninety-nine per cent sure Picea *wasn't* a courier. What she did have stuck to her body must have been something else, travel documents perhaps, as we've talked about before. The Samurai are furious that they've been tricked, as they think. They take out their fury on Picea. She's stabbed to death. It must have been a terrible sight because I know now there was blood all over the kitchen in the house. The murder might have taken on a ritual character or the bastards thought she must have swallowed the bags of dope and started cutting her open, but realised it was a waste of time.'

'It bothers me that we still don't know who she was.'

'Me too, you can't imagine how much,' Stribolt sighs. 'There are some indications that she was Russian, but that's all I have. I don't completely understand Øystein Strand's role in all this, even if he found what apparently was her bag.'

'Isn't Strand a classic example of a guy who knew too much or sang too loud in prison?'

'I think there's more to it than that. There's a missing link in this case somewhere.'

'The person who's threatening Thygesen?'

'To be frank, Vaage, I think that's a red herring. But I forgot to ask you if Larsson caught anyone.'

'Larsson's brooding in his brother-in-law's old banger while Thygesen's climbing trees in search of fungus.'

'Fungus? Mushrooms? In trees? At this time of year?'

Vaage spells out Thygesen's state of mind. He is suffering from acute fungal neurosis, bordering, in her opinion, on paranoia.

*

Gerhard Ryland has found what he is looking for and what he feared he would find. In Natasha's chaotic photo collection there is one picture, a slightly grainy colour photo, of two women standing with their arms around each other's shoulders. One is his wife. The other is very similar to the newspaper sketch of the murdered woman. In the background you can glimpse hairdryers, the kind that are used in salons.

So his suspicion that the foreign woman was one of the staff at Holywell Hotel in Athens is borne out.

Ryland turns the photo over. Natasha always writes on the myriad of photos she takes or has taken. This one is no exception. Natasha has written in pencil, in that slanting style she has when she writes Norwegian letters:

'Katka (Orestovna Grossu) and Natasha (Blagodarjova Ryland), Athens, Christmas holidays 2000, Holywell Hotel. Great girl, terrible perm. We spoke Russian. Her favourite book is Solzhenitsyn's *1814*.'

Katka is the usual abbreviation of Yekatarina. Russian abbreviations have become common girls' names in the West. Katya rather than Katka. Katinka, from Katarina, Tanya from Tatyana. This is how the great Russian bear influences an otherwise Americanised western world.

'But Grossu?' Ryland says, lighting up his pipe, a

smaller crooked one than Stalin's. Grossu is a Latin name, it occurs to him. Romanian? There is something familiar about Grossu. Could a Grossu have been one of the butchers during Ceauşescu's time?

Ryland gets up from the chair in his office and walks over to the shelf where he has his volumes of the Encyclopaedia Britannica. He checks the 1988 edition and the 1989 edition. No Grossu. In the 1990 edition, which deals with events that took place in 1989, there is one, a gentleman, or rather a 'comrade' by the name of Semyon Grossu. In fact, he was a leading politician. But not in Romania. In Moldavia, as the region was called when it was a Soviet republic.

The Encyclopaedia says: 'On November 10 the republic's Ministry of the Interior was attacked and set ablaze. Over 2,000 MVD troops were flown in, and calm was restored after the hard-line party leader, Semyon Grossu, was dismissed.'

The country is called Moldova today. It has received its independence, but the former granary and the great wine cellar of the ex-Soviet Union has sunk into deepest poverty. Moldova has become the poorest country in Europe and exports almost nothing except prostitutes.

Was she one?

Perhaps the hairdressing salon in Holywell Hotel was only a front, as they say, for prostitution?

Katka Grossu. Yekaterina Orestovna Grossu.

It strikes Ryland that he may be the only person in Norway, in the whole universe for that matter, who knows about this person, in the sense that he can attach a name to a photo, and knows about her fate in Norway. Natasha will know the name as well, of course, but a veil of oblivion has been drawn over the meeting with this Katka.

The Norwegian police, who were responsible for the identikit picture in the newspapers, perhaps don't even know who she is, Katka Grossu. He should inform them. It can be done anonymously. He could ring and say: 'I'm Mr X. I know that the woman who was found in Thygesen's garden was Yekaterina, known as Katka, Orestovna Grossu, probably of Moldovan origin. Hope this information will be of use to you. Goodbye.'

The problem is that all telephone conversations can be traced back to the caller. Whether he uses a landline or a mobile makes no difference in this regard.

He could ring from a phone box. A phone box! In Bærum? Only decrepit people nostalgic for the past would even think of using a phone box near Haslum. And if they did, they would soon find out it has been vandalised. Even if there is a phone and a cable, there won't be a dialling tone and if, contrary to expectation, there is a dialling tone, it won't be possible to insert a card or a coin because the slot has been sealed with chewing gum.

A better solution would be to write a letter on a diskette at a computer and have the text printed in a specialist office somewhere. He will have to do this, but it will have to wait until the weekend.

He is at war with the Finns; he is at war with Peterson and Kingo. He can't wage war on all fronts like some Napoleon or Hitler.

Gerhard Ryland goes into the garden to get some fresh air. The garden is overgrown and needs some attention. The pine hedge bordering his plot – *Natasha's and his plot*, he shouldn't forget that – has taken on a brownish hue. Several of the branches have brown needles. There is bound to be a practical, scientific explanation for this phenomenon, but it doesn't interest him in the slightest.

'Katka Orestovna,' he says in a low voice. 'May peace be with you.'

Ryland turns on his heel, fetches a chisel from his toolbox in the cellar and breaks open a drawer in Natasha's bedside table, where she keeps her diaries. They are a secret to this whole nasty world, but not to him. She has often asked him to read them aloud to see if he is keeping up his Russian, a female wile.

He finds her diary of 2000 and leafs through to 18 December, the day they arrived in Athens, finds nothing, thumbs further to 19. And sees the name Katka.

In his office, with the help of his Norwegian-Russian dictionary, he notes down: 'Beautiful, brown-eyed Katka Orestovna from the salon told me she has to flee for her life. The Kishinev mafia have come to Athens. They want to force her into prostitution. They are especially cruel to her because she comes from a "bad family". A relative (uncle, great-uncle? I don't remember) was supposed to have been a big wheel during the old (good old! Better than today anyway with everyone starving in what used to be the Russian granary) regime. "I don't want to be a whore," Katka said. "Come to Norway," I said. "We – I, my husband and the whole nation – protect women." She took my address and a hundred US dollars (disgusting money!), so she had something for the journey. I daren't ask Gerhard for more. He wants to see the Acropolis even though it's raining and we've been there before. Pops is as stubborn as a mule! He's been on one of his rare shopping trips! He's bought two records by Mikis Theodorakis and a tie. So boring, but it suits him. I shouldn't eat so much Turkish delight.'

Ryland opens *The Times Atlas 1986* and sees that Kishinev was the biggest town in what was known as Moldavia in those days.

The pieces are falling into place. He should hand them over to the police, but can't bring himself to do so. Now the nation's interests are not his primary concern, Natasha is. He doesn't dare imagine how she would react to a police interview.

20

THYGESEN SWEEPS HIS HAND along some pine branches; the brown needles fall off in a shower as soon as he touches them. He sees a man, a young man, wearing a leather coat and a captain's hat on his head walking along Bestumveien. The wind lifts the skirts of his long coat and makes them flutter.

'Possible target approaching,' Thygesen says into the walkie-talkie, thinking that sounds like pseudo-military language.

'Him in the Gestapo coat?' Larsson asks.

'Yes.'

'I'll hold on until I see him put something in the post box.'

The man heads straight for the post box on the gate, doesn't stop to look around, doesn't see Thygesen high up the ladder in the clump of pines, takes out an envelope, opens the lid of the post box and pops it in with a nonchalant flick.

Larsson is out of the van. There is a metallic glint of something in Larsson's hands. He sneaks up from behind.

Before the young man realises what is going on he is attached to the wrought-iron gate by a pair of handcuffs.

Which Gunvald Larsson did in a surprisingly nimble and professional fashion, Thygesen thinks.

'What the fuck!' the arrested man shouts and turns to Larsson, who is standing with his hands on his hips, grinning. 'Are you a bloody terrorist or what?'

'Police,' Larsson says. 'If anyone's a terrorist here, it's you.'

Thygesen decides he can allow himself a shouted 'Gotcha' into the walkie-talkie as he clambers down the ladder.

'Have you got officers in the *trees* as well?' asks the cuffed man, tugging at the chains and kicking out behind him. Larsson performs an elegant sidestep.

Thygesen pushes the gate open, perhaps with unnecessary force, causing the wire netting to hit the man cuffed to it amidships; he groans and curses.

'Shut up, you imbecile,' Thygesen says. 'I'm Vilhelm Thygesen and I live here. So who the hell are you?'

'ID,' Larsson shouts in the arrestee's ear.

'ID yourself. If you're a bastard cop I want to see evidence.'

Larsson flashes his ID and frisks the man. All he finds is a Leatherman sheath on his belt.

'Tell me who you are,' Thygesen orders.

A mumbled name passes his lips.

Larsson flicks off his captain's hat, grabs a handful of brown hair and forces the man's head backwards. 'You're a bit of a scally, aren't you?'

'I said Thomas Gierløff, and that is actually my name. You'll find a driving licence in the wallet in my inside pocket.'

Larsson finds the wallet and studies the licence. Thygesen opens the envelope that was put in the post box.

'What sort of morbid shit have you delivered today then, Gierløff?' he says.

'I repeat my offer on behalf of PP Productions of a role in a documentary video.'

'Thanks a million,' Thygesen answers. 'Are you Captain Paw-Paw or Dr Papaya, or perhaps you're one and the same person?'

'I'm Paw-Paw, Captain. My father was a captain on Wilhelmsen Lines. My girlfriend is Papaya. She lived with her mother in Africa for a while and knows all about tropical fruit.'

'You don't say,' Larsson answers, taking the letter off Thygesen. 'I can see a drawing of tropical fruit here, yes. But I can also see a drawing of a naked woman with a knife in her belly and I can read that you're armed and want five kilos of amphetamines.'

'Same sick shite as last time,' Thygesen says.

'I think we should confiscate the knife,' Larsson says, removing the Leatherman from his belt. 'I note that you've stuck a colour photo of a woman who was killed on the paper.'

'It's a different picture from last time,' Thygesen says. 'This is a close-up of Picea.'

'You owe us an explanation,' Larsson says.

'I'm an artist,' Gierløff says.

'That explains nothing. We choose to regard you as a lowdown blackmailer. The basest of all criminals.'

'I'm a video artist and live in the art colony in Ekely.'

'Living in an art colony doth not an artist make,' Thygesen says.

'I invoke the freedom of art.'

Thygesen slaps Gierløff around the face.

'He hi…, he hit me!'

'That was just a little softener to help you think straight,' Larsson says.

'You, you fucking numbskull,' Thygesen shouts. 'You, with your accursed video nonsense drove an innocent woman to her death. And then her picture's in the papers and you want to try and *profit* from her death. You can take your artistic freedom and stuff it up your arse.'

'I hadn't expected such language from a lawyer,' Gierløff says, trying to assume a superior expression. 'The incident with the woman was for me an excellent opportunity to make a documentary. I had unique footage of her while she was alive, on the train from Copenhagen. Then it transpires she's been murdered, she was the woman who was found in the garden here. Not many filmmakers have footage like that.'

'Did he say *fetish*?' Larsson asks.

'No, *footage*. It's English for film material, as far as I know,' Thygesen answers. 'Who let a dilettante like you into Ekely?'

'We're renting an atelier at my girlfriend's aunt's – she's on long-term sick leave,' Gierløff says. 'I beg you to keep my girlfriend, and her aunt, out of all this.'

'Edvard Munch would turn in his grave,' Thygesen says.

'What's Munch got to do with this?' Larsson asks.

'He owned Ekely until his death in 1944. After the war an art colony moved in. It's just up there. Hey, Gierløff, what gave you the brilliant idea that I cut kilos of amphetamines from the stomach of the dead woman?'

'She looked the drug-mule type. That was one of the reasons I devoted so much photographic and filmic attention to her. When the customs officials came she disappeared into the toilet. I assumed she went there to swallow bags of drugs.'

'If anyone swallowed drugs on that train,' Larsson says, 'it was your girlfriend. She had to be taken to A&E and pumped and given an antidote because she passed out on arrival in Oslo. Or have you forgotten?'

'They were just sedatives,' Gierløff says.

'All right, Thygesen,' Larsson says. 'I think we'll have to get the uniforms in, have Monsieur Video-Artiste here put in a bare cell and tell the lawyers to prepare a charge.'

'I also have a right to legal assistance,' Gierløff says.

'You could try hiring me,' Vilhelm Thygesen says.

*

Ragnhild Skammelsrud, who is prouder of coming from a family of smallholders in Rakkestad than being distantly related to one of Norway's all-time great footballers, drives in through the gates of Trøgstad Prison. It is Saturday, a quiet afternoon in the institution where she works. A big fork-lift truck moving planks is working overtime and blocks the way to the building where she, as a social welfare officer, has one of the better offices. A one-man office, as it says in the prison manuals. A one-woman office, as Skammelsrud calls it.

She is in low spirits. The news of Øystein Strand's death has hit her hard. Trøgstad is a prison full of young men from the streets of Østland's towns and the occasional older drunk driver or cheque counterfeiter. She is conscientious with everyone who comes to her, but over the years she has had a strong sense that her efforts are the labours of Sisyphus; she rolls a stone up a slope only for it to come rolling back down and fall even deeper.

Øystein Strand had seemed to be an exception to this rule. He was a fantasist and a clown, yes, but also open-minded and a receptive soul. If you spend your days casting pearls before swine you are happy when the pearls hit a bird, even if the bird is an imitative parrot.

After recovering from the shock of the news of Strand's death she remembered the envelope he had placed in her hands, with an expression that was both mischievous and serious, and said 'To be opened if anything happens to your banzai.'

Skammelsrud unlocks her filing cabinet. She finds the letter under S, takes a silver penknife which she uses on solemn occasions, slices open the envelope which Strand had taken the trouble to seal with wax, and puts on her reading glasses: 'Dear Ragnhild S(ocialist)! I have to go now, as they say here, out into freedom. You warned me about the dangers of freedom, and there are more dangers than you are aware of. If anything bad should happen to me you should know that I've played a high-risk game to ensure a just distribution of certain goods to a circle of my friends. The Samurai, you know. But they may have misunderstood my zeal, my positive-minded creativity and my energies. Accordingly they may try to "waste" me because they consider me a "grass". If they do, strictly between you and me, Ragnhild S, I presume Leif A Borkenhagen, the Samurai chief, will be the instigator. You should also know that my game involves a high-ranking member of society by the name of Gerhard Ryland, the MD of the State National Oil Fund. He may feel pressurised to wish me harm. If anything happens, you should inform the police I can document that Ryland has a skeleton in the cupboard and was trafficking women, which I think you will find repugnant. Probably though everything will run smoothly/turn out fine. Bye, Øystein S(uperboy).'

Isn't there a single decent person left in this country? thinks Ragnhild Skammelsrud as she dials a number on the phone. Gerhard Ryland, a fellow member of the Socialist Party in the sixties. He joined the Labour Party when the Socialist Alliance was formed in 1973 because he didn't want to be in the same party as ex-communists even if he was a Soviet friend. But he held more of the fundamental beliefs than most of his new friends and had enough integrity and independence for Bondevik's government – to the annoyance of *Aftenposten* and the financial newspapers – to appoint him – the Social Democrat – MD of the new oil fund. A fund which wouldn't invest money in eco-unfriendly mining in New Guinea, but would try to secure Norwegian industry.

'Is that the Kriminalpolitisentral?' Skammelsrud enquires.

'Kripos, yes, it is,' answers a youthful voice.

'I work in Trøgstad Prison, but I'm not used to ringing the police. I believe I have some important information and need to talk to the duty officer.'

'Chief Inspector Vaage's at the desk. Just a moment.'

*

Vaage has thrown on her uniform and chosen to drive what the police call a uniformed car. She sweeps into Anton Tschudis vei in Haslum with the blue light on to frighten the opposition. As Stribolt is in Halden and no one else knows the case as well as she does, she has put a replacement at her desk and taken the job herself.

She doesn't have time to ring the bell before a man she recognises from the papers is standing in the doorway.

'I saw you,' says Gerhard Ryland. 'It ought to be possible to be more discreet.'

'My apologies,' Vaage says, 'but we're up to our knees in a murder investigation, a case involving a number of deaths, and we're pressed for time and can't be too fussy with formalities.'

'My apologies too,' Ryland says. 'I should have contacted the police earlier. But I had greater priorities to consider.'

'Not any more you don't. Now the truth's the greatest priority.'

'I may be able to help you there. I think I know who she was, the woman who was found murdered in Vilhelm Thygesen's garden earlier this year.'

'Who was she?' Vaage asks. 'We've been searching for this piece of information for months.'

'We don't need to stand here talking on the doorstep. Come in.'

Vaage hesitates. If the MD of the oil fund murders women she ought to step warily. She acted on impulse when she set off. It was foolish of her to be on her own, without any back-up.

'I'm not violent,' Ryland says.

'That's what all violent men say before they swing an axe. In a little while there'll be more cars and officers here. Who was the woman and how did you know her?'

Vaage steps into the hall where there is a rug that looks suspiciously like an authentic Persian.

'Let's go to my office,' Ryland says. 'Or the library, as my wife calls it.'

'So that I can be throttled by the butler?'

Ryland laughs the way a man who is not used to laughing does, with clenched lips: 'I may be a kind of missing link in your investigation.'

'You betcha.'

'Does the name Katka Orestovna Grossu mean anything to you?'

'No,' Vaage answers. 'Not in the slightest.'

'Then I may have important information. By the way, is it a punishable offence not to report blackmail against your own person?'

'You'll have to ask the police lawyers. Did you say Katka?'

Ryland answers in the affirmative.

'Katka,' Vanja says. 'That's a pet name in Russian, just like Vanja.'

'How so?'

'Did I forget to introduce myself?' Vaage asks as Ryland opens the office door.

21

Vaage and Stribolt are sitting on the second-floor terrace in the Kripos building. Norway's capital is festooned with flags on the occasion of Independence Day, 17 May.

Stribolt fetches a jug of fresh coffee from the empty canteen. The man they have to meet at Gardemoen Airport doesn't land until 16.10. They thought he would arrive at 12.50, but that was down to a misunderstanding in one of the faxes from Kishinev. 12.50 turned out to be the *departure time* from Moscow for the Finnair flight to Oslo via Helsinki. They have spent the interim time reviewing the Picea case, or the Katka case, as they should call it now.

'I still insist Ryland was obstructing our investigation,' Stribolt says, pouring the coffee. 'He deserves to be charged for trying to hide evidence.'

'On the contrary,' Vaage says. 'He deserves a medal for *providing* decisive information that gave us an identification of the victim. No one's obliged to report an amateur attempt at blackmail. We should be glad that not everyone who's blackmailed and cheated immediately runs to the police and that some are adult enough to tackle the situation themselves.'

'He just sat on the information he had about Katka for an eternity.'

'That doesn't fit the facts. He reacted as fast as he could, he was observant and wondered whether the woman who'd been killed in Norway could be the one he'd glimpsed in a hairdressing salon in Athens. He can't be blamed for taking all the time necessary to verify that the photos were in fact of her.'

'You, Vanja, as a feminist – as a *kind* of feminist – should react with disgust at the way Ryland treats his wife. What sort of man tries to stop Kripos interviewing his wife when she's a witness in a murder case? He treats her like a domestic *animal*.'

'Natasha Ryland's a fragile flower. You mustn't forget she's a war victim.'

'Was *she* fighting in the trenches around Leningrad?' Stribolt counters.

'A million people died in the besieged town. Don't you think hunger and disease ravaged women and children as much as bullets and shells did the guys defending the front line against the Germans? That's a typical male notion that only soldiers on the front line suffer war injuries.'

'I cede the point.'

'We'd better let the lawyers argue about any potential legal measures against Ryland,' Vaage says.

'You're just saying that because for once our nitpickers are tending to your view.'

'Shouldn't we say a *skål* for what we've achieved?'

'I never *skål* with coffee,' Stribolt says.

Vaage conjures up a yellow bottle and two paper cups from her bag.

'And what plinkety plonk is that?' Stribolt asks.

'Egg liqueur. You should drink egg liqueur on 17 May. We always did at home in Træna. Mum made eggnog and dad tapped the moonshine in the outhouse, and then we all celebrated, each in our own key signature.'

'It says Advocaat on the label. You bought this for Thygesen, didn't you?'

'No, I'm going to buy a decent bottle of whiskey for Thygesen in recompense for ungrounded suspicions of murder and the pain and suffering.'

Vaage fills the cups.

'Here's a *skål* for Colonel KO Grossu and hope he has a happy landing in Norway,' she says. 'Who pays his pension do you think, by the way? My money's on the KGB or the old Soviet army. Signing with two initials instead of full names seems so old-fashioned and Soviet.'

'We'll have to ask him. But I think we should leave him in peace until he's identified her.'

'A *skål* for the colonel's daughter, Katka, who sadly had an unhappy landing in Norway.'

'*Skål*.'

'It's dreadful that a girl who studied social anthropology at university ends up as a hairdresser abroad because her home country is destitute,' Vaage says.

'What's wrong with hairdressers?'

'You know what I mean. Do you think that Katka really ended up on the streets in Athens or she got away before the gangsters managed to push her into it?'

'All we can go on is what our Greek colleagues tell us. When they claim the girls in the salon serviced the guests at Holywell, in all ways, we have to take them at their word. Does the title *No One Writes to the Colonel* mean anything to you?'

'Nope.'

Stribolt tells her it is a novella written by Gabriel García Márquez. He read it again when Kripos eventually managed to contact Katka Orestovna Grossu's only known relative in Moldova, and it turned out to be her father – and he was a former colonel.

'I visualise him as a colonel no one writes to any more,' Stribolt says.

'We'd better give him a warm welcome whoever he is.'

'Has the interpreter been told the correct arrival time?'

'Everything's hunky-dory. She'll show up, and she's one

of the better ones who don't try to steal the whole show. I have to confess I'm really excited to hear what he says about his daughter.'

'Got any more of that sweet stuff?'

They say another *skål* for Bård Isachsen getting four weeks in prison. It should have been eight, according to the prosecution, after Isachsen also confessed carrying out surveillance on Øystein Strand and Terje Kykkelrud under orders from Leif André Borkenhagen.

'A *skål* for Larsson whose stint in the plumbing van led to a remarkable success,' Stribolt says. 'And I suggest we raise our cups to the judge who sentenced Thomas Gierløff to two well-earned weeks in prison.'

'Gierløff's defence counsel did us a great favour by allowing him to keep repeating that the threats against Thygesen were a practical joke, of course,' Vaage says.

'What pleased me most was that all that cool defence crap about artistic freedom didn't cut any ice with the judge. The day violent threats are raised to art we can all pack our bags. What about a *skål* for the excellent witness Hege Dorothy Rønningen?'

'Dotti de la Motti,' Vaage grins. 'Have you found out what *motti* means?'

'In history there's an expression the Finns used during the Winter War about pockets where they'd surrounded the Russians. Originally the Finnish word *motti* meant "a storage place for logs". Dotti Rønningen said she invented the word for the rhyme.'

'Let's not digress into her private domaine,' Vaage says.

'We've as good as solved a murder case, but we haven't arrested a murderer. The Samurai we have every reason to suspect has disappeared like a will o' the wisp,' Stribolt says, looking towards the mountains west of Oslo as if Terje Kykkelsrud were hiding there. Kykkelsrud's name has spread so far that he can be considered one of Europe's most wanted criminals. But he has vanished into thin air.

*

The man who emerges from passport control at Gardemoen Airport really does look as though he has been a colonel in the Soviet military. He has brushed his white hair up, perhaps to increase his height – he is not tall. He is wearing sunglasses. His suit is as dark blue as Stribolt's 17 May outfit, but square.

When the Finnair flight came up on the arrivals board as landed Vaage said they should have had a little cardboard sign saying 'Welcome, Mr Grossu'. They hardly had time to make one before he was there and any need for it was redundant.

He must be used to picking out police officers in civilian clothes because he makes a beeline for Vaage and Stribolt, sticks out a big paw, gives them a firm handshake and lights a brown cigarette with a white cardboard holder. The interpreter turns up in the nick of time. She was nervous that Grossu wouldn't speak Russian but Romanian, as Moldova has been a geopolitical football between Romania and Russia. She gestures that he has to extinguish his cigarette.

KO Grossu speaks Russian so well that even the two Kripos officers, who can't speak a word to save their lives, realise it is Russian. The colonel seems to have unleashed a formidable salvo on his arrival in Norway.

'He says he can't understand why smoking isn't allowed in such a big, well-ventilated hall,' the interpreter says.

'Tell him we think he has a point,' Stribolt says, 'but let's go out and have a smoke.'

Once outside, Grossu stands to attention. The interpreter says he wants to make a short announcement:

The colonel says: 'My daughter, Yekaterina, who has been missing for more than three months, appears from all accounts to have been murdered in Norway by bandits. I've come here to identify a body that is presumed to be hers. If it's my Katka in the mortuary in Norway, I'm sure she didn't allow herself to be taken without a good fight, she would have resisted to her dying breath. Unfortunate circumstances, which require a political analysis I cannot go into here, forced her to flee her homeland to find a living abroad. The Kishinev mafia tried to force her into a shameful occupation. The gangsters would never have succeeded. I swear Katka would have taken their lives, or her own, rather than become a prostitute. If the Norwegian police ever have anything to do with "our" mafia you should know that it was created by the bourgeoisie, it is made up of bourgeois elements along with the dregs of the proletariat, it nourishes itself at the bosom of the bourgeoisie and deserves to be annihilated. I'd like to thank the Norwegian police for the work they have done to solve the case and hope that the perpetrator or perpetrators will receive the severest punishment the law will allow.'

In the midst of this tirade Stribolt's phone rings. As quick as a flash, he turns it off. As they walk towards the barriers of the Oslo train he checks his call log. The Kripos desk has been trying to get hold of him. He rings them.

'Terje Kykkelsrud, the wanted man, has been found,' says Haldorsen at the desk.

'Alive?'

'Severe injuries, maybe life-threatening. He's in the hospital in Mora, Sweden, and has just come out of a coma.'

Haldorsen thinks it wise for Stribolt to go to Mora as fast as possible to interview him. The Swedish police have been informed by the doctors that Kykkelsrud could relapse into a coma at any moment.

Stribolt explains the situation to Vaage.

'Best if I take our car and set off right away,' he says.

'Just go,' Vaage answers. 'You'll probably drive better with a few milligrams of Advocaat in your blood.'

Stribolt says to the interpreter: 'Explain to the colonel that our chief suspect has been caught in Sweden and I have to interview him at once.'

Colonel KO Grossu receives this news with a thin smile and runs a hand across his throat. He can see that the Norwegian police also understand the international sign for death.

*

Stribolt has driven from Kongsvinger to Torsby, through the Tiomila Forest from Torsby to Malung and through another hundred kilometres of forest when he finally sees Mora ahead of him from the hills over Lake Siljan. Late in the evening, the town looks like a glittering jewel cast into the wilds by a giant fleeing through the Dales.

He rings his contact in the Mora police, an officer called Krantz, and is put through to the station in Millåkersgatan. Krantz is waiting outside in a police Volvo and drives in front of Stribolt to Mora Hospital.

Before they go in, Stribolt wants a smoke and asks a few questions.

'Why did it take you so many days to report that you had the man we were after?'

Krantz answers that he has been on holiday and knows only what is written in the daily logs. The police in Mora turned out early in the morning on 12 May after receiving news of a serious accident near Lake Fågel on the R45 between Mora and Sveg. At the scene a lorry carrying logs was on fire. The driver explained that a motorbike had gone straight into the parked lorry from behind, skidded under the lorry and started burning. The driver had dragged the apparently dead biker away from the fire and tried to put it out with a hand extinguisher, to no avail.

When the badly injured, unconscious biker was taken to A&E they found some ID in his wallet. His Norwegian driving licence said he was Henrik Lindberg and he was a resident of Drammen.

Accordingly, Drammen Police District was contacted. The Norwegian police reported back that the Henrik Lindberg living at the respective address in Drammen had died several years ago.

It proved difficult to supply any further information to the Norwegians. The plates on the burnt-out bike actually belonged to a Kawasaki Ninja reported stolen in Karlstad on 10 May.

It was only when the patient woke up and told them who he was that they checked his name against the wanted list and raised the alarm.

At the reception a doctor introduces himself as Dr Khan and tells the two police officers that the Norwegian patient has broken his spine in two places and cracked his skull and a cervical vertebra which in all probability will paralyse him from the waist down.

'Is Kykkelsrud aware of the situation?' Stribolt asks.

Dr Kahn answers that he is, and that he can thank his solid constitution that he survived his encounter with a lorry-load of logs. He warns Stribolt to take care when interviewing him.

Stribolt is led into the intensive-care unit.

Kykkelsrud's head, resting against a white support, is framed by steel rods. The red-bearded face is reminiscent of an old icon. The icon's eyes are open and staring at the ceiling.

'Are you Terje Kykkelsrud?' Stribolt asks.

The swollen lips open. An arm with a cannula attached moves a fraction.

'Yes. And you're a Norwegian cop?'

'Chief Inspector Stribolt from Kripos in Oslo.'

'You'll have to moisten my mouth with a wet cloth if you want me to talk.'

Stribolt does as he is asked, and says: 'As yet there's no charge against you, but this is a formal interview because you're under suspicion of committing the premeditated murder of Øystein Strand and the wilful murder of a Moldavian woman by the name of Katka Orestovna Grossu.'

'Never heard of her.'

'She was probably murdered in Halden. Found in Oslo.'

Kykkelsrud tries to nod. He grimaces.

'You will also be questioned about the murders of your friends Richard Lipinski and Leif André Borkenhagen,' Stribolt says.

'Let's get this over with so that I don't snuff it before I've finished talking.'

'Just say stop if you need a break.'

'I got Lips with a grenade. It was self-defence. I shot Borken. They wanted to kill me.'

'Why?'

'Because I didn't throw the woman in the lake and I didn't bury Beach Boy in the marsh.'

'Describe the scene of the murders of the two you call Lips and Borken.'

'Deserted area by the lake. Mälaren. Got Lips on the tarmac, Borken in a rental van close by.'

'The murder weapon, the one you claim you shot Borken with?'

'Heavy pistol. Walther, belonged to Lips. Dumped it in the river afterwards.'

'Do you admit disconnecting the brakes on a Ninja motorbike Strand rode to his death on?'

'Yes.'

'Where did it happen?'

'Middle of Nowhere. Våler Forest. Reckon he knew… more water.'

'I'll give you some, but quickly tell me if you were involved in the murder of the woman in Halden.'

'Not the murder. Transporting her away from Aspedammen.'

'Who killed her?'

'Borken. He had a knife.'

'Motive?'

'He thought she was a mule and was cheating him and Lips.'

Stribolt moistens Kykkelsrud's mouth. It creates an intimacy between them which he doesn't like, but he supposes it's advantageous for the interview.

Kykkelsrud closes his eyes.

Stribolt makes notes on his pad. If Kykkelsrud died in a mist of blood now, at least he would have clarified most of the elements of the case before he took his leave.

The hospital surrounds them with its noises. A dull scream comes from somewhere in the building.

'Let's go on,' Kykkelsrud says without opening his eyes.

'You deny murdering Katka Orestovna, but my understanding is you moved her body. Where to?'

'Thygesen's. His garden.'

'Why?'

'A joke. An old score between us.'

'You said you were supposed to dump her in the lake?'

'Those were Borken's orders. But I wanted her to be found.'

'It's easy to put the blame on someone you know is dead.'

'Rubbish,' Kykkelsrud says, opening his eyes. 'For Christ's sake, you know I've decided to confess. Whatever I *can* confess.'

'Did Borkenhagen order you to kill Strand?'

'Yes.'

'Why?'

'Grassing on us. Some crazy plan about blackmailing a rich man. The boy's plan could have revealed the murder of the woman and our smuggling.'

'Smuggling what?'

'Amphetamines.'

'Big quantities?'

'You kidding? Smuggling's a drop in the ocean.'

Dr Khan comes in to see whether the interview can continue. Kykkelsrud says he *wants* to go on until he blacks out. He asks the doctor to give him a shot which will both dull the pain and liven him up. After some fuss he gets it.

The large body under the white sheet trembles. Stribolt thinks the suspect is about to die, but Kykkelsrud comes out of the shakes more focused than before.

'I have an alibi for the night of the murder in Halden,' he says. 'I don't want the stabbing of a woman pinned on me.'

The alibi Kykkelsrud comes up with is that he was at the new leisure centre in Askim. To Stribolt's question of whether the centre was open in the evening he answers you can swim there until midnight, to attract kids who want to snog in the pool.

He was there because he likes swimming.

'*Liked* swimming, I should say. I like nothing better than a pair of wheels, but now I'll have two under my arse. Kykke the Cyclops will be a centaur in a wheelchair. They'll remember me in Askim because another guy and I fished up a kid lying on the bottom and they had to revive him.'

After the swim in Askim Kykkelsrud got a call from Borkenhagen. And instructions to go to Aspedammen to pick up something from the house the Seven Samurai were borrowing. When he arrived on Brontes to find that what he had to pick up was a woman's body, he rang back and protested.

'Borken said if I didn't remove her body he'd ring the cops in Halden and give them the address. And then I'd be found with a dead woman on my hands. He had me nicely snookered there. There's only one road through Aspedammen. The other ways out are paths blocked by barriers when you get into the forest.'

'So you acted out of loyalty to your biker gang and a certain amount of pressure?' Stribolt says.

'You could put it like that.'

'I'll make a note that there are mitigating circumstances.'

'I don't need any mitigating circumstances.'

'Really?'

'I'm going to get life. For me that's as clear as crystal. You can't deny it.'

And indeed Stribolt can hardly deny the punishment the suspect himself puts forward. In the USA Kykkelsrud would be given two or three life sentences or worse.

'How did you transport the woman?' Stribolt asks.

'I went to Halden and stole a little van close by Brødløs. I didn't have a clue what to do with her and then I thought of Thygesen. Seemed to work, confused the police anyway.'

'But how did you imagine you'd get away with killing Strand? Fixing the brakes was bound to be discovered. All the evidence would point to you.'

'Truth is I'd started to give up. We were going to set ourselves up in Estonia with the money from the smuggling. But I wanted out. To escape from all this shit. When I crashed I was on my way to fucking Finnmark to live alone on the plateau.'

'Before you hit the truck by Lake Fågel you'd killed two friends along the way.'

'They deserved to die. They tried to lure me into a trap

and kill me, but I saw through them. So it was an eye for an eye and a tooth for a tooth.'

'I think we can stop now and continue later,' Stribolt says. 'Anything you want to add?'

'The lad, Strand. I reckon he knew what I'd done to the Ninja. He knew he'd gone out on a limb and the limb was going to break.'

'You mean Strand knew he was going to ride to his death?'

'Maybe. But I'll take responsibility for it. A question from my side. Who was that woman, Katka, actually? Borken said she almost clawed his eyes out.'

'Katka? She was a refugee from Moldova. Circumstances were such that she had to get out and she thought she would find safety in Norway.'

'What sort of circumstances?'

'Threats from the mafia,' Stribolt answers.

'Borken said she was a cheap whore.'

'There's no evidence to support that claim.'

'Have you contacted her family?'

'Yes. Her father's in Norway to identify her body. By the way, has anyone contacted your family to say you're here?'

'No family worth contacting.'

'You've been very honest in your statement. That will play to your advantage.'

'I'm not after any poxy advantages. Except for one. If things go badly for me and I end up in a wheelchair I reckon I'll be better off in prison than outside. They say the new high-security prison in Ringerike, where the Kosovo-Albanian drugs ringleader, Prince Dobroshi, is doing time is well adapted to wheelchairs. Could you put in a good word for me?'

'I'll see what I can do,' Stribolt says.

'I go in for Zen Buddhism. You can imagine what the

boys in Ringerike are going to call me when they find out, can't you?'

'No.'

'The Lame Dalai,' Terje Kykkelsrud says.

*

Vanja Vaage has driven to Bestum to hand over a bottle of Jameson's whiskey.

Vilhelm Thygesen comes on to the doorstep, takes the bottle and frowns with disapproval.

'Why are you giving me this, Vaage?'

'We have a closed case to celebrate. You helped, and we at Kripos did our bit.'

Thygesen asserts that, in his opinion, competent police work was not the primary reason the case of the frozen woman was solved. No, it was the internal antagonisms in a group of men that caused them to crack.

'You've got a point,' Vaage concedes. 'But who remembers defeats when you carry the day?'

'I don't drink Irish whiskey,' Thygesen says.

Vaage has already mused that taking whiskey to a man who has had alcohol problems is like pouring petrol on a fire. However, she couldn't come up with any other ideas for a present. Perhaps she has offended him by bringing spirits?

'Just joking,' Thygesen says. 'I've got ice cubes in the freezer. Step inside, you trumpet of Nordland, you dusky cherub of the Helgeland coast.'

'Oh, shut up,' Vaage says, wiping her feet.

Jon Michelet has been one of Norway's leading authors for five decades. He made his debut in 1975 with the crime novel *He Who Is Born to Be Hanged, Shall Never Be Drowned.* He has since published numerous novels, plays and non-fiction books, and co-authored five bestselling reportage books from the Football World Cup with Dag Solstad. Michelet has also worked as a sailor, a docker, a journalist, publisher and newspaper editor. He is renowned in Norway for his strong commitment to a number of political and cultural causes.

Michelet was awarded the Riverton Prize for Best Norwegian Crime Novel twice, for *White as Snow* and *The Frozen Woman,* both part of his long running Vilhelm Thygesen series. He has also had phenomenal success with his epic series, *A Hero of the Sea.* Telling the story of the dramatic experiences of a Norwegian merchant navy sailor during WW2, the five novels published so far have been topping the charts since 2012, and have sold well over half a million copies, making Michelet a household name in Norway.

Don Bartlett lives with his family in a village in Norfolk. He completed an MA in Literary Translation at the University of East Anglia in 2000 and has since worked with a wide variety of Danish and Norwegian authors, including Jo Nesbø and Karl Ove Knausgaard.

About Us

In addition to No Exit Press, Oldcastle Books has a number of other imprints, including Kamera Books, Creative Essentials, Pulp! The Classics, Pocket Essentials and High Stakes Publishing > oldcastlebooks.com

For more information about Crime Books > crimetime.co.uk

Check out the kamera film salon for independent, arthouse and world cinema > kamera.co.uk

For more information, media enquiries and review copies please contact > marketing@oldcastlebooks.com